JOCELYN MILLER

Tanglewood Plantation

A Novel

Cover Graphic: Annie McCoy

Annie McCoy paints from her home on Maryland's Eastern Shore. She is a member of the Cider Painters of America, Mid Atlantic Plein Air Painters, and is an Associate Member of the Oil Painters of America. Visit her website at <u>AnnieMcCoyArt.com</u>.

ISBN: 0-6154-4980-8
ISBN-13: 9780615449807

"Time does not bring relief; you all have lied
Who told me time would ease me of my pain..."
Edna St. Vincent Millay

Descendant Chart for
Joseph Woodfield Family Slave

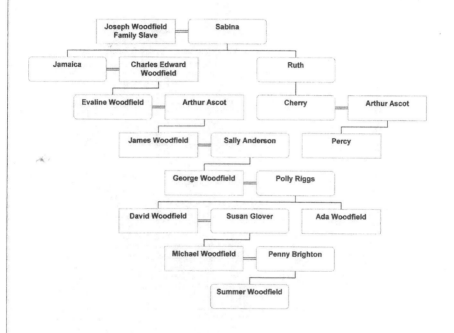

1

She didn't see it until a slight splash and rustle of saw grass caught her attention. In the dusky light her eyes focused on the peaks and valleys of the creature's rough hide as it lay along the riverbank, its thick body half submerged in the dark water. An ominous pair of eyes stared blankly ahead, unmoving; a docile creature—or so it seemed.

The sudden twitch of a claw shot a current of panic through her, causing the hairs of her neck to bristle.

Run!

It was an instinct fine-tuned through the ages of time and she took heed; her heart a jackhammer as her legs took flight across the terrain.

A thunderous explosion reverberated from behind and she knew then, without looking back, that the creature had propelled itself out of the water with its great tail and was in pursuit. It was close. She could hear the whoosh of its body across the stubble of growth, and sharp pains filled her chest in exertion. It couldn't run far on land—but neither could she, for just ahead stood a massive growth of brush, so tangled and knotted that escape was impossible. She was trapped. *This is how I die!*

Without recourse, she turned her back to the knotted mass and faced the horrid creature, its prior docility replaced by a ferocity of reptilian girth and length, and burst of speed; its intent clear.

"No!" she shrieked, as it knocked her to the ground with a powerful swing of its tail. "No!" she screamed as the teeth of the alligator tore through the flesh of her thigh....

✳ ✳ ✳

"Miss? Young lady?"

Summer Woodfield woke in a cold sweat. The man sitting next to her on the flight to Savannah sat forward in his seat, his neck craned to better see her face. "Are you all right?"

Summer focused her eyes on the stranger. Had she really screamed? The dream was so real, so terrifying. It took a moment to collect her breath—and her dignity. This was out of character for the *'heiress hauteur'*, as her coworkers back in Chicago mockingly called her.

"I'm fine," she assured the man, as well as the flight attendant who appeared suddenly in the aisle. "I...I guess I had a nightmare."

"Must'a been a doozy. Can I get you a cocktail to settle your nerves?" the attendant asked.

"No thanks, I'm fine," she lied.

The flight attendant continued down the aisle, while the man sitting next to her lifted the book off his lap and read, leaving her to her thoughts.

She was shaken by the dream. She had never experienced such a frightening nightmare and could not imagine what brought it on; perhaps the trip to Savannah? Or, had she read of an alligator attack recently? The memory of the gator's teeth in her thigh sent a chill down her spine.

Perhaps the death of great aunt Ada Woodfield brought on the ominous dream. Ada was her paternal grandfather's sister. She wasn't close to her aunt, as she only remembered meeting the woman once at the age of ten, and that was twenty years ago. The memory was vague, but she did recall when her father first told her of Aunt Ada, and how she lived at the family estate, Tanglewood Plantation, in Bluebell, Georgia.

"One day, when you're grown up, you'll inherit Tanglewood Plantation and be its new mistress, just like Aunt Ada is now."

Of course, that meant nothing to her back then, but the older she grew and the more she listened to her parents rave about Tanglewood Plantation, the more she envisioned herself a modern day Scarlet O'Hara, mistress of the manor house, barking orders at servants and entertaining the 'in' crowd of Bluebell. Visiting Tanglewood and Great Aunt Ada was on the proverbial 'list of things to do' in her lifetime, but, unfortunately, Aunt Ada's lifetime ran its course before the opportunity arose.

Disembarking the plane in Savannah, she noticed a few curious looks from fellow passengers—obviously the ones within earshot of her death shriek. Finding herself the reluctant highpoint of the flight, she ran her fingers through her cropped, tussled head of blond hair, raised her chin and advanced to the baggage claim. *Let them look. What do I care? I'm a blueblood of Bluebell, the heiress of Tanglewood Plantation!*

'SUMMER WOODFIELD'. A black-suited, sun-glassed limo driver, waiting in line with the other drivers near the baggage claim, held the placard.

"I'm Summer Woodfield," she said, and the man followed her to the carousel. This was getting better by the minute. *Just like in the movies!*

"Where is Mr. Ascot?" The estate lawyer was supposed to meet her at the airport.

"He had a phone call just as we pulled up. He's in the limo."

Summer followed the black suited driver as he wheeled her Louis Vuitton luggage through the baggage claim to the black limo waiting at the curb. She was glad she spent the money on the luggage; it cost plenty, but an heiress should look like an heiress. A day of shopping at Neiman Marcus for a new wardrobe put a small dent in her trust fund, too. Her navy blue white-trimmed jacket complemented a navy fitted skirt; *cute and sexy*, she thought.

She pictured Mr. Ascot just as the name sounded, aged and dignified, with silver temples to complement a silk suit. She wasn't expecting the disheveled young man smiling at her from the luxurious interior of the limo, a cell phone pressed to his ear.

"Hello, Miss Woodfield," he said, setting the phone aside.

She shook the hand extending outward from the rolled sleeves of his white shirt. His collar was unbuttoned and his tie loosened and askew.

"I'd stand up like a proper Southern gentleman but, as you can see, I'm hopelessly encumbered at the moment."

"Hello, Mr. Ascot."

A shock of dark hair jutted from his forehead and beneath that, alert and intelligent eyes. A briefcase sat on his lap, papers and folders spilling outward onto the seat.

She sat opposite him in the limo, all the while aware of him watching her every move. She busied herself settling in, but his eyes remained fixated on her. *Why doesn't he say something?* He continued to stare, which began to raise her anxiety level; was he a sexual deviant? She didn't know him from Adam. Should she even be in the limo with him? He was nearly catatonic.

"Mr. Ascot, you're *staring* at me. Is something wrong?" No reply. *The most exciting time of my life and I end up with a psycho lawyer!* The continued intensity of his gaze was now such that she was tempted to ask the limo driver if something was wrong with Mr. Ascot. Two bizarre incidents in one day were enough for her, but before she could catch the attention of the driver, Mr. Ascot blessedly awoke from his trance.

"I'm sorry, Miss Woodfield. I don't know what came over me except... except that you seem so familiar somehow. Have we ever met?"

"Not unless you've spent time in Chicago, and I think I would have remembered you." Indeed, she would have remembered the boyish face that dimpled with a smile. He looked much too young to be a lawyer.

His gaze lingered a moment more, and then he shook his head as if trying to dislodge himself from his thoughts. "Let's get down to business. You want to hear about Tanglewood Plantation. Have you ever been there?"

"No, I haven't, but I've heard about it all my life. My parents were very proud of the Woodfield heritage, and my father had wonderful memories of Tanglewood. I've seen photos, and it's beautiful!"

"Well, hmm. It certainly *was* beautiful in its day. It has quite a history. There wasn't a plantation around to equal its grandeur, or its rice production. Even my Ascot's Royal Palms Plantation couldn't hold a candle to the splendor of Tanglewood."

"Did your people have property here?"

"Did, and still do. We're neighbors, Miss Woodfield, for about 200 years."

The town of Bluebell was disappointing. Gas stations, fast food chains, banks, and a small shopping center were the sum of it. *So much for mingling with bluebloods.* "It's not much of a town, is it?"

"Don't be fooled by its appearance. It takes a while to get to know a place."

"You'd think with all the money that was here once—the plantations, the slaves—you'd think Bluebell would be as pretty as its name."

Mr. Ascot didn't reply, and she wondered if she had offended him. She had a habit of doing that, which is precisely why they called her '*heiress hauteur*' at the office. She knew they talked behind her back. They thought she was stuck-up, thought she had a chip on her shoulder.

She gave notice when she received the news of her inheritance. She didn't have much of a career anyway, just a glamorized secretary in a fancy office. She'd be a fool *not* give up *that* for *this,* even though she wasn't quite sure what *this* was, yet. It wasn't like she was a doctor or lawyer with a lengthy clientele to keep her in the three 'M's for the rest of her life; Money, Mercedes and *more.* Her parents left her a small trust fund. She didn't know if Aunt Ada left her financially secure, along with the plantation, and that's where Mr. Ascot came into the picture.

"We're nearly there," he informed her.

Summer pictured Tanglewood Plantation as she had seen it in a photo once. It was an old photo, as her father was a very young child then. He sat on a pony in the foreground, while behind him the manor house rose, imposing and grand. Her anticipation ran high as she crossed over to Mr. Ascot's side of the car in order to view the plantation as they approached.

As she remembered from her parents' incessant bragging, giant live oak trees lined the long entrance drive. Spanish moss draped gracefully from the limbs of the trees, promising true southern hospitality at the end of the road. She swelled with pride as the limo made its slow approach. What could be more perfect? Summer Woodfield, the mistress of Tanglewood Plantation, was home at last!

When the magnificent moss-draped oaks subsided, the view expanded to include crumbling shanties on the left side of the drive. Summer counted nine small structures in deplorable condition.

"What are those horrible shacks?"

The driver slowed the limo.

"Slave cabins." Mr. Ascot informed her. "They're made of tabby, a concrete made of lime, sand and oysters shell. There were once twelve tabby cabins where these stand. There are more down that way." He pointed to the right where a narrow road disappeared around a curve.

"Strange place for slave cabins, isn't it?"

"Not at all. In those days, plantation gentry loved to show off their slave populations. The more slaves, the more wealth they boasted."

Summer was shocked that Aunt Ada would have such a disgraceful, rotting scene on display at the end of such a charming entrance drive to the estate.

"Why didn't Aunt Ada tear these down?"

"Your Aunt Ada was attached to the family history. She realized that the cabins have great historical value. It was Ada's wish to restore Tanglewood to its antebellum state. Perhaps we can discuss a few ideas on the restoration of Tanglewood Plantation once you've had a chance to settle in a bit?"

"Perhaps...." Summer's voice trailed off as the limo approached the manor house by way of a circular drive, stopping in front of the looming three-story structure. Before she allowed herself the first scrutinizing look at her new home, her eyes focused on the fountain, a gnarled, twisted and grotesque bronze tree that rose twelve feet out of a moss covered pond in the middle of the circle. Its blackened limbs reached out across the pond in a hideous fashion.

"Someone had a macabre sense of humor, I see."

"Charles Edmund Woodfield, your ancestor. However, it didn't always look like that. Lore has it that it was quite splendid in its day."

She shivered against the memories of the day; the horrifying alligator dream, the strange trance of Mr. Ascot, the dilapidated slave cabins, and now a disturbingly ominous fountain greeted her. Her initial elation quickly deflated as her eyes turned to the manor house. She knew before she focused that her luck would not change. It stood three stories high, fronted by a massive double stairway which arched its way parallel across the front of the portico allowing entry from either side. Four enormous fluted columns, topped by ornate Corinthian capitals, braced the paint-chipped overhang that shaded the immense porch. Despite its basic grandeur, the mansion did not do the old photograph justice. Shutters hung catawampus on end, the brick façade crumbled in places and the paint was chipped and worn by neglect and time. The lawn, which ran as far as the eye could see, sported grass and weeds at least knee high. She found it hard to believe that Aunt Ada lived here until a short time ago.

Stepping out of the limo, Summer was hit with a furnace-like blast of high heat and humidity. Sweat immediately formed rivulets and traveled down the sides of her face to her chin. The jacket of her Neiman Marcus suit no longer felt cute and sexy, but more like a suit of armor worn in a sauna. No bluebloods of Bluebell to enchant, no servants to order about, just Summer Woodfield, *heiress hauteur* of disaster! She felt cheated. Her anticipation melted along with her mascara. She left a good job for *this?*

"I hope this is a joke, Mr. Ascot."

Mr. Ascot slid out of the limo and faced her on solid ground. He wasn't much taller than she, perhaps 5'10" to her 5'6".

"Why don't you call me Blaine?"

Blaine? It figured. There was nothing normal about this day.

"What kind of name is *'Blaine'?*"

He laughed. "What kind of name is *'Summer'?* May I call you Summer?"

"Oh certainly, *Blaine.* By all means, do call me Summer, and tell me that I'm having a nightmare...*another* nightmare...my second of the day."

"I beg your pardon?"

The heat and humidity didn't seem to affect Blaine in the least, while Summer, on the other hand, was a wet and soppy rag. Her hair fell flat, while the armpits of her jacket turned dark with sweat. Meanwhile, Blaine stood cool as a cucumber, the grotesque arms of the dreadful tree fountain reaching out to him as he stood between her and the murky pond. It gave her the willies to see the tree rising like a bad omen behind him. *The heat is getting to me.*

"I think I need to find someplace cool to sit down, Mr.—uh, Blaine."

"Let's go inside. It should be nice and cool in there."

He held her elbow as they made their way up the left side of the wide stairway to the portico. Already it was cooler in the shade. Summer turned to look out over her land and the beautiful oak-lined drive. The contrast between the dark portico and the bright acreage beyond created a stunning vision—a vision destroyed by the ominous fountain, the horrid, grotesque tree reaching out for what, she didn't know.

"I don't understand why anyone would want such an ugly fountain. Certainly it scared off any travelers or guests back in the old days."

"There's a story to that fountain and I think the one to tell you about it is Jesse."

"Who's Jesse?"

"Jesse works for me as a paralegal, but she also has roots in Tanglewood Plantation. She's waiting inside." He opened the great door to the manor house, and Summer's spirits brightened a bit. The entrance hall was immense and still held an ambiance of what it must have been in its days of grandeur. The wooden floors needed work to bring back sheen, as did the double stairway leading to the second floor, but just the expanse and charm of the room alone spoke volumes of its past.

Blaine led her into another room. "The parlor,' he said.

Summer was surprised at the modern décor of Aunt Ada's parlor. The atrocious fountain in the driveway gave her the impression that the rest of the house would follow suit. Aunt Ada may have ignored the outside toward the end of her life, but the parlor was warm and inviting. A deep brown leather sofa sat on a Persian area rug facing the width of a white marble-mantled fireplace. Flanked by matching armchairs on either side, the fireplace setting signified the epitome of comfort and hospitality. Even in the oppressive heat, Summer wished it were winter outside so she could enjoy a crackling fire.

"Jesse!" Blaine called "Jesse!" he called again, with no reply. "Have a seat, Summer, and I'll see if she's in the kitchen."

Alone in the parlor, Summer was drawn to the fireplace mantle and a display of photographs. She was surprised to find sitting amongst the other photos, the photo of her father riding the pony. Next to his image, was a tintype of a young soldier in a Confederate uniform, posed and unsmiling. She moved closer for a better look at his face, most of which was hidden beneath a kepi-cap. His eyes, dark and intense, stared out from beneath the brim of the cap. There was something about him...something nagged at her. He was familiar, somehow.

A second tintype caught her eye; a middle-aged woman sitting in a high-backed chair. Her light hair was parted in the middle and pulled back into a bun. A small bow closed the tightly fitted bodice at her neck, while loose-fitted sleeves gathered at her wrists, baring hands neatly folded in the lap of her full skirt. The sternness of her eyes and sharpness of her face gave Summer the creeps. It was no wonder the black woman standing behind her looked miserable. *They must be slaves,* she thought and looked closer. The older woman was very dark, her hair hidden beneath a bandana. The camera caught the weariness in her face, the sad, melancholy eyes.

The younger woman, perhaps in her late teens, was not nearly as dark of skin. Soft black curls outlined her pretty face. Summer was struck by the contrast of the trio; the white, fair-haired woman appeared stern and foreboding, the older black woman was tired and resigned, while the younger woman held a spark in her eyes that was missing in the others. *Not resigned to her destiny.* Summer was captivated by the pretty young woman with the sparkle. Again, she felt something very familiar about her just as she had with the soldier. Her eyes returned to the soldier, then back to the young woman in the tintype. She stood mesmerized, glancing from one photo to the other, until a chill ran through her. "Evaline," she whispered, not having a clue why.

"How did you know her name?"

Summer's heart skipped a beat at the sound of the voice behind her. She turned to find a tall black woman standing with a tray of drinks in her hands.

"Did your Aunt Ada tell you about Evaline?"

"No...uh, I don't know why I said that name. It just came to mind. I...I don't understand."

"The woman in the foreground is Elizabeth Woodfield your great-great-whatever- grandmother, and Charles Woodsfield's wife, mistress of the house. The two women standing behind her are my great-great-whatever grandmother Ruth, and her niece, Evaline. Are you sure you never heard of Evaline?"

"I'm positive." *But how did I know her name?*

"How strange." Jesse muttered, and looked at the tray in her hands. "Iced tea?" she asked, and set the tray down on the coffee table in front of the fireplace. "I'm sorry if I startled you. I'm Jesse Williams. Blaine's in the kitchen, on the phone—as usual—but that'll give us a moment to get to know each other."

Summer sat on a leather chair and took a sip of her tea—then a gulp. She was parched. *How did I know the woman's name was Evaline?* That was a bothersome question. *This is such a strange day.* She looked at Jesse, still standing at the fireplace. French manicured toenails peeked out from beneath the hems of her white slacks. Her lime green silk shirt was unbuttoned just enough to show a hint of cleavage, the color a nice complement to her mahogany skin. Jesse wore her hair cropped short, exposing small ears adorned with gold and pearl earrings. She was stunning.

"Your people were slaves on Tanglewood Plantation?" Try as she might, Summer could not picture Jesse in the rice paddies of Tanglewood.

"Yes, indeed. Joseph, my ancestor, was bought by Charles Woodfield in 1825 and brought to Tanglewood—only it wasn't called Tanglewood then, it was called Magnolia."

Summer was surprised at this comment. In all the years her parents spoke of Tanglewood, they never mentioned it having a different name.

"Did you notice the fountain out front?" Jesse asked.

"Did I? How could anyone *not* notice the fountain? It's grotesque!"

Blaine appeared in the parlor doorway. "Jesse, I told Summer you would fill her in on the fountain story but first, let's give her the grand tour of her new home."

The tour of the first floor, aside from the parlor, consisted of a library, old, dusty, and sure to intrigue both the historian and antique collector. One wall was covered floor to ceiling with books, and some looking quite antiquated from the condition of the spines. An old, ornate desk—obviously from a prior century—sat alone in front of a tall rectangular window, one corner of a catawampus outside shutter visible through its pane.

From the library, they moved across a hallway into the kitchen. Summer noticed the porcelain sink was dingy, with dark stains encircling the drain. A short, white refrigerator sat against one wall. Jesse stopped at the large, wooden table in the center of the room.

"This table was here at Tanglewood before the War between the States. It was in the original kitchen, which was a separate building."

"The Woodfield's didn't cook in here?"

"The Woodfield's didn't cook at all," Jesse snapped. "They had slaves to do the cooking."

Summer felt her face flush, but was determined not to let Jesse William's attitude get to her. She had enough aggravation for one day without a hotheaded slave descendant giving her a royal headache.

They passed through a kitchen door and entered the dining room.

"Cooking was a fire hazard in those days." Jesse continued, apparently over her flash of anger. "It was a lot cheaper to rebuild a kitchen than an entire mansion."

The late afternoon sun filtered in through a long rectangular window in the dining room, casting a mystical ambiance to the four portraits which hung on its walls. In the first portrait, Summer recognized the fair-haired, middle-aged stern-faced woman from the tintype on the mantle. "That's Elizabeth, isn't it?"

"Yes, and next to her is her husband, Charles Edmund Woodfield." Jesse nodded to the next painting of a white-haired gentleman. Directly across the room were two other portraits, one of four children, and the other of the young black woman from the tintype on the mantle.

"These are the Woodfield children; John, Margaret, Edmund and Su-sannah." Jesse turned to Summer."Who do you come down from, John or Edmund?"

"Why, I don't know." She wasn't aware of them until this moment.

"It had to be one or the other for you to have the surname of Wood-field."

Summer was now the *ignorant* heiress hauteur. From whom did she de-scend? Funny, her father never mentioned it, and now the only other person who might know the answer was gone. In fact, it now appeared that Jesse and Blaine knew more about her heritage than she did!

"My father's name was Michael, and his father's name was David but that's all I know." *At least I know something.* "We weren't that close with the relatives because there were so few." She looked closely at John and Edmund Woodfield in the portrait, but they shed no light on the mystery. It was strange feeling, standing in a room with her ancestors and not knowing which one was solely responsible for her existence.

"And this one..." Jesse put her hand on the bottom of the heavy frame hanging next to the Woodfield children. "This is Evaline."

Summer was again mesmerized by the light-skinned slave girl, this time adrift in a sea of grass, the image of a stately and impressive Tanglewood Plantation manor house faint in the background. Evaline's scoop-necked, white blouse rested suggestively on mocha-colored shoulders, while her skirt blew gently in a breeze frozen forever in time. A teasing smile curled the corners of her lips.

"I don't get it. How does Evaline rate a place on the dining room wall? Wasn't she just a slave?"

"Yes," Jess answered curtly. "Evaline was a slave, but she was also the daughter of Charles Woodfield and the slave woman, Jamaica."

"Wow." Summer raised her eyebrows and glanced at Blaine, who had been quiet throughout the downstairs tour. "I wonder how Elizabeth felt about that portrait hanging in her home?"

"You'll see that the portrait is not signed or dated, and it's questionable as to how Charles could have paid for a painting of that quality during the war, and he died before the end of the war. The painting remains a mystery."

"Was Charles a soldier?"

"Uh, no." Blaine replied, casting a short glance in Jesse's direction.

"How did Elizabeth die?"

"She had an accident. She fell down the stairs and broke her neck," Blaine said.

"What an end for the mistress of the manor."

"Evaline disappeared the night the Yankees burned the fountain. She was twenty years old." Jesse said.

"*Burned* the fountain? How can you burn a fountain?"

"Look closely at the painting. In the background you can see the fountain in front of the double stairway entrance, but it doesn't look like the fountain out front."

Summer stood on tiptoe, balancing with her palms against the wall. Sure enough, far in the background was the fountain. It looked like a tree, but not the hideous monstrosity out front. "What is it?"

"It's a magnolia tree," Jesse answered. "Charles Woodfield's father had it cast in bronze in Italy and shipped here. It was the most impressive fountain in the entire state of Georgia, right down to the bronze magnolia blossoms. Of course that was long before the Yankees came and Charles Woodfield lost everything."

"Maybe Evaline ran off? What year would that have been?"

"It was 1864. Susannah Woodfield wrote the date in the family bible."

"Maybe Evaline went north. After all, she was a free woman, wasn't she?" This sounded perfectly reasonable to Summer.

"I don't think it was as cut and dried as that." Jesse snapped. "Evaline disappeared before the end of the war, and freed slaves didn't just up and head north. They didn't have money, didn't have work, and had no roots except for the plantation they were born on or sold to. Most of them couldn't read or write. It wasn't an easy world for a free black." Her dark eyes grew darker.

Summer's knowledge of the history of slavery and the emancipation appeared even more limited, and she felt intimidated by Jesse Williams. Jesse not only knew a tremendous amount about the Woodfield family but also expressed strong feelings over slavery issues. Because it was Summer's people who enslaved Jesse's, she somehow felt that Jesse was putting the responsibility of slavery on *her* shoulders. Unfair! Summer came to Georgia to be the lady of Tanglewood Plantation, nothing more, and here she was in a dusty old dining room surrounded by paintings of people she didn't know, but *should* know, and on the cusp of a debate on freed slaves with the slave descendant her own ancestor's slaves!

"How about we head upstairs?" Blaine saved the moment.

The grand staircase creaked as they made their way to the second floor. Aunt Ada's bedroom was impeccably furnished and feminine, not to mention huge. Brocade drapes fell lavishly on either side of an immense doorway that opened up onto a veranda.

"This was actually a ballroom before the demise of slavery." Jesse said, opening one of the tall doors for a peek of the veranda.

A thick and fluffy bedspread covered an elaborate four-posted full-sized bed. The dressing table, Jesse said, was an antique. It was Elizabeth's own dressing table, as were the dresser and the four-poster. Obviously, the furniture was well cared for since the War Between the States. Summer could not recall ever seeing a bedroom as beautiful as this one.

Built into one corner of the immense bedroom was a modern bathroom, the fixtures old fashioned, and the tub clawed, complementing the ambiance of the bedroom.

"There were no closets built in the old days, or indoor plumbing, either. One of the later Woodfields added the bathroom, and this large closet." Jesse opened a door, exposing a closet with empty hangers. "Not a walk-in, but it sufficed."

The other three bedrooms would have been a shock had it not been for the fountain and dilapidated slave cabins to foretell the true state of Tanglewood. Dust and cobwebs found good company in each other, as the rooms obviously had not been cared for, for quite some time. The window sills of all three rooms were rotted and splintering, and looked as if they hadn't been painted or opened in years…maybe decades? A few of the panes were missing and some patched with clear vinyl and duct tape. Wallpaper peeled from walls. The wood planking on the floor was warped in some places and missing in others. These rooms had little in common with Aunt Ada's lavish bedroom and bath. It were as if Aunt Ada's rooms were misplaced—as if they belonged elsewhere in a fine mansion, but were placed here as a rude joke. It seemed a personal affront to Summer, whose dreams of grandeur were so abruptly destroyed that day.

The third floor held a nursery and two other rooms. "All the Woodfield children spent their early years in the nursery before moving down to the second floor." Jesse said. She opened a door adjoining the nursery. "This was Ruth's room. She cared for the Woodfield children. She was also Jamaica's sister."

"So you and Evaline are related?"

"Distant cousins."

Crossing Ruth's room, Jesse opened yet another door. "And this was Evaline's room. Charles Woodfield insisted Evaline be raised in the house."

"Where was Jamaica?"

"Jamaica was a house slave, until Miss Elizabeth realized Charles Woodfield visited Jamaica's bed more often than her own. After Evaline was born and weaned, Elizabeth forced Charles to send Jamaica to the rice fields."

"How do you know all this?"

"Oh, Evaline's story is folk-lore in my family, passed down through the generations. She was half white, the master's favored child, and she was beautiful—too good a story to let go."

Another door in Evaline's room led to the attic. Blaine opened it to a cloud of dust.

"Achoo!" Summer sneezed. "Achoo! Sorry. I'm allergic to dust."

Blaine closed the door quickly. "Guess we'd better not take you up there. That's the attic, by the way. It's full of neat old stuff if you ever want to take a look. It's a real history lesson in itself."

"You've been up there?"

"After Ada's death, I had a peek."

Summer followed Blaine and Jesse back to Ruth's room. "This always fascinated me." Blaine opened a door to a narrow circular stairway. "This was the servant stairway. Think your nose can take it?"

Summer peeked into the dark abyss—a tubular stairwell that faded downward into blackness.

"Why the heck would anyone build stairs like this?"

"For the slaves to travel." Jesse answered. "They weren't allowed to use the grand stairway. They traveled this stairway night and day, sick or well, winter or summer, at their master's beck and call."

With that remark, Summer was determined to walk the stairway, dust or no dust. "After you," she gestured to Blaine, who took a small flashlight from his pocket.

Following his lead, the trio made their way downward guided by the narrow beam of light. The journey required extreme caution, as the treads were narrow and footing unsure in the darkness. Summer hadn't realized she was claustrophobic until this moment, as her heartbeat quickened and her breath came in short gasps. She fought hard the urge to push Blaine aside and race to the landing. Instead, she focused on his head below her on the stairs. At the second story landing, she regained her composure to some degree, with a narrow slit of light coming from beneath a door. *One more floor,* she repeated silently until, at last, Blaine opened a door, which entered into the foyer.

The manor house was impressive in history and size, but she felt overwhelmed by its deteriorating condition. Aunt Ada utilized very few rooms, leaving most of the mansion to ruin. Summer did not have the funds or the desire to revitalize an aged plantation house. Did Aunt Ada leave money too? If so, Blaine hadn't mentioned it. She only knew that Tanglewood was hers, but was there something else? Why hadn't Blaine read her the will?

Returning to her seat in the parlor, she took a sip of her tea and fought the urge to cry. She hadn't felt so alone since her parents were killed. The day grew long and she grew weary. She came to Georgia with such anticipation. She came as the only surviving Woodfield, and now she had family—dead family, none-the-less—but they seemed alive now that she had learned a small fraction of their story. Her ancestor, Charles Woodfield, lusted after a slave woman. Elizabeth banished the slave woman from the house to the rice paddies. Jesse Williams was as tied up in this story as she was, and she couldn't shake the feeling that Jesse held her in contempt.

"I hope there's a hotel in town. I can't stay here tonight," she blurted. "This day has been a disaster for me and I don't think I can stay here alone."

"We didn't think you would want to." Blaine said. "Jesse is prepared to spend the night. Bluebell doesn't have a hotel that I would recommend. We've stocked the kitchen, so you won't run out of food for quite a while. The linens are clean, and we even had a prepared meal sent up for tonight. But, if you're determined to not stay here at all, we can take you back to Savannah."

Summer glanced at Jesse, hoping to find encouragement either way. After all, the poor woman had to disrupt her own life to babysit the new heiress. Jesse's face registered a blank, except for a slight look of impatience.

"Well, I can't see you driving me all the way back to Savannah. If Jesse doesn't mind, then I guess I can stay the night. I don't know what I'm going to do about tomorrow night or all the nights after that."

"I don't' understand," Blaine said. "Aren't you interested in Tanglewood?"

"I was interested before I saw what a dilapidated mess it is. I was interested when I thought there might be some kind of social life in Bluebell—may as well call it *Deadbell*, for all the charm it has." She stood out of her chair. "What am I supposed to do with this place? I don't have the kind of money it takes to bring it back to livable condition. Did Aunt Ada leave money to maintain it? Why haven't you read me the will?"

"I thought we could do that tomorrow. You seemed so excited about Tanglewood over the phone. I thought you'd like to see it first, before we got into the paperwork."

Summer envisioned herself the lady of the manor house, the new gem of Bluebell society, the sole owner of Tanglewood Plantation. What a fool she was to think she would waltz right in and charm the local society. What society? What did she have now but a broken down over-sized house with an ugly fountain out front and a bunch of dead ancestors staring at her? The horrid fountain may as well be reaching out to choke the life out of her, for all the anxieties she felt at this moment.

Blaine stood and put a hand on her shoulder. "Why don't you get some rest tonight? You're right, it *has* been a long day and things always look different in the morning. It's an old cliché, but true."

With her outburst over, she was embarrassed. This always happened to her. She always opened her big mouth before thinking, and always ended up insulting someone or making a fool of herself.

"I'm sorry. I just wasn't expecting this…this wreck."

Blaine sighed. "I'm really sorry you feel that way about Tanglewood. It does have its charm, if you'd give it a chance."

He was obviously disappointed, but Summer couldn't help the way she felt; this wasn't at all what she expected! Blaine was headed for the door with Jesse following, and she fell in behind the two, employer and employee. *Master and slave. Good grief, what made me think of that?*

A full moon cast a spell of silver on the fields of tall grass and weeds, as she and Jesse stood in the great entrance hall doorway of Tanglewood

Plantation. They silently watched the limo pull around the circular drive and disappear into the silvery folds of Spanish moss, eerily visible in the moonlight. Summer could not avoid the wretched tree fountain, which looked more gnarled and menacing in the moon's glow than it did that afternoon.

As she and Jesse turned to reenter the house, a moan—a sad, pitiful moan—drew their attention, and they turned to the fountain again. They never spoke of it—the fact that they both, simultaneously at that moment, reached for the door and slammed it shut against the night.

2

"I find it comforting to think my ancestors may have sat at this very table," Jesse confided later, while sitting in the kitchen eating the dinner that was prepared for them.

Remembering Jesse's short fuse in reference to her enslaved ancestors, Summer remained silent, enjoying the delicious roast beef that came au gratis in celebration of her first night as mistress of Tanglewood Plantation. *Such an honor,* she thought, envisioning the catawampus shutters, and acres of grass-gone-haywire. She couldn't imagine why Aunt Ada hadn't kept the place up, at least to the quality of the few rooms she lived in.

After a minute of food-chewing and the clinking of silver and glassware, Summer broke the silence. "S o, tell me about that god-awful fountain out there."

"The fountain." Jesse took a sip of tea and dabbed at her mouth with a napkin. "The fountain you see out there now is the sorrowful remains of the magnificent magnolia fountain, for which the plantation was once named. In December of 1864 a troop of Yankees rode up to the manor house. They terrorized the family and servants before gathering most of the furniture in the house, except for Miss Elizabeth's bedroom set and the library desk, and piled the collection up in the fountain pond, which was empty of water at the time. We don't know why Elizabeth's furniture was spared, but they set the furniture in the pond afire and, as the story goes, it was the biggest, brightest bonfire anyone had ever seen. It burned so hot and so long, that the beautiful magnolia fountain began to melt. When it was all over and done with, what you see out there, is what the Woodfield family saw about a century and a half ago."

"How horrible!"

"And that is the night Evaline disappeared."

Summer was silent. One would never have known the drama involved in her family history had they judged by the perfectly boring and mundane existence of her childhood. "What about Elizabeth? How did she fall?"

"Elizabeth died before the fountain fire. Nobody knows exactly what happened. She fell and died at the bottom of the stairs."

A shiver shot up Summer's spine. To think she walked up the very steps that had killed her ancestor. Why, she may have placed her foot on the very spot Elizabeth Woodfield drew her last breath!

"According to family lore, Charles' personality changed after Elizabeth's death—even though it's told there wasn't a great love story there to begin with. He totally withdrew from the family and from the remotest effort at keeping the place going. The slaves were freed by then, and without slave labor, the rich, white plantation owners were nothing but a bunch of common farmers."

Summer felt the jab, but it was true. Would Tanglewood have existed at all without slave labor? Would she be sitting in this ruin tonight, were it not for slavery?

"Evaline had a baby." Jesse continued.

"Whose?"

"Some say it was Charles Woodfield's child. You see, Charles loved Evaline—possibly in ways he shouldn't have. She was his own child, but he was captivated by her. She had special privileges in the house, and Elizabeth was jealous of her from day one. It was an embarrassment that the slave girl would have her own room, nice clothes, and even learn to read and write. It was hard for Elizabeth to hold her head up, when all of Bluebell whispered about the way Charles Woodfield carried on over Evaline—how he treated her equal to, if not better than his other children."

"Jeez." Summer was beginning to wonder what kind of crazy family she came from. "How do you know all this stuff?"

"Hearsay from my granny." Jesse paused. "Evaline's son was nearly white, which is probably why they pointed the finger at Charles Woodfield. Nobody knows for sure. Evaline kept mum about it. All we know is that she had a boy and named him James. Charles Woodfield's daughter, Susannah, raised him after Evaline disappeared."

"What happened to the Woodfield boys? Why am I the only living Woodfield descendant?"

"That's a good question. As far as I know, John and Edmund were both killed in the war. As I recall, John married before he went off to war. You should check marriage and death records at the courthouse and see if you can find the missing link. I guess Granny knew, but I've never looked."

The missing link. How did I get from 'heiress hauteur' to the missing link? This sure was getting complicated. She came to Georgia to claim her beautiful mansion, which in truth was nothing more than a crumbling ruin. It seemed such a simple thing that morning; fly to Georgia, claim plantation, accept inheritance, hob-knob with social elite, live happily ever after.

So far, an alligator (hypothetical, but it seemed real) had attacked her; the estate attorney suffered a mysterious trance due to her mere presence; her dreams were shattered by a dilapidated and antiquated house; a descendant of her ancestor's slaves put her on the defensive; she discovered her ancestor, Charles Woodfield, was a lustful, incestuous, man who forced himself on a slave woman, and may have forced himself on his own daughter! Her ancestor, Elizabeth Woodfield, mysteriously suffered death by stairs and, to add insult to injury, she didn't even know which one of the revered Woodfields to call her own! To top it off, *she heard the bronze fountain groan.* She suddenly felt very tired.

"Thanks for the history lesson, Jesse. I think I need to go to bed and soak this in. Where are we sleeping?"

"You have your Aunt Ada's bedroom and I can sleep down here on the sofa."

"Please, you take the bedroom and I'll take the sofa."

"Don't be ridiculous. This is *your* house and Aunt Ada's bedroom is your own now. Your luggage is there, and I'm prepared for the sofa."

"I insist."

"No, I insist that I sleep on the sofa. I do *not* take orders from you!"

✳ ✳ ✳

Aunt Ada's bed proved as comfortable as it looked, and Summer woke refreshed. She opened the double doors leading to the veranda, where a hazy morning sun foretold of the oppressively humid day to come. She pulled on her pink bathrobe and traversed the stairs to find Jesse already at the kitchen table sipping coffee.

"Blaine called. He'll stop over after breakfast and show you the rest of the place."

"What about you?"

"I'll be heading back to Savannah. I do have a life there."

"No doubt." Summer answered, attempting to sound as cool and aloof as she. Regardless, she felt a twinge of fear at the thought of Jesse leaving her. Odd as it was, even though Jesse appeared to dislike her, she felt somewhat safer with her around. She didn't plan on spending another night here anyway, and certainly not alone! The place gave her the creeps, but why? Nothing odd happened overnight. In fact, she slept like a newborn babe.

"I'll come back tonight. Blaine said he would read the will then." Jesse sipped her coffee.

Not wanting to infringe further on Jesse's peaceful breakfast, Summer poured a cup of coffee and opened the door to the back steps. As yesterday, the stifling hot air greeted her as she stepped onto the landing. It was going to be wickedly hot today, for sure. The thigh-high grass stretched a distance of nearly 1000 feet to the Savannah River. Summer could see the patch of water through the trees at the river's edge.

"I wouldn't walk that, if I were you." Jesse stood behind her, cup in hand. "That grass is probably crawling with ticks, not to mention some nasty snakes. Blaine said he has Guy Mason coming today to cut it. You'd better wait."

The back steps were nearly as impressive as the front. The double stairway led to either side of the brick landing below. Summer chose the left stairway and stood on the landing looking up at Jesse. "I guess this was pretty fancy in its day."

"You bet. This was actually the main entrance to the house. People traveled by the river in those days, since roads were not what they are today. Most visitors came in this way. Of course, there was a different door back then—much bigger and nicer. I think they did some adjusting when they added the kitchen."

Even from the back of the house—the old front—the house looked worn and weary. The catawampus shutters on the other side, matched the ones here, in their angled disarray.

"Whew." Summer wiped at the sweat gathering on her forehead and fought the urge to tear the robe off her body. "I can't imagine what brought people here—this climate is something else!"

"Guess it's in our blood. After all, we slaves had to work the fields no matter what the climate."

Summer flushed with embarrassment at Jesse's sarcastic insinuation. That, and the sudden vision of slaves toiling in the fields in this sultry sweatbox just to keep her ancestors living the high life, made her want to hide in the tall grass, tick and snake infested or not. Jesse gloated above her—or so Summer thought—like a proud overseer, glad to have her servant humbled at last, at the bottom of the stairs.

The growl of a motor caught their attention.

"Oops—that must be Guy, the gardener," Jesse said.

It was a welcomed intrusion.

Jesse gathered her things, while Summer retired upstairs to dress for the day, sans Neiman Marcus. This was a shorts day. Again, she traversed the grand stairway, her slender legs carrying her lithe figure to the foyer, where Jesse had piled her overnight things at the doorway.

"I didn't see your car. Where is it?"

"In the garage—the old carriage house. We wanted the circle free yesterday. Blaine will give you the grand tour today."

"Guess my eyes were glued on the fountain yesterday." She didn't recall seeing any other buildings aside from the slave cabins.

Jesse gathered her belongings and opened the door. "It was nice to meet you, Summer."

Yeah, right. "Thanks for staying with me last night."

"My pleasure. Enjoy your new home."

While Jesse crossed the great veranda to the double stairway Summer's nerves balanced at the edge of panic at the thought of being left alone here—even for a moment. Guy, the grass man, could be seen outside in the distance taming the field, but couldn't help her should she need it...*help me from what?*

"Jesse!" she called out, not knowing what to say when Jesse turned at the top of the veranda stairs. She shuddered at the sight of the ugly fountain rising behind her.

"Uh..." *What a crybaby I am,* she thought, while frantically conjuring up something to say.

"Uh...yes?" Jesse asked.

It was in this state of mute confusion, while searching for words to hold Jesse a moment longer, that she saw *it*. She shook her head as if to clear her vision, and as the reality of the vision registered, a blood-curdling scream resonated under the veranda roof. It was her own voice, sharp and shrill, for beyond Jesse, hanging by his neck from the uppermost branch of the burned magnolia fountain, was a body—a white-haired man dangling over the empty pond. His eyes were not visible beneath the shock of white hair that halfway covered his face, but his tongue—his horrid tongue, grotesquely swollen and black—protruded from his parted lips as if someone had placed a huge and rotted banana there as a joke.

Summer screamed again, ran toward Jesse, and then back through the front door. It was a blur—a blank—she was gone into total darkness. She awoke on the leather sofa in front of the fireplace. A man stood over her, and behind him, Jesse.

"You alright Summer?" Jesse asked. "What the heck happened? You scared the life out of me!"

"Me too," the man said.

Summer focused on the deep brown eyes of the stranger.

"I'm Guy." He answered before she could ask. "The landscaper."

"Oh, my god!" She sat bolt upright. "The man! He was…." She swung her legs to the floor, forcing the stranger to step backward. A wave of nausea punched her in the gut, but she moved quickly from the parlor to the foyer, and opened the front door a crack. "Where is he? What did you do with him?"

"With who?" Jesse and Guy asked simultaneously.

"He's gone!" Summer swung the door open. "He's gone." She turned to the quizzical faces behind her. "He was there…I swear he was."

"Summer, girl, we don't know what the heck you're talking about." Jesse said, crossing her arms over her chest.

"Jesse, I swear…this is going to sound strange…but I swear there was an old man hanging by the neck from the fountain. It was awful! His tongue was hanging out!"

Jesse's mahogany skin went pale.

"Turn around and look out there now," Guy said. "There's nobody there. It's all right." His voice was deep and reassuring, a voice well suited for the tall and masculine frame before her. He stood over six feet with power-ful arms suspended from broad shoulders. Veins protruded from the skin of his forearms as if the muscle beneath needed space and shooed them to the surface. His hands rested at his sides, curved, ready to make fists. Those arms must have carried her effortlessly to the sofa in the parlor. She was suddenly intimidated. The dark eyes continued to penetrate her own; dark eyes that peered from a chiseled face, where a stubble of beard pricked his chin—a comic book hero. He was familiar—like the tintypes on the mantle—she knew him, somehow.

Summer pried her eyes away from the gardener and focused on Jesse. It gave her the willies to see Jesse's eyes fixed like a bayonet over her shoulders—fixed on the fountain. *She knows something.* "What is it?" She was afraid to look herself, for fear the vision had returned.

"Nothing." Jesse said, turning to Guy. "Thanks. I guess the emergency is over."

Guy nodded to the women. "Take care,' he said, and descended the steps that led to the lawn, his tractor, and the monumental job ahead.

"You *know* something," Summer accused. She leaned against the doorframe. "You know something, so tell me."

"Okay," Jesse exhaled. "This is creeping me out. Charles Woodfield hung himself on that fountain out there. Did you know that?"

Summer's jaw dropped. "I didn't know anything about anything until I got here. I never heard of Charles Woodfield, or Evaline, or Elizabeth...or any of them! I came to collect my inheritance, that's all!" She threw her arms into air and passed Jesse, headed for the kitchen. She needed coffee, or tea—or booze. If Jesse thought *she* was creeped out, how about herself? *Good god, what kind of people do I come from? They're all insane!*

3

Summer watched the white Jeep Wrangler approach beneath the moss-draped oak trees as she sat on the large veranda outside Aunt Ada's bedroom. Earlier, she dragged one of Aunt Ada's chairs outside so she could put her feet up on the balcony, sip her iced tea and try to forget the morning's encounter with the hanging ghost. She reluctantly sent Jesse on her way to Savannah. Just knowing Guy was out there on the tractor helped to settle her jittery nerves. Of course, it didn't hurt to have the daylight. Everyone felt safer in daylight, even though the ghost of Charles Woodfield didn't know that he was supposed to show himself *only* at night. She shuddered against *that* prospect, too.

"Hello, Blaine," she stood and called down as he stepped out of the Jeep. He looked sporty in a yellow polo shirt and khaki green slacks. Here was the high-society of Bluebell, right under her nose. She tried to avoid looking at the fountain, but it was inevitable, as its dark arms tenaciously invaded her peripheral vision.

"Hey, Summer! How are you feeling?" He craned his neck and shaded his eyes with one hand. "I had a strange call from Jesse a while ago."

"No doubt. You didn't tell me this place came with a ghost. Meet me in the kitchen."

"You look good as new," he said, plunking a fat manila envelope down on the kitchen table.

"Okay for having seen a ghost this morning, right?" She poured him a glass of tea.

"Okay, tell me about it." Blaine sat and took a swallow of his drink.

"Jesse was leaving, and I called out to her. She stopped, turned around, and off to the side of her—my right side—I saw a white-haired man hanging from the fountain. It was horrible. I did not make this up, I swear. I came here to get my inheritance. That's all. I did not come to present myself as another Woodfield screwball. I saw what I saw."

"I know you're upset, Summer, and I don't know what to say. I've been here many times and I've never seen a man hanging from the fountain. I don't recall Ada ever mentioning a hanging man. Maybe you're just tired from the trip? Maybe it was too much yesterday…meeting your ancestors."

"That's all good and fine, but what am I supposed to do here? I'm terrified to stay alone! I shouldn't tell you this, but last night while you were driving away, I heard a terrible groan—like someone in agony—and I think Jesse heard it too. It sounded like it came from the fountain. Jesse and I were standing in the doorway when that happened—just like today—I was in the doorway…" She paused. "How strange, both times I was standing in the doorway."

"I tell you what. Let's take a grounds tour. Looks like Guy has much of the lawn under control. I think Jesse told you to not walk in the tall grass, right?"

"She did."

"*Especially* in shorts. You wouldn't want ticks over those lovely legs now, would you?" The dimples puckered his cheeks when he smiled.

It was roughly 500 feet from the main gate to the first slave cabin. Summer was very curious about these and insisted they start their tour here. The tabby cabins still stood, but in grave disrepair. The roof of the first cabin had caved in at some point in time and remained concave, dipping into the structure.

"Careful!" Blaine warned, as Summer stepped to the doorway.

"Darn. Can't see a thing with the roof in there." She went back to the yard and stood on tiptoe checking to see if one of the cabins had at least part of a roof still intact. "Okay, number five looks good," she said, walking toward the cabin. "This is much better."

It was a simple room with a fireplace. Hazy sunlight filtered through a dingy window illuminating the worn wooden floor. There was no furniture, just the empty stillness of memories muted in the passage of time. A straw broom leaned in a corner, the only reminder that the cabin was once inhabited. She watched Blaine through the window, fanning the air against the gnats that hovered relentlessly about his face.

A sudden gush of warm breath on the back of her neck caused the hairs of her arm to rise. When she turned to see no one standing behind her, a rash of gooseflesh sent her out the door to solid ground. "There's something odd about this place…it gives me the creeps."

Blaine shrugged his shoulders. "It's just an old plantation, nothing more."

Directly across from the slave cabins, and across the driveway, stood the carriage house. A few stalls remained toward the back, but the front was converted into a three-car garage, with a small apartment overhead where the hayloft had once been. Behind that, a small house.

"The overseer's cabin," Blaine said.

Crossing the yard toward the manor house, he pointed to a fenced section of land that obviously had, at one time, a purpose. "That mangled mess was the garden. It was very pretty in its time. Ada kept the garden up until the past few years. Guy said he'd love to get his hands on it. He has a knack for that kind of stuff, which is why he's in the landscape business in the first place."

"Have you known Guy a long time?"

"Sure have. We went to school together, from kindergarten until I went away to high school."

"And then?"

"And then I went Ivy League, and he went agricultural."

"Does he live around here?"

"He lives a couple miles down the road, which is nice and handy. He does the yard and gardens at my place, too."

"I should ask how much he costs, before I let him loose on this mess."

"This is covered, don't worry. I think he'd do it for free. He can't stand an eyesore, and he loves this old relic—the plantation."

"Don't tell me his people were slaves here, too."

Blaine laughed, and there went the dimples again. "No, but I think his ancestor was the overseer here during the Civil War. You should ask him sometime. He's really into that history stuff."

"This is like old home week, right?"

Blaine laughed again. "Enough of buildings. Let's go to the river."

The trek to the river from the back steps of the manor house was much longer than it appeared that morning while she was having her coffee. As the sun climbed higher, it tightened the vise on heat and humidity. The gnats swarmed around their faces as they trudged across the newly cut lawn. The grass smelled good, but the gnats kept their arms busy swatting the critters away.

"Damn things!" Summer exclaimed.

"I should have known better than to come without bug spray," Blaine answered.

At last, the river was only a few short feet away. The trees and tall azaleas along the riverbank blessedly shielded them from the oppressive sun. It was cooler here, and the gnats let up a bit. They stood on the small dock that jutted off the riverbank.

"This is it, the Savannah River, right in your back yard."

"Front yard," Summer corrected. "That's a heck of a long walk for guests to make. I just can't picture women in hooped skirts making that trek for a neighborly visit."

"Well...they did it. The river was the way to travel back then. It was quicker, and safer."

"Safer?"

"Sure. There were plenty of sleazy characters on the roads waiting to make a buck or two off a traveler."

They followed the overgrown remains of a narrow path along the river.

"Watch out for the saw grass," Blaine warned. "It'll cut you to shreds. You don't want to cut up those lovely legs of yours, do you?"

She stopped, her back to the river. "I guess you don't think I should be wearing shorts on this venture?"

"To the contrary! I'm glad you did."

He smiled, and Summer couldn't be offended. At least she had one friend in this strange place.

"Don't move," he said, the dimpled smile suddenly gone.

Her natural instinct was to run at those words, but he repeated himself through gritted teeth this time. "Don't move."

"You're scaring me!" she whispered.

"Let's back up to the tree line."

It crossed her mind that he was playing a joke, but he was dead serious. He held her hand as they stepped slowly backward until they reached the brush and trees.

"What the devil was that about?"

"Look!" Blaine pointed. Her eyes followed his finger, but saw nothing.

"There, on the bank. It's old Bruno, the biggest, meanest alligator on the Savannah River."

"Oh, no!" Summer collapsed against a tree, visibly shaken as the sinister form registered. "It's him!"

"It's who?" Blaine asked. "You're trembling. Come on, let's get out of here."

This was her dream! This was surely an omen! She fought her way through the trees and brush until her feet touched the grassy lawn, Blaine following behind. He deserved an explanation. *She* deserved an explanation!

"I don't know what's going on here, Blaine," she gasped. "This is crazy. Yesterday, on the plane, I had a dream that an alligator chased me; it bit my leg and wouldn't let go. I woke up screaming—it was very embarrassing. What's happening to me? Alligators, ghosts...I'm scared. I have to get out of here. It's like this place hates me."

"I don't blame you for being scared over Bruno. He scares all of us, but he's a local legend. We let him be, as long as he leaves us alone. It doesn't hurt to be cautious."

"I've got to get out of here before I wake up and find that thing on my bed."

He laughed, as though he found her anguish amusing.

"It's not funny!" she yelled, stopping halfway between the river and the house. "I'd sure like to know how you'd react if you saw an old man hanging from that damned fountain out front—or had an alligator sink his teeth into your leg!" She walked off toward the house, while Blaine ran to catch up to her.

"I'm sorry, Summer. *Really*. Please accept my apology. I can see you're suffering, and this is not how it's supposed to go. This was to be a happy day and here I've gone and ruined it."

In the kitchen, Summer poured another glass of tea. "Would you like one? You look flushed."

"Sure," he said, sitting at the table in front of the manila envelope. "This is the will. I want Jesse here when it's read."

Summer sat across from him and eyed the envelope. "I hope there's something good in there, because so far, it stinks."

"Why don't I drive us into town for lunch? I know a great restaurant."

"Is there a library, or a place that has the old records from when the Woodfields lived here—the Charles Woodfield's?"

"Actually, the library has some amazing records from the old cotton and rice days."

"Is it open on Sunday?"

"No, but I'll show you where it is."

Despite herself, Summer enjoyed the lunch in town. On a closer look, Bluebell wasn't as bad as it first appeared—it just wasn't Chicago. The restaurant Blaine took her to was quaint and cozy. Murals of the good old days of rice and cotton covered its walls, and Summer wondered what the local black population thought of the slaves depicted here, hunched over in the fields against a backdrop of opulent Georgian architecture. She leaned in toward Blaine. "It's kind of strange in this day and age, isn't it?"

"What's that?"

"Having slaves painted on the walls."

"This is our history, darlin'. We don't have slavery anymore." He winked.

"I wonder what Jesse thinks of this restaurant. She certainly has an attitude when it comes to slavery."

"You can ask her later."

Sure. "What am I going to do about tonight, Blaine? I can't stay in that house alone, it's too creepy."

"I don't mean to undermine your fears, Summer, but your Aunt Ada lived in that house for seventy-six years and never once spoke of ghosts, goblins, hanging men or anything of the sort. I can't say as I understand what's happening, either. Ada loved that place with all her heart."

"I did not imagine the hanging man."

"Listen. Jesse says she'll spend the night again, and if you still feel the same way tomorrow, why...we'll get you a place in Savannah if it will make you feel better."

"Good."

Blaine pointed out the library on their way out of town. She would plan a research trip and look up any information she could find on the Woodfield family.

❋ ❋ ❋

"I, Ada Elizabeth Woodfield, residing in Bluebell, Georgia, being of sound mind, do declare this instrument to be my last will and testament... .I give all the rest and residue of my estate to my heir, Summer Rosalind Woodfield, providing she remain in residence at Tanglewood Plantation for the period of not less than one year."

"What?" This was incredulous. "What?" Summer repeated. "I would like to know *exactly* what's included in this estate. Are we talking about more than a falling apart mansion?"

"In plain English," Blaine interjected, "if you live at Tanglewood Plantation for the period of one year, not leaving for more than one week during that time, the estate—including the monetary inheritance—is yours. If you cannot fulfill this prerequisite, then the estate will be gifted to the Bluebell Historical Society, and all debts procured within that time period paid. It's quite a sum. I'm not disclosed to tell the exact amount, but if I were you, I'd stick it out."

"This is not at all what I expected. It's like I stepped into a giant cobweb the moment I walked off the plane." She was weary. It seemed years ago she saw the dangling body of Charles Woodfield hanging from the burnt fountain. Tears formed in the corners of her eyes, and she sniffled. Blaine was quick to hand her a tissue. He put his arm around her and she cried onto his shoulder.

"I'm...I'm scared to stay here."

"Let's find you a live-in housekeeper. Try it, for Aunt Ada's sake—rest her soul—and for yours. Give it a good old college try."

4

Once again, Summer and Jesse stood at the front doorway and watched Blaine's car disappear beneath the moss-draped oaks. Summer avoided looking at the fountain and closed the door immediately.

"I appreciate you staying with me, Jesse. I hope Blaine can find someone, quick."

"Me too. Otherwise, my boyfriend will have to start visiting me here."

"That's fine with me, really." *Just don't leave me alone.*

"What now?" Jesse asked, after an embarrassing moment of silence.

"As long as it's still daylight, why don't we take a look in the attic? If I'm stuck here, I want to find out who I descend from in the Woodfield family. Maybe there are some clues up there."

"That's a good idea, girl."

"You'll come with me?"

"Not without a flashlight."

The women climbed the two flights of stairs, passing through the nursery and Ruth's room to Evaline's room, to the attic door. When the expected poof of dust dispersed itself upon opening, they climbed the steep stairway, Summer in the lead.

"Have you been up here?" Summer asked as they ascended.

"No…and on second thought, maybe I don't want to. This is creepy."

The fading light of day filtered in through the windows. Summer pulled the string of the overhead light bulb and they perused the far darkened corners in the yellow glow.

"Wow, what a pile of junk. Look at this stuff!" Toys, trunks, mirrors, furniture, books, beds, everything imaginable to fill a house, filled the attic "An antique junkie's dream." Jesse said, and eyed herself in an oval mirror leaning against a wall.

"Let's get serious." Summer walked across the creaking floor to a small trunk resting beneath a window. "We may as well start here, the proverbial trunk of lost treasure."

The window faced the approach road. From here, she looked over the treetops to patches of the roadway beyond. A car passed in a rapid blur between the foliage. "It's a different time zone, between the attic and the road. Such a short distance, yet two different worlds." She felt far removed from Chicago, from the life she left but two short days ago.

The trunk was padlocked shut.

"Well, darn. Shot down already!" Jesse was disappointed.

"We'll take it downstairs and open it later," Summer said, scouring the attic for another target. There was enough to keep them busy for days, if not weeks.

Fortunately, a larger trunk, sitting unobtrusively in a dark corner, was unlocked. They pulled it away from the wall, and Summer sneezed as the lid clunked open against the floor.

"Wow." Jesse fingered the light blue taffeta of a gown. A black lace fan lay across its muted sheen.

Summer opened the fan, sending a poof of dust up her nose. "Achoo! Achoo!" slapping it shut, she was surprised that it folded so nicely. "It still works," she said sniffling, setting it on the floor. "Let's see the dress."

Jesse lifted the gown carefully, and found it to be in two pieces, a bodice and a skirt. The sky-blue taffeta shone duly through the dust, but, alas, moth holes and time had taken their toll. An overlay of black lace on the skirt nearly crumbled with its journey from the trunk tomb into the dim attic light. Beneath were more clothes, neatly folded.

"Look how tiny the waist is." Summer held the skirt for Jesse to see.

"Bet you'd fit."

"No way."

"Try it."

"You mean without an asthma attack?"

"Here." Jesse reached into her jeans pocket and pulled out a tissue. "It's clean, just in case."

"Shake the dress out first."

Jess took the bodice and skirt to a far side of the attic and shook gently.

Summer pulled her t-shirt over her head and stood in her bra. "Okay, don't laugh. I'm not endowed like you."

Jesse held the bodice out while Summer slipped her arms through the armholes and turned for Jesse to fasten the back.

"Hold still. There are a gazillion buttonholes back here and not enough buttons. I can just picture some big-fingered planter trying to button his wife up into this contraption. Oh, silly me, they had slaves for that! There." Jesse patted her back. "You're done."

Summer pinched the front of the bodice between thumbs and forefingers and pulled it outward. "Whoever wore this dress filled it out nicely. Not me, that's for sure."

"Now, the skirt. Darn, we don't have a hoop...or, do we? Wait, I saw a dress dummy back there wearing something mighty strange looking." Summer accompanied Jesse back to the corner where she had shaken the dust from the gown. A mannequin of undeterminable age stood in the shadows, a hooped crinoline tied around its waist. "Aha, view the relic!"

"It looks like it will disintegrate if we're not careful," Summer said, as Jesse untied the bow at the waist of the mannequin. As they lifted the petticoat, with it's expanding rows of hoops, over the headless dummy, dust found its way to Summer's nostrils, sending her into a sneezing fit. After a dozen sneezes in a row, Jesse handed her a tissue. "You need an antihistamine, girl, if we're going to be antique hunters."

Returning to their station by the mirror, Summer climbed into the petticoat, and brought the skirt over her head while Jesse secured the crinoline at the waistline.

"This is amazing." Summer was temporarily soothed from the busted dream of her new life in Bluebell. For this moment in time, she truly *was* a Southern belle, the Mistress of Magnolia, even if her antiquated attire was showing its age.

"See, I knew you'd fit, except for the boobs—but we'll overlook that." Jesse stood back and eyed her. "Wow, dust never looked so good," she said, handing her the black lace fan.

Summer stepped to the ornate mirror that leaned against the wall. She was speechless! She *knew*—she saw for herself—that the gown was moth eaten. She *knew* the black overlay was in shreds. She *knew* her small breasts did not fill the bodice, and yet, in the mirror, the gown came to life; the blue of the taffeta sparkled even in the dim light of the attic. The black lace overlay was now scalloped prettily at arms-length to the skirt, with nosegays of tiny pink roses. At her throat was a black velvet choker looped through a cameo, and the hands that held the black lace fan were gloved in white. The bodice, which moments ago lay limp across her chest, was now plumped with full, soft breasts. A chill ran up her spine as she dropped the fan and turned her back to the mirror.

"What's wrong?" Jesse asked, startled.

Summer turned again—slowly—to the mirror, afraid to look, yet needing to. Again, the dress was like new in her reflection, only this time a man stood behind her, his eyes locked on hers.

"Evaline", he whispered, and smiled.

Were he not the fine and handsome figure that he was, she would have run shrieking from the attic then, at that moment, but his stature held her; the broad shoulders, the chiseled jaw, the powerful arms—the familiarity! She stood momentarily enraptured by the vision, before the reality set in. *A ghost!*

"What's wrong, Summer?"

"Get it off of me!" she whispered, turning from the mirror. "Get it off...now! Hurry!" Her trembling hands tried unsuccessfully to unbutton the skirt.

"Hold on," Jesse said, and unbuttoned the waistband, then the crinoline, letting them fall at Summer's feet. The bodice was a different matter, since she had previously buttoned at least ten tiny buttons. All the while, Summer trembled beneath her fingertips. "What the devil is the matter?" Jesse asked, but Summer could only tell her to 'hurry...hurry...hurry'.

When the gown and its pieces lay crumpled on the floor, Summer stepped out of its circle and grabbed her tee-shirt, pulling it back over her head. "I need something to cover the mirror," she said, searching wildly through the opened trunk. "Here." She threw a long black dress in Jesse's direction. "Cover it!"

"You're creeping me out, girl!" Jesse caught the dress, and did as instructed. "Okay, now just what was that about?"

Summer stood by the trunk, a safe distance from the pile of blue taffeta and black lace. "Put it back," she ordered, motioning with her hands.

"Jeez." Jesse reluctantly picked the mess off the floor and threw it haphazardly into the trunk. "Help me close the darn thing...Massah," she added.

Summer gingerly lifted one end of the trunk lid off the floor, and Jesse did the same. The trunk slammed shut.

Summer sighed with relief. "It...it wasn't the same in the mirror."

"*What* wasn't the same?"

"The dress. It was different. It was *new*. There were no holes, and the black lace was all together—not ripped." She shuddered and placed a hand against her throat. "There was a choker around my neck with a cameo, and I...I had *boobs*."

Jesse stared at her a moment. "Maybe it's the lighting in here—or lack, thereof. I didn't see anything different in the mirror."

"I *saw* it, it wasn't the same, but that's not all—there was a...a man standing behind me. I gotta get out of here." She said abruptly, and headed toward the stairs. "I can't stay here. There's something here—something... something not good."

"Wha...? A man? I didn't see a man. Hold on, let's get that little trunk."

"I'm afraid to. I don't know if I should touch anything up here."

"Come on, let's take it downstairs where the ghosts *aren't*."

"It's not funny, Jesse. Damn. I'm still shaking."

Jesse picked the small trunk up off the floor and groaned. "This thing is heavier than it looks!"

Summer was already in the kitchen by the time Jesse set the trunk down on the table, where it landed with a thud. "Whew! This better be good!" She said, rubbing her elbows. "There must be a hammer or a screwdriver here somewhere." She opened and closed the drawers along the kitchen counter. "Come on Summer, give a hand."

"I don't like this place. I came here for my inheritance, and this is what I get, hanging ghosts and haunted mirrors." Summer leaned against the sink. "How will I stay here a year? This house hates me!"

"You really are shaken, girl. Sit down. We need some tea."

Summer sat at the table staring at the dusty trunk. "You'd be scared too, if you'd seen what I did. I'm afraid to look in there."

Jesse found a hammer and screwdriver and set the tools on the table. She put the kettle on and set tea bags and cups out. "Don't be silly. It's only a trunk, and I'm too curious to stop now. I'll open it, if it's okay by you, and you don't have to touch a darn thing in it."

When the kettle whistled, the teabags steeped, she filled the cups. "Here, drink this. Maybe it'll help settle your nerves." Jesse went back to work with the tools and opened the trunk by removing the hinges on the back of the lid. She looked at Summer. "Are you ready?"

Summer set her cup down and stood up out of her chair. With trepidation, she stood next to Jesse as she slowly opened the lid, back to front. She shielded her eyes against its mysterious contents, feeling silly, but helpless to act otherwise. In lieu of her recent experiences at Tanglewood, it paid to be cautious.

A few envelopes neatly tied in a pink ribbon sat atop the unexplored paraphernalia. The letters looked harmless enough.

Jesse gently lifted the small bundle out of the trunk. "My God, these were written to Evaline!" She untied the ribbon and counted three yellowed envelopes, beautifully addressed to *Miss Evaline Woodfield, Magnolia Plantation, Bluebell, Georgia*. She turned the top envelope over in search of a return address, but there was none, just a name, Robert Mason.

"Robert Mason," Summer said aloud, running her finger over the name. "This is odd." She took the letters from Jesse and filed through them. "The letters are sealed with some kind of lumpy glue. They've never been opened." The women looked wide-eyed at each other.

"Are you thinking what I'm thinking?" Jesse asked.

"I don't know...should we?"

Jesse set the letters on the table. "Later." There was more in the small trunk.

With new found courage, Summer reached in and pulled out a tintype that rested beneath the letters. "Look, it's Charles and Elizabeth together, in happier days, obviously."

"Younger days, too, I think." Jesse said.

"Elizabeth looks pretty here." Summer set the tintype on the table and reached for another one. "Oh, God!" she exclaimed, taking a few steps backward. "This is the man in the attic! I think it's the man in the tintype on the fireplace, too!" It was the same handsome face, the same strong square jaw line and high cheekbones. Startled, yet mesmerized, she ran a finger over the Confederate jacket that stretched across his wide shoulders and felt a strange tingle run up her thighs. Turning the tintype over, her stomach flip-flopped; written in dark lead was the name 'Robert'. She showed it to Jesse. "This must be him, the one who wrote the letters!"

Jesse reached into the trunk, pulled out a third tintype and gasped.

"What is it? Let me see."

"I don't think you want to see this."

Summer's skin prickled at the words. "Let me see," she demanded.

Jesse slowly turned the tintype toward her. Summer stared in shock at the image—the image of Evaline—a dark choker around her neck, looped through a cameo; white gloves, one holding a black fan; full breasts filling a bodice with capped sleeves, and a hoop skirt with a black lace overlay an arms-length down, attached with tiny nosegay rosettes.

5

The small trunk sat on the kitchen table—untouched—for three days. Summer tiptoed around the mysterious box, mystified, yet terrified of its contents—terrified of the tintypes of Evaline and Robert. How did she see the man in the mirror? He wasn't *really* there and yet she was so attracted to him. How could the mirror have mended the ball gown? How did the cameo appear around her neck? How many years had the letters sat in the box? Why hadn't Evaline opened them? Was this *her* trunk? Or, were the letters kept from her?

These questions haunted her throughout the three long days she spent unpacking and organizing her new life. She would stick it out…maybe. It depended on a few things, such as, the hanging ghost of Charles Woodfield. If he behaved himself, perhaps she could make it through the year. She would have to avoid the attic at all costs and broke out in goose bumps at the thought of Evaline's ball gown taking on a life of its own, not to mention the mysteriously captivating man in the mirror.

Blaine was still trying to find her a live-in housekeeper, Jesse continued to spend the nights with her, and Guy spent a great deal of time manicuring the grounds. She watched him from the balcony at times, as she did on this day. *He's so familiar.* She couldn't place him, but it was almost as if she knew him.

"Darn." She ducked her head behind the balcony door of her bedroom when he caught her looking again.

Twenty minutes later, she heard several loud knocks at the front door.

"Oh, hello, Guy," she said, feigning surprise as she opened the door to the grand foyer. The smell of him made her tingly. A red bandana tied around his forehead kept the sweat from his eyes, but his tee shirt was soaked. It smelled good; maybe not in Chicago, but here on the veranda it smelled darn good.

"Hello, Miss Woodfield. I was wondering if you had any ideas for the gardens. I'd sure like to bring them back to life. They were quite beautiful once."

"Would you like some iced tea, Guy?"

"Sure."

"Come on in and we'll talk about the gardens. And, *please,* call me Summer. 'Miss Woodfield' makes me sound like the next old spinster of Tanglewood."

It was good to have company. It was lonely in the big rambling house. Summer was nervous, too, afraid to look at the fountain for fear of the return of Charles Woodfield. She hoped Blaine would have a live-in housekeeper for her soon, but she had no place to put her. She needed to spruce up one of the bedrooms, but her recent experience with 'other-worldly' apparitions put a damper on her plans, making her afraid to spend any time in the forgotten rooms. She was plain scared. If Guy was not out there mending fences and grooming the grounds, she didn't know if she could stay in the house at all without a twenty-four hour case of the heebie-jeebies.

They sat at the kitchen table, tall glasses of iced tea in their hands. The small trunk sat between them, a strange centerpiece.

"That's an interesting thing." Guy said.

"You can say that again."

"Is it yours?"

"It is now. It came with the house."

"What's in it?"

"Letters. *Old* letters. And...tintypes." Summer shuddered.

"A lot of history, I guess."

"We—Jesse and I—found it in the attic."

"Anything interesting in the letters?"

"They've never been opened. We were tempted, but didn't."

"What about the tintypes?"

Summer rubbed her hand over the trunk's lid. With Guy here, she felt courageous. "Would you like to see?"

"I sure would."

She gingerly opened the trunk, back to front, exposing the bundle of letters wrapped in pink ribbon. She untied the ribbon and handed a letter to Guy. "These are addressed to Evaline. Do you know of Evaline?"

"No...I don't think so."

"She was a slave here—the daughter of Charles Woodfield and a slave woman named Jamaica."

Guy turned the letter over. "Robert Mason," he said under his breath. "Strange."

"What's strange?" *What isn't strange?*

"My last name is Mason, and Robert Mason was my...let's see...great-great-great-great grandfather."

"Blaine said one of your ancestors was the overseer here before the Civil War."

"Yes, he was. Mick Mason. I know overseers historically don't have a good reputation, but I don't know much about Mick, so I can't vouch for him. I know Robert was his son. My parents are gone, but they kept a pretty good family bible."

Summer lifted the three tintypes out of the box. "This is Robert Mason." Again, upon viewing Robert's face, that strange tingle crept up her thighs. Shaking off the sensation, she handed the tintype to Guy, but not without catching the resemblance first. Her flesh prickled. *No wonder he looks familiar!* The broad shoulders of the soldier in the tintype were duplicated before her across the table, as were the chiseled face and penetrating eyes.

"You're very like him," she said, handing him the tintype. "This must be your Robert. You should keep it." She watched the surprise in Guy's face as he viewed his ancestor for the first time.

"Well...this certainly sparks my interest."

"Maybe you want to join me at the town library. I'm going to look up records of Tanglewood and see if I can find out who my direct ancestor is, John or Edmund Woodfield, Charles' sons. It looks like you and I are in the same boat—the 'USS Missing Link.'"

Guy chuckled. "Sounds like a good idea to me. How about Monday? Why don't we do it then? I usually take Sundays and Mondays off."

"It's a date." Summer was happy to have a social event scheduled, her first as mistress of the manor. "Oh, you may want to see Evaline." She reluctantly looked at the tintype of Evaline, beautiful in the ball gown, the fan held seductively at her chin. "She's pretty, isn't she?"

Guy took the tintype from her and sat mute, staring. He laid the two tintypes together, on the table. "I can see why Robert wrote her letters."

"Jesse says Charles Woodfield treated Evaline better than his own white children. I don't think Mrs. Woodfield harbored any love for her, though."

Guy picked up the envelope she had given him from the stack. "Are you going to read these?"

"I'd like to, but I feel like a peeping Tom."

"If you do, I hope you'll share. This is very interesting." He stared again at the two tintypes, side by side. "She really is beautiful. Robert never married her, though. He married a woman named Julia. Evaline *is* very beautiful," he repeated.

Evaline was suddenly a great annoyance. Summer snatched the tintype out from under his nose and put it back into the box. "I want you to have the one of Robert. He most definitely belongs to you. Evaline belongs to me, figuratively speaking."

"We didn't speak of the garden."

Summer totally forgot that *that* was the purpose of this afternoon's tea party. "You're talented at what you do. Just fix it, the way you see fit. I'm sure it will be beautiful again." She didn't know a darn thing about plants. "I'm a city girl, no green thumbs," she said, flashing a double thumbs-up.

Guy laughed. "You're easy to work for," he said, rising out of his chair.

Shoot. That distracting tingle crept up her thighs again with just the sight of him standing tall and planted before her. She was disappointed he was leaving so soon. She would have to face the loneliness again, but she did have their library date to look forward.

"I'll pick you up at 9 a.m. Monday morning, okay?"

"I'll be ready."

✻ ✻ ✻

"May 10, 1863

My Beloved Evaline,

If only you knew how much I miss the sound of your laughter. How I wish to be in your presence again, to laugh at your little stories and to comfort you when Miss Elizabeth lays a heavy hand.
The war rages on, but it is a futile war. God cannot grace the South with victory. I pray the end to this carnage is near, so that I may return to you, my heart. I will return to you. I promise, my love.
Robert "

Summer sighed. Curiosity got the best of her. The letters she showed Guy that afternoon ended up on her nightstand, and she now lay in bed reading one. The aged paper threatened to tear at the folds, and she made a mental note to pick up sheet protectors in town. She wondered if any man living today could write such a beautiful passage. She would have to show Jesse in the morning. After all, Jesse carried the trunk down three flights of stairs out of uncontrollable curiosity. She would have to show Guy, too. Robert was his ancestor, and that ancestor loved a slave on her plantation. She turned out the light and lay in the dark thinking of love, and how it transcended time—how a letter such as this would turn her to mush, had she found it in her mailbox.

✻ ✻ ✻

"Evaline...my beautiful Evaline." He held her cheeks between the palms of his large hands. She felt the heat of his face close to hers. It was heavenly, this love; warm, deep, reassuring. She pulled him to her, their lips but a breath away. He had a unique and masculine odor about him that she couldn't place.

"It's been so long, my love. I could not find you."

"Mm?" Summer woke from the warmth and joy of her dream. Someone was talking. "Jesse?" she mumbled, opening an eye. It was still pitch black outside, as the slit in the drapes did not show daylight.

"Where have you been, Evaline?" It was as clear, deep and virile a voice as she had ever heard and the hairs on the back of her neck shot up in alarm. It certainly was *not* Jesse in her room at this hour!

"Oh, my God!" She sprang bolt upright. Someone was in the room with her! "What do you want? Who are you? *Where* are you?" It was a petrifying moment; alone in the dark with…*with who?* She was too terrified to get out of the bed, and too terrified to stay. Pulling the covers up to her eyeballs she tried to calm the violent trembling of her body.

"I've waited so long, Evaline."

The voice was beside her, now. She tried to whack it, *it*—whatever *it* was—with a fist, a foolish weapon that battled nothing but air. "Where are you? What do you want?"

"I've missed you so much, my love." A hand spread wide against the base of her skull and pulled her forward. She reached behind to grab the hand and, again, there was nothing but air. Still, her head moved forward, slowly, until her lips pressed against the invisible force.

It was riveting—the kiss. Her power of resistance was slowly diminished by surrender as the entity's lips traveled from hers down the tender stretch of her neck to the crook of her shoulder. *Swoon. I could swoon,* she thought, understanding for once the gist of the old word.

She felt her nightgown slip from her shoulders, then a hand on her breast—then two hands that gently pushed her back against the pillows. He was weightless, whoever—*whatever*—he was, and, as her legs involuntarily spread with ease beneath the comforter, his mouth—his voracious, luscious, invisible mouth—traveled up her neck sending shivers to her core. How she wanted him, but she could grab nothing of him, nothing to pull him to her!

"Summer? Are you okay?"

The moment shattered. He was gone—gone into the darkness.

"Wha..?"

"I heard you yell. What's going on? Can I come in?" Without waiting for a reply, Jesse entered, flipping the switch for the overhead light. "Are you okay?" she asked

"Jesus, Jesse," Summer said, squinting in the sudden brightness. "Turn that light off!"

"What the heck is going on? You scared me half to death."

Summer sat on the edge of the bed, her legs dangling over the side, her shoulders slumped. "Jesse, you won't believe this. I think I nearly had sex with a ghost."

✳ ✳ ✳

"The plot thickens," Jesse said, the following morning, gently folding the fragile letter and slipping it back into the envelope. "Robert Mason and Evaline; this little part of history I know nothing about. I didn't tie Guy and Robert together either, but now that you mention it, I can see the resemblance and, of course, the same last name." She took a sip of her coffee and looked at her wristwatch. "Don't look so glum, you were just dreaming last night. There's no such thing as sex with a ghost, and you haven't broken any laws of nature. Cheer up, your date will be arriving at any moment."

Summer was ready to run out the door when Guy arrived. "I hope I find some helpful information today." She was pinning her hopes on the library trip. "Guy, too. He's hoping to find out more about Robert Mason."

"Sounds like you've got a thing going with Guy. Tsk-tsk, the lady of the manor doesn't hanky-panky with the overseer's son."

Summer didn't know how to react to that remark. Sometimes Jesse was so sensitive that any reference to the 'slave days' set her off on a lecture.

"We must bury the past, mustn't we," Summer said, taking the letter. "Hey, why don't you invite your boyfriend over, and I'll ask Guy if he'd like to have dinner here tonight?"

"Sounds like a plan, girl. I'll check the fridge and do a little shopping in town."

Things were looking up at Tanglewood. The Bluebell social calendar had begun, and she needed to put the ghost business behind her. When Summer mentioned dinner to Guy, he jumped at the invitation. The thought crossed her mind that perhaps he was married, but she stole a glance at his ring finger on the way to the library and was relieved there was not a ring. She would take that as proof.

✷ ✷ ✷

"We have a large genealogical department," the librarian said, showing them a corner of the library where the genealogical gems were stored. "Much of it is donated by local families whose history dates back prior to the War Between the States. If you have anything to donate, we'd sure appreciate it."

"I'm hoping you'll be able to help *me* this trip around. I'm curious about my Woodfield ancestors."

"Oh, well, there should be plenty of information on the Woodfield's, since they owned the largest rice plantation in the area."

Summer was relieved. For a moment she thought she would come up empty-handed if nary a Woodfield before her had donated records.

"You might try the county clerk at the courthouse, too. They have a better collection of births, deaths, and wills."

"What about slaves? Do you have information on them?"

"We have an ongoing slave recovery project. Again, we depend on information contributed from families who have been in this area for the past two centuries. Most of our African-American population is descended from the slaves of the surrounding plantations."

Summer wondered if anyone had contributed information on Magnolia slaves.

"Look up the surname you're searching for in the card file there. That's where you begin." The librarian left them standing in awe at the project before them.

"The USS Missing Link is on a mission. Let's dig in," Guy said, pulling out the 'Ma—' drawer on the index file. "Mason...here we go. Mason-Dixon. No, I don't think I'm connected to that." He shuffled through the files. "Here. Robert Mason, MF 30098."

"MF stands for 'microfiche'," the librarian explained later as she led them to another room, where a microfiche reader sat on a folding table. After a short lesson in using the equipment, they sat head to head reading a February 1863 edition of the Bluebell Banner.

"Like a needle in a haystack." Summer said.

"At least the newspapers are only a couple of pages and not like ours today. I'm surprised they had a printer at this point; the South was demolished." Guy continued to turn the microfiche knob. "Here it is, under the heading 'Returning Soldiers'. Robert Mason, son of Mick Mason." There was no further mention of Robert Mason in the index drawer, so they moved their search to the Woodfields.

"This will take a lifetime," Summer exclaimed, fingering the multitude of index cards representing Woodfields. "Here's mention of Edmund Woodfield, another MF selection."

Once more, they turned the microfiche knob searching for Edmund's name, and found it under 'Soldier's Killed in Battle.'

"Oh, oh, it doesn't mention a widow." Summer was disappointed.

"Look, here's Arthur Ascot under 'Returning Soldiers'. He's related to Blaine."

Summer continued searching the wartime MF selections. "And here's John, fallen in battle. My hopes dwindle. Let's hit the courthouse," she said, grabbing her purse. "I want an answer—today! Maybe we can find some birth and death records."

✳ ✳ ✳

"I have a ton of Woodfield papers," the county clerk said. "Give me a minute."

"Could you bring 'Mason' files too, if you have them?" Summer asked. "Mick Mason was the overseer at Tang…Magnolia Plantation before the war. His son's name was Robert."

The clerk returned with a fat manila file, and a slim one. "It wasn't required by law to keep birth and death records in those days, but being that the Woodfields were such a prominent family, there is a lot of information on them, such as wills, a very good source. I found some information on the Masons, too, Guy."

They took their treasures into a room the clerk indicated would be free for a while.

"Let's do Mason first," Summer said, opening the Mason file. "The Woodfield file looks like a challenge." Three pages filled the Mason folder. The top page was the will of Robert Mason.

"It looks like Robert had some property."

"The same property I live on today. It used to be part of the Ascot plantation. As I understand it, Robert made a deal with the Ascots after the war to manage the so-called 'hired help' in exchange for a piece of property. It's been in the family ever since."

"He lived a long life," Summer said, pointing to his death date of 1898. Let's see, three children living when he died; Ann, Michael and Stephen."

"Stephen is my line."

"Wow." *How strange life is.* She came to Georgia to claim her inheritance, and here she was, sitting in a courthouse with a descendant of the plantation overseer, tracing their common ancestry! Yes, truth is stranger than fiction, and she was snared, hook, line and sinker.

She turned her attentions to the Woodfield file while Guy contemplated the findings of his ancestry. She wished she could take the Woodfield file home with her, as there were too many papers to view in one afternoon. She knew how to organize, though, having worked as a secretary all her adult life. Channeling her search to the descendants of Edmund or John Woodfield, she shuffled through the pages searching for those names in particular.

"Jackpot! It's a good thing the Woodfield boys thought to write wills before they went off to war. Looky here," she said, holding up several legal-sized pages. "The Wills of Edmund and John Woodfield. How lucky can I get?" She read a few moments then looked at Guy. "Darn. Edmund wasn't married; he left all his possessions to his father. I guess John is my man." She looked forward to studying the painting of the Woodfield children—especially John—when she returned home, now that she knew her connection.

"Well?" Guy asked, as she intently studied John's will.

"This doesn't make sense. I've read the will three times and John's wife, Mary, was his sole beneficiary. There's no mention of children. How can that be?"

"Let's look through the file, maybe the answer lies there."

After shuffling through dozens of papers, Summer closed the file. "Maybe I'm not a Woodfield? Maybe Tanglewood isn't mine after all?" Despite ghosts, moaning fountains, magic mirrors, and a dilapidated mansion, Summer was surprised to feel saddened at the thought of losing the place. "I think I'll have Blaine join us for dinner tonight. Hopefully he has some answers."

Summer photocopied the Woodfield and Mason wills. Over lunch at the very same café Blaine had taken her, she showed Guy the love letter. "It's beautiful, isn't it?" she asked, wondering how many times he was going to read it. "I want to cry, thinking of him returning home to find Evaline gone."

"It would be interesting to find out more about them."

"I was just thinking the same thing. Maybe there's more in the attic. Jesse and I should take another look around—if I can get my courage up."

"What do you mean by that?"

"It's spooky up there."

✳ ✳ ✳

Later that night, Blaine looked over John Woodfield's will as the group sat in the parlor over cocktails. "We'll have to trace the deed, Summer. Tanglewood has been in the Woodfield family since the early 1800's. It's never changed hands, that I'm aware of, but this is a bit of a mystery."

"Guess I know where I'll be tomorrow—at the courthouse looking up Woodfield deeds." Jesse sat on the leather sofa next to her boyfriend, Raymond Taylor. He was a tall, good-looking black man, a lawyer, with an office in the same building as Blaine.

"I just don't understand this. My father was a Woodfield. Ada was a Woodfield. My grandfather, David, was a Woodfield. Look at the pictures on the mantle. That's my dad sitting on the pony. Why would he be here, if he didn't belong? It's back to the missing link. Mary and John *must* have had a child. He's been overlooked, somehow."

"I'm sure that's the case." Blaine said. "We'll find him."

"I forgot to mention that we came across one of your ancestors today, Blaine. Arthur Ascot. He returned from the war alive."

"He did, indeed, or I wouldn't be sitting here. Arthur was my great-great-great-great grandfather."

"There must be a record of Evaline's child, somewhere too," Summer added. Especially since Susannah raised him after Evaline disappeared. Evaline and Robert were in love, and I wonder if her child was Robert's child?"

"A regular Civil War soap opera," Raymond piped in.

"All we need is for your people to have been slaves on Tanglewood, too, to complicate things further," Summer said.

"Nope. My folks are from Mississippi. I guess they have their own tangled webs back there."

"Good, one less problem to solve!"

Summer shoved the Woodfield mystery out of her head. She wanted to enjoy her first social event at Tanglewood. Tonight, she was the mistress of the manor, no holds barred. As long as the photo of her father stood on the mantle, she was surely a part of this place.

"Are you going to read the other letters?" Guy asked, as she walked him to his truck. The dinner party was over and the guests were leaving. Blaine's Jeep already headed down the drive. He left with promises to resolve the ancestral mystery.

"I think I may read another one tonight, and I will be sure to share them all with you the next time we're together." She hoped it was soon.

"It's been quite a day," he said.

Indeed. One day together, and she felt as if she'd known him all her life.

"I'll be back on Wednesday...the garden." He nodded in the direction of the overgrown bushes and weeds hidden in the dark of night, and opened the door to his truck. "It was a good day, Summer. I really enjoyed it."

"Me, too." It was no lie. She desperately searched her head for something to say that would keep him a moment longer. "Uh...well, I guess this is goodnight!" She turned to go but was stopped by a hand on her arm.

"Can I kiss you goodnight?" With barely time to reply, his powerful arms drew her to him and she was immersed in the folds of his embrace. His lips were at first warm and tender, then pressed harder and deeper as his tongue invaded the chasm of her mouth. His hands slid to her hips pulling her to him. The innocent tingles he'd wrought of her prior fanned a raging fire within, leaving her breathless as he stood back at his release. "I'm sorry, Summer. I didn't mean to be so—so aggressive! I'm very drawn to you. I don't quite understand it."

"Whew," was all she could muster, trying to regain her composure. She couldn't lie, she felt the same. "I know what you mean. I feel like I've known you a long time. Strange things are happening here, and I guess this is one of them."

"*More* strange things?"

It was bad enough he had to lift her off the floor when she fainted over the vision of a dead man hanging from a fountain. *How absurd!* How could she possibly explain Evaline and the man in the mirror? What about nearly having sex with a ghost? Would he think her nuts? She didn't want him to leave with *that* impression, and certainly not after that tantalizing kiss!

"Whew," she said again, ignoring his question. "I guess we'd better call it a night."

As Guy drove away in his truck, she turned to the fountain; it was unavoidable. Jesse was already in the house after saying goodbye to Raymond, leaving Summer to walk past the dreaded fountain alone to reach the stairs. She wondered if Jesse would hear her if she yelled. *Oh, but that's silly, I'm a big girl!* If only she could calm the goose bumps sprouting on her flesh. There was not a full moon on this night, and the only light came through the windows with the haphazard shutters. She would ask Guy on Wednesday if he could fix them. They made the place look creepy, and especially now, when she had to pass the fountain in the dark. She focused her eyes on the stairway as her feet crunched across the gravel. Her hair stood on end with just the thought of Charles Woodfield hanging from it, his tongue swollen and protruding...*stop it!* She certainly knew how to torture herself! When she reached the stairway, she lost all control and ran the rest of the way to the front door, ever fearful that something...something evil, was close behind. As her hand turned the knob, she heard it—the groan, the mournful groan that she heard the first night, only this time she understood..."*Evaline.*"

6

Still shaken by the cursed fountain, Summer laid beneath the fluffed comforter in the four-poster praying she could get through the night without the occurrence of another supernatural event. She did not mention the latest fountain episode to Jesse, for fear Jesse would conclude that she was truly nuts. After all, she was the *only* witness to the hanging ghost of Charles Woodfield, *and* the trick mirror in the attic. Could it be that her imagination had run wild?

"*November 1863*

My Beloved Evaline,

I fear that you do not receive my letters. I realize Miss Elizabeth's anger at my attentions to you, and I am suspicious that she intercepts them. You fill my thoughts, my heart, my soul, in every breathing moment and I want so desperately for you to know this.
I leave a thumbprint on this page. Press your thumb to mine, dear Evaline, and feel the love I send to you. When you are afraid and lonely, press your thumb to mine and I will be with you. Distance and time cannot separate us, for our love transcends the evil circumstance of our world. Wait for me, my dearest, I shall return.
                                                                Robert"

Summer stared at the faded thumbprint beneath Robert's name. Her eyes welled with tears and she wished for a box of tissues. It was so beautiful—the letter, the thumbprint, the *meaning* of the thumbprint. To imagine Evaline and Robert as living, breathing people in this place was difficult to grasp, yet here was the proof. They lived, they died, and saddest of all, distance and time *did* separate them. Robert returned from the war, and she was gone. How heartbroken he must have been.

Summer grew drowsy, her head molded comfortably into the fluffed pillows. She could not put the letter to rest, and especially now that it was safely contained in the sheet protector. Her eyes rested on Robert's faded thumbprint at the bottom of the page. The temptation to touch it was great; *but he doesn't want me, he wants Evaline.* How odd that after nearly 150 years, Robert's desire seemed timeless. He was waiting for Evaline, still, for *her* touch. Would it be a sacrilege for her to come between them, to taint the thumbprint with her own?

Yet, she wanted him. She wanted to feel the love and desire that seeped through the words he wrote on the fragile page. She wanted to be on the receiving end, for once, of something as timeless as Robert's love.

Temptation got the best of her. "Forgive me, Evaline," she whispered, and placed her thumb over the print that Robert Mason left for Evaline in 1863.

❉ ❉ ❉

"Get up now, Evaline! Miz 'Lizbet's gonna whup you good if you ain't der wid her breafas'."

"What? What's wrong?" Aside from a flickering yellow glow in one corner, the room was pitch black. "Is the electricity off? Did we have a storm?"

"I don' know what you's talkin' 'bout, Evaline."

The yellow glow hovered toward her until two black eyes set in white globes stared through the golden orb of light. She could smell the hot wax. "Who the heck are you?" Summer pulled the covers up to her chin and tried to appear calm—not an easy task considering the strange events that had occurred since her arrival. "Where's Jesse? What are you doing in my room?"

"Who is I? You lost yo' head, gal?"

Have I lost my head? Could it be another ghost? "Git!" It was worth a try. "Shoo!"

"Don' you shoo me, chile. You must be sick. Dis is yo' Auntie Ruth speakin'. Enough o' dis nonsense. Git yo'self to da kitchen 'fo Miz 'Lizbet come lookin' 'fo you."

"Enough of this nonsense is right!" Summer threw off the covers—thin covers, compared to plump quilt she remembered going to bed with—and stood. "What are you doing in my room?"

Funny, she didn't *feel* like herself. Her breasts felt heavy, and when she touched them...*oh my god!* They were huge compared to her normal A-cup size! "Wha...what have you done with Jesse?"

"You's makin' my hair stand up, gal. I don' know no Jesse and you don' neither."

Her rump felt different too. Her hands shook as she reached behind to touch her buttocks. Two perfectly rounded, solid mounds of flesh filled her palms. *What's happening?* She wished for this behind all her life, and here it was—in a nightmare!

"Jesse. Jesse!"

"Cut dat out, Evaline! You wants to get us in trouble wid Miz 'lizbet? Git yo dress on and git to da kitchen. You ain't too big for me to whup, and you ain't gonna like Ol" Mick beatin' you fo' not having Miz 'Lizbet's breafas' on time."

"You're crazy. I'm going to find Jesse."

"Who da devil is Jesse?"

"Who the devil are you?" Summer carried her new and strange body toward the bedroom door—or so she thought—and walked straight into a wall. "Turn on the lights!" she demanded, rubbing a rising bump on her forehead.

"I got dis light right here," the woman replied, waving the candle.

"Where's the light switch?"

"Da switch...? De only switch you be knowin' is da one on yo'behind if you don' git yo'self to da kitchen!"

This is a dream! "Wake up!" she screamed.

"You's scarin' me to death, Evaline! You stop dat right now, baby, you heah?"

"Wake up!"

"Jumpin' jehosephat, I don' know what you's up to."

Summer flattened against the wall as the strange woman approached, the candle illuminating the dark pupils against the whites of her eyes. "Jesse!" she screamed.

"Lordy, Evaline."

"Evaline is *dead*! I'm Summer Woodfield!"

"Sum...I never heard of no Summer Woodfield. What's you talkin' 'bout? Evaline ain't dead. Don' go scarin' me like dat. And, what's you doin' in Evaline's room if you ain't her?" The woman held the candle so close to Summer's face, she could feel the heat of the flame. "You don' sound like Evaline, but you sho looks like Evaline...'cause you *is* Evaline!"

The room fell silent as the black eyes peered into hers.

"What year is this, Ruth? Your name *is* Ruth, right?"

"O'course I'se Ruth. Maybe you have da fever...." Ruth put a hand on Summer's forehead.

"What year is this?" she repeated.

"You know what year dis is. Miz 'lizbet had dat New Year cel'bration. 1861. Don' you 'member?"

"1861? Oh, God!"

"I don' know how's you kin forgit. Massah give you dat pretty blue gown and you done gone to da white folks party!"

"The blue gown...."

"See, you 'member. Come on now," Ruth said, taking Summer's hand. "I don' know what's got into you today, but you gotta git Miz 'lizbet her breafas'." Ruth opened a door that led to the servant's stairway. "Git your dress on, and git on down der 'fore you have more trouble den you need."

This is a nightmare. "Okay...okay. Where's my dress?" She obviously had to appease Ruth, or she would never leave her alone. Surely, she would wake up from this horror any minute now and be Summer Woodfield again.

She followed Ruth and the candle to pegs on a far wall, where a dress and petticoat hung. The limp homespun resembled a potato sack. "I can't wear that thing! I thought Evaline had *nice* clothes."

"You's a strange one today, Evaline. You gots fine clothes when Massah let you. When he aint here, Mis 'lizbet don' want you lookin' like no more'n a plain' niggah slave. You know dat." Ruth held a full-length petticoat in one arm and the dress in the other.

"Without a bra?"

"A what?"

"You know, a bra—to hold these gigantic breasts up." She cupped the two solid torpedoes in her hands, which sent Ruth into peals of laughter.

"You stop that, chile!" Ruth laughed until she had to wipe the tears from her eyes. "It's a good day dat starts wid a smile. You 'member dat."

Summer took the petticoat and dress and waited for Ruth to turn her back, but she stood steadfast, holding the candle, waiting.

"Hurry up, now."

She pulled the nightgown over her head and was tempted to look at her new body, but instead finished dressing while Ruth waited.

"There. Ugly as all get out."

"Here's yo apron."

Summer cinched the apron around her waist and tied a bow in the back. "Shoes?"

"Ain't no shoes."

"Jesus."

"Don' be talkin' 'bout Jesus like dat."

"I'm ready."

"Follow me. I don' know what's wrong wid you today."

Treacherous! It was unimaginable how anyone thought the narrow, circular stairway was wide enough, or safe enough for the servants to manage in the dark—by candlelight, none-the-less. The narrow treads, spiraling downward under the glow of candlelight, surely were not made for adult feet, and it was all Summer could do to keep from toppling over onto Ruth. She braced her hands against the narrow walls.

"I don't have to bring Miss Elizabeth her breakfast on this stairway, do I?"

"Course you do!"

The thought was frightening. *Good thing this is just a dream.* "What time is it?"

"Sun gonna be up and Miz 'lizbet gonna be waitin' fo her toast and tea."

"I'd like to cram the toast and tea down *Miz 'lizbet's* throat!"

"Shhh. She gonna hear you! Dat woman gots ears like a fox."

At last, Ruth opened a door to a large room, separated from another by archways. It was cool and dank, their shadows cast eerily against its whitewashed walls.

"What is this place?" Summer whispered. Jesse and Blaine had skipped over this room in their tour.

Ruth stopped in her tracks, the candlelight glowing yellow against her dark skin. "Da basement, like you don' know. You gots to stop dis game."

Ruth opened another door and they were outside. Summer recognized this as the river side of the house.

"Where are we going, Ruth?"

"To da kitchen, where d'you think?"

A glimmer of daybreak sparkled on the river in the distance as they approached a tidy brick building, smoke blowing from its stack. She didn't remember seeing the building on the grounds tour, but followed Ruth through the threshold where a large black woman, her hair hidden beneath a bandana, stood over a stove. A white-haired man sat at a table eating from a bowl.

"Lucy, Evaline don' think she Evaline today. Don' know what come over her, but you gots to tell her what to do 'bout Mis 'lizbet's breakfas'. She don't 'member nothin'."

Lucy wrinkled her brow and glared at Summer. "What's yo problem, girl."

Where should I begin? She just wanted to get this dream over and done. Surely, she would wake soon, the sun would shine through the balcony doors and she would wake up in Aunt Ada's splendid four-poster. "Is Miss Elizabeth's breakfast ready?"

"Say dat agin."

"Is Miss Elizabeth's breakfast ready?"

Lucy's round wrinkled face broke into a toothy grin, and from that, a hearty laugh. "Hey, Pompey, listen to Evaline! She's talkin' like dem white folks up north!"

The white-haired man obeyed, raised his eyes from the bowl and stared blankly at Summer.

"See, I tol you she don' think she's Evaline today." Ruth said. "She don' sound like Evaline, but she sho look like her."

The kitchen door flew open, followed by a young boy. "Mis 'lizbet rung da bell!" he yelled.

"Good boy, Percy," Lucy said, looking Summer's way. "Miz 'lizbet's up now." She quickly set a teapot, toast, jam and a bowl of porridge on a tray. Next to the bowl, she lit an oil lamp. "You best get goin' now, 'fore she rings dat bell agin."

Summer reached for the tray. "Aren't you coming with me?" she asked Ruth, who in turn gestured at Lucy.

"See? She don' know nothin' bout bein' a po' slave today."

"How am I going to get up that treacherous staircase carrying this tray and wearing this...this potato sack?"

Lucy chuckled. "You's full of da devil today, Evaline!"

Summer followed Ruth across the lawn and through the basement door to the servant's stairway.

"Wait," she said when Ruth opened the stairway door for her. "Where *is* Miss Elizabeth's room?"

"Git off at the second landin'. When you open dat door, Miz 'lizbet gonna be waitin' for you."

"Ruth," Summer whispered at the first step. "Lift my skirt and tuck it under my hand, okay?" Ruth obliged, and she was able to begin the climb without fear of tripping over her hem. When the door closed behind her, it took every ounce of courage she could muster to keep from screaming her lungs out in the dark cylinder. The dishes rattled uncontrollably on the tray as she made her ascent. *Oh, God in heaven, wake me up!*

Her breath came hard as she fought to maintain her footing on the narrow treads, and she turned her head so that her heavy exhalations would not extinguish the flame of the oil lamp in the dark and sadistic passage. Her thoughts turned to Robert; *"When you are afraid and lonely, touch your thumb to mine...."* How she wished she could do so now. *Wake up!*

7

"Is that you, Evaline? It's about time!"

The voice startled her. She stood at the door on the second landing wondering how she could open it without dropping the tray. "Yes…it's me." She answered, not knowing what else to say. Perhaps Miss Elizabeth would open the door for her. Moments passed.

"Get yourself in here, girl, before I take a switch to you!"

Jesus. Balancing the tray on her inner left arm, she turned the knob. She was nervous—so nervous! The door creaked open, and she entered the room she knew just yesterday as a bedroom in desperate need of repair. Not today, though—not in this, her dream. On this day, it was pleasantly painted, the windows unbroken, the sills intact. The bed she slept in last night—until Ruth so rudely awakened her into this nightmare—stood in this room, polished to a shine, a lace coverlet rumpled at its foot. Summer wished she were in it and waking to another day as herself, instead of Evaline, the slave girl.

"It's about time, you lazy girl." Elizabeth sat at the dressing table, brushing her thick honey-blond hair. She was softer in appearance than in the tintypes, except for chilling blue eyes that glared at her in the mirror. "What are you staring at?"

Summer was shocked, yet she could not take her eyes from the mirror. She stood mesmerized by the reflection staring back at her; the dark hair softly curled around her face, a face the color of a latte she could have ordered at Starbucks. She moved the tray up and down, and the figure in the mirror moved with her. *I really am Evaline!* Gooseflesh chilled her, and she felt faint.

"Evaline!" The sharp voice of Elizabeth Woodfield broke the spell.

"Here's your breakfast." Summer held the tray out.

Elizabeth stopped mid-stroke. "What?"

"Your breakfast…didn't you call for your breakfast?"

Elizabeth stood up from the dressing stool. She was short, perhaps 5'2", and slender. Summer remembered later, the cold, blue, hypnotic eyes that came at her like a demon.

"How dare you speak to me like that!" Elizabeth swung the brush with a mighty force, hitting Summer full on the check with the back of it.

The pain was riveting, causing her to drop the tray, sending it crashing to the floor at Elizabeth's feet. To her horror, the oil lamp spilled and caught fire from the flame, sending a burst of hot orange up Elizabeth's robe. Despite the excruciating pain in her head, Summer quickly ripped the robe off Elizabeth, who screamed bloody murder. Summer had the fleeting thought that if she did not put the fire out, she would not have a future home in the 21st century. "Get something...a blanket...anything!" she yelled.

Elizabeth ran in her nightdress from corner to corner and finally returned with the rumpled coverlet, which Summer threw over the fire. In seconds, the room was full of thick, black smoke. "Get on the floor!" she yelled to Elizabeth, who was simultaneously gagging and screaming. Summer grabbed the hysterical woman and pulled her to the floor where the air was clear. Spotting an oval rug by the side of the bed, she dragged it across the room to the burning mess. Mercifully, it was thick enough to smother the fire. She lay on her back a moment, wondering when she would wake from this horrible nightmare. Her hands hurt. They were red and puffy. Would they hurt if this were just a dream? "I'm burned," she said.

"You insolent tart," Elizabeth coughed. "I should beat you for starting a fire in here."

"I saved your life." It was clear who the insolent tart was in this situation; the woman obviously had a screw loose.

"Don't talk back to me," she spat. "Wait until the master hears about this." Elizabeth was on all fours now, her long hair, parted in the middle, hung like a lion's mane to the floor. "Open a window and let the smoke out," she coughed.

Summer bit her tongue and crawled to the nearest window, a difficult task with hands tender and sore. As the window slid upwards in its track, the black smoke was sucked through the opening like a vacuum. When it cleared, the morning sun shone on a surreal scene below. The fountain, hideous when her eyes last saw it, rose from a clear pond, its branches spread beautifully across the water, bejeweled with pink bronze magnolia blossoms. The water spewed upward from its spout, sunlight reflecting off the fountain mist, creating a spray of rainbow diamonds. It was a breathtaking sight, peaceful, serene, so contradictory to the busy life around it. A few able-bodied men swung scythes as easily as if they were playing a round of golf; some weeded a fenced vegetable garden, some rode in an opened buckboard down the dusty dirt entrance road that was just yesterday, paved. The impressive giant live oaks which first greeted Summer on her arrival, stood half their size, not even meeting at the tops across the drive to block the sky. Dark skinned children laughed and shrieked as they chased one another around the fountain.

"Clean this mess up and bring Ruth!" Elizabeth broke the silence. "I've had enough of you for one day."

Summer was bone weary. When would she wake up? She didn't like this place, Elizabeth was wicked. This was her ancestor, and Summer *hated* her. She was confused and faltered a moment, feeling the burning throb of her hands.

"I'm going to sic Mister Mick on you for your insolence. Get out of here!" Elizabeth scowled. She was a sight; her nightdress singed, her hair hung in stringy strands and her face smudged with black.

Summer imagined that she, herself, looked in the same state of disarray, and felt worn and exhausted. She was a stranger here. This was not her world, and yet she knew no escape.

Before Elizabeth could bark at her again, the servant stairway door flew open and Ruth entered, out of breath. "The chillin' say der's a fire in here! Dey seen da smoke comin' out da window. Oh Mercy," she added, spotting the remains of the fire disaster.

"Get this cleaned up, Ruth, and get Evaline out of here. Bring me breakfast, and have Mr. Mason come this afternoon." She glared at Summer.

"Y'sm," Ruth replied, and cast a worried glance in Summer's direction. She bent to gather the charred remains, while Summer fought back tears.

"Give her a hand, Evaline." Elizabeth snapped.

Summer could do nothing more than hold out her arms, her swollen, pink and tender hands protruding from the homespun sleeves.

"Po chile,: Ruth whispered. "I'se fix you up when we's outta here." She gently laid the charred rug across Summer's arms, gathered the tray, lamp, food dishes, and told Miss Elizabeth she would return shortly.

In the darkened stairwell, Ruth led the way with a small candle balanced on the cluttered tray. Summer followed through a veil of tears. "I can't believe how cruel that woman is!" she sobbed. "Can't she see I'm hurt? I saved her life and all she did was yell at me!"

"You's a strange one today, Evaline. You know Miz 'lizbet don' have a kind bone in her body—not when it come to you."

They passed young Percy sitting against a wall in the basement, and crossed the yard. When they reached the now empty kitchen, Ruth set the tray down. "You sit," she ordered. She removed two bottles from a cabinet on the far wall, and proceeded to mix the contents together into a bowl.

"What are you making?" Summer asked, suspiciously eyeing Ruth, busy stirring the contents of the bowl. *Not even a damned hospital to go to for help.*

"I'm makin' de burn potion."

"What are you making it out of?" Summer wondered if she should be leery of the 'burn potion,' but set that thought aside as the pain in her hands intensified

"What I always makes de burn potion from, linseed oil and lime water. Stop playing dis game, Evaline!"

"I wish this *were* a game," she replied, and winced as Ruth smoothed the thin oily paste over her hands and forearms. "Looks like I'm stuck here," she moaned, as Ruth retreated with the bowl. Her hands throbbed, her jaw ached and she fought the urge to cry. "Do you have any aspirin?"

"Asprin?"

"You know, to kill the pain from a broken cheekbone, headache... burned hands...whatever else ails me in this god-awful place."

Ruth scurried to a shelf and reached behind a stack of plates. She returned with a brown bottle. "You take a couple swallows o' dis, and you's be feelin' good in no time."

Yes, that's what she needed—to feel good. This day, so far, was a disaster. Without question, she took two swigs from the small brown bottle and enjoyed the glow that quickly spread through her veins. The pain in her hands subsided, along with the throbbing jaw. She didn't notice Ruth busy at the counter. In fact, she forgot about Ruth, about Evaline...about the nightmare. She laid the good side of her head on the table and didn't flinch when Ruth set a wet cloth on her aching jaw. She reveled in a dreamy peace and drifted away.

✳ ✳ ✳

"What's happened to Evaline?"

A deep, masculine voice woke her. She could not place the voice, or herself. Her eyes were glued shut and she strained to open them. When she did, her head still flat on the table, she viewed a hat sitting a few inches from her nose, and beyond it, the lower torso of a man.

"Mis 'Lizbet give it to her good dis mornin'." Ruth said in the background. "Den Evaline drop de break'fas tray and de oil lamp starts a fire and near burned da big house down! Evaline save Mis 'Lizbet from burnin' up wid it, but God knows why. Dat woman's meaner 'an a meat ax. Poor Evaline done save her and what does she get but burnt hands and a black cheek. I jes don' know why God makes dis misery."

"Amen." Summer whispered. She gingerly raised her head to catch a full view of the stranger standing beside her. He was very sturdy; his shoulders broad and muscular, his hands large, made for heavy work. His face— despite her extreme discomfort—nearly brought a gasp. Never, in the thirty years of her life, had she felt such an instant attraction. *Masculine;* the word came to mind. No wimpy Chicago yuppie playing with his Blackberry on the subway. No business suited CEO wannabe sucking up to the big boys… no, this was a man, and by his stature, a man to be reckoned with. She knew who he was, the man in the mirror—Robert Mason. He was nearly the image of Guy.

He bent over and looked at her through warm brown eyes, dark hair falling across his forehead. "You alright?"

"I give her some laud'num for da pain."

Summer was speechless, captivated by his presence. *The man who wrote the letters!* "Maybe I'll live," she murmered.

He reached out and gently touched her wounded cheek. "I wish…I wish I could make it better for you." Contrary to the tortured love in the antiquated letters, Robert seemed concerned, but removed from his passion for Evaline. Summer was confused. *Maybe he doesn't want to let on in front of Ruth.*

"It will mend."

"I don't mean just that, I mean everything…your life."

But this isn't my life, it's Evaline's life.

The moment was broken, as Lucy entered with a basket full of produce. "Massah Mason!" she said in acknowledgement.

Robert straightened up and cleared his throat. "I've come to say good-bye. President Lincoln has declared war against the South."

Lucy and Ruth gasped, their eyes wide in surprise. Even Summer was astonished, only for a different reason; it was hard to wrap her mind around a war that occurred nearly a hundred and fifty years prior.

"You's goin' to war?" Lucy asked.

"Yes, I am. I came to say goodbye," he repeated. He nodded to the servant women, and turned to face Summer. "I'll see you again, Evaline," and, putting on his hat, he walked out the door.

"God bless you, Massah Mason!" Ruth called.

"Amen." Lucy added.

Summer lifted herself painfully off the chair. She felt old and creaky. Miss Elizabeth certainly did a job on her. Her body ached from crawling on the floor, and her hands were tender from the burns. She was surprised the hands didn't pain her more than they did. Ruth's paste was a miracle. If she were at home in Chicago, she would have run to emergency, and even then she wondered if the treatment there would have matched Ruth's fix. Of course, if she were home in Chicago, she wouldn't have had the altercation with Elizabeth Woodfield in the first place!

Standing in the doorway, she watched Robert walk out of sight around the side of the big house. It was easy to see how Evaline could fall in love with him.

"Don be lookin' at him dat way," Ruth said over her shoulder. "Ain't nothin' but trouble when a slave gal gots a fancy for a white man. 'Member what you is...*a slave.* Dat's how it's always gonna be, 'less Massah Lincoln set us free."

Summer made a mental note to somehow explain to Ruth that she really wasn't Evaline, and she, Summer, was really not here. This was a dream, and a bad one.

At that moment, Percy flew out the basement door and ran across the yard toward the kitchen. "Miz 'Lizbet callin' you, Mama Ruth! She's ringin' dat bell!"

"How does he know, Ruth?" Summer was curious how Percy could know anything, sitting in the basement.

"Dat's his job, to listen for da bell—like you don' know."

"Does he sit in the basement all day?"

Ruth looked exasperated. "In da mornin' he sit in da basement next to da bell. In da afternoon time he help Lucy in da garden gettin' things for supper. He ain't big enough for da fields, and maybe he be a smart boy and gets to work in da big house, or da livery when he grows up. I gots to go see what Mz 'Lizbet want now."

"But...wait! What do I do, Ruth? Where do I go?"

"Have sometin' to eat. You ain't had no breakfas' and now it's dinnertime. I'll tell Miz 'Lizbet you can't do no work today for a while cuz of da hands. She ain't gonna like it." Ruth trudged across the yard, Percy jumping at her feet like a playful puppy.

Without Ruth to guide her, Summer was paralyzed. This place was foreign to her. She looked like Evaline, but she didn't sound like Evaline and she had none of Evaline's memories. Surely, Elizabeth would question the accent and what then? She wanted to be Summer again—run to the safety of her old life, but where was it? She was trapped in this nightmare!

"How's dem hands?" Lucy asked, stirring a steaming pot.

"They're better, thanks," Summer sat again at the table, recognizing it as the one upon which she and Jesse ate their meals. Jesse had said she was 'comforted' knowing her ancestors probably ate here. What a shame this wasn't Jesse's nightmare instead of her own!

Lucy's pot smelled good. "Is this lunch? I'm starved."

"Evaline, git off yo'behind and git over here. *Is dis lunch?*" She mimicked. "Since you's special dumb today, dis here is dinner for da big house. Go to da smokehouse and bring da ham for supper tonight."

Summer felt her face flush. The last thing she wanted was to get on the bad side of the only people in this nightmare who were nice to her. Ignoring her tender hands, she jumped to her feet. "Where's the smokehouse?"

The looks of exasperation were becoming familiar. Lucy pointed to a door at the back of the kitchen and scowled. Without further ado, Summer crossed the threshold into a dark, windowless room, lit only by the daylight creeping through the frame of another doorway. This small room led her to the outside, where she stood bewildered. She dreaded having to ask Lucy again about the smokehouse. A gasp caught her attention, and turning, she saw a young black couple against the kitchen house wall, disheveled, and obviously caught off guard.

"You snoopin', Evaline?" the young woman asked, pulling her skirt down. "Don' you tell Mama, or I'll have yo' hide." She was a pretty girl with dark, sassy eyes. Her counterpart was a muscular, shirtless man and, by his demeanor, not at all embarrassed by the intrusion.

"Uh…I won't. I'm going to the smokehouse. Which way is it?"

The man snickered.

"Wha…? What's wrong wid you? You know where da smokehouse is." The young woman buttoned the opened flap of her blouse and rested her hands on her hips. "And why's you talkin' so funny?"

"I'll show you where da smokehouse is," the young man said, stepping toward her.

"No you ain't, Juba." The young woman put a hand on his bicep. It looked to Summer like a doll's hand against the massive muscles of Juba's arm. "She know where it is, alright."

"Let go, Cherry." He shook her hand loose. "You don' own me, too," he said, and motioned Summer to follow.

His broad, dark shoulders dwarfed her as she followed behind. She couldn't resist a peek back at Cherry, glaring at the two of them, and wondered if Cherry was a child of Ruth or Lucy.

"What'sa matter wid you?" Juba asked. "You don' sound like yo'self. You get hit in da head?"

"You might say that," Summer replied, remembering the hairbrush slamming against her cheekbone.

Juba stopped in front of a small brick building. "Da smokehouse," he said, opening the door.

Summer entered, adjusting her eyes to the darkness. She noticed Juba scanning the surrounding property, before stepping in.

"I ain't s'pose to be here. Ole' Mick find me wid Cherry, he'll whup me good."

"Well, mercies then, go! Go wherever you're supposed to be. I have enough troubles of my own to contend with."

"I miss you, Evaline. How come you don't like Juba no mo'?"

If only she had Evaline's memory! Did Evaline have a relationship with this man? "You go, Juba. I like you just fine. Now go."

"I ain't goin' til you kiss me."

"What?"

"Kiss me, and I go."

"Didn't you have enough kissing with Cherry?" Summer's nerves tightened. Here she was in a time warp, with a Magnolia slave—a giant Mr. Atlas—making a pass at her, and no one to help!

Juba put a huge hand on each of her arms and drew her to him.

"One little kiss," she said, closing her eyes against the absurdity of it.

In a fraction of a second, Juba's lips covered hers and he held her to him, rubbing her newly acquired buttocks with his large hands. His arms were a vise of steel. She tried to wriggle free, but was helpless to do so until he released her. This would be trouble if she couldn't get rid of him.

"Now go!" She was breathless. "Lucy's waiting for the ham and she'll come looking for me if I don't' hurry up."

"Now you got me all worked up."

The bulge in his trousers caused her alarm. "Go!"

Juba backed off. He opened the door a crack and peeked out. Without another word, he was gone. It crossed her mind that she may have caught something from that kiss, and she wiped at her mouth with a corner of her apron. She didn't know anything about these people, but she did know that Juba was kissing Cherry only a few short minutes before. Her new life was getting more complex by the minute. When was she going to wake up as Summer Woodfield?

Getting back to the business of fetching a ham, she was surprised to find several hams hanging on hooks suspended from the ceiling. With the heat of Juba gone, it was the first time she noticed the still and thick air in the smokehouse. Was the meat well preserved? So much had happened in such a short time, that it was only now becoming apparent to her the advantages she enjoyed in the 21st century.

She chose the ham nearest to her, and then struggled to get it off the hook overhead; it was a difficult angle for one of minimal upper body strength. If only she had taken advantage of Juba's height and strength while he was here! Finding a wooden box in a corner, she placed it beneath the hanging ham and gingerly placed a foot atop the box to test its strength. "Go for the gusto!" she said aloud, as she put all her weight on the box. This action placed the ham in front of her nose. With her hands on either side of the lump of meat, she was able to slip it off its hook. The box creaked from the extra weight, and she groaned, surprised at the ham's heaviness. It seemed a much longer trip back to the kitchen.

"Where you been? Miz 'Lizbet gonna be out here wid a switch looking for da dinner, and I's gonna point at you when I sees her comin'."

The wooden table, which only minutes ago stood empty, was now covered from end to end with food; pea soup, biscuits, corn bread, yams and roast chicken. "How did you do that so fast?" she asked Lucy.

"I ain't been sittin' on my fat ass all day like some peoples I knows."

Cherry, who was now busy cleaning the kitchen mess, grinned over Lucy's shoulder.

With two trays loaded with the afternoon meal, Lucy sent the two young women on their way. Summer followed close behind, taking advantage of the chance to give Cherry the once-over. She looked sassy, even from behind. A red bandana covered the bulk of her tight black curls. Broad, straight shoulders narrowed to the apron tightly cinched around her small waist. Her small waist gave way to hips that swayed an invitation to (Summer supposed) all the young men enslaved at Magnolia. She could see why Juba was smitten, and she wondered if Robert Mason ever gave the girl a thought.

By the time they reached the servant stairway, Summer's sore and tender hands were weakening under the load of her tray. "Stop! I have to set the tray down a moment!"

"Such a baby, Evaline. A spoiled baby, livin' in da big house. Percy! Git over heah."

Out of the shadows, young Percy appeared.

"Go on. Res' da tray on his head."

Summer stood in place, trying to comprehend the order.

"Go on!" Cherry yelled again.

Percy took the lead, and stuck his head beneath the overloaded tray, straightened his slender body to lift the tray an inch, which gave Summer a chance to rest her hands and strained muscles. He was just the right height, and Summer assumed Cherry herself used the child's head just for this purpose— only would never admit it.

"Dat's enough. Let's go." Cherry said after a few seconds.

The weight of the tray fell again into Summer's hands as Percy stepped out from beneath. She resumed her place behind Cherry on the dark stairway and was relieved when Cherry pushed the door open at the first landing. The weight of the food was straining her muscles to the limit and to drop the tray was a great temptation. The memory of the hairbrush cracking against her cheekbone quickly erased that temptation from her mind.

8

In awe, she scanned the room. It was surreal, as if she had entered the stage in the middle of a scene. The four women sat at the meticulously set dining table, dressed in unaccustomed refinement. She recognized Elizabeth at the head of the table from their dramatic meeting that morning. She now wore a dress of slate gray trimmed in purple, high to a neck trimmed in lace. Long pagoda sleeves covered white under-sleeves, while tiny buttons lined the front of her bodice from neck to waist. Her hair—hair that just this morning resembled that of a mad lion—was parted in the middle, pulled neatly to the back, rolled up at the base of her skull, and secured by netting. Summer did not recognize the three younger women, but assumed that at least two were Woodfield women. They too, were dressed in refinement, visibly covered from neck to wrist in paisley, plaid, and hunter green.

Summer followed Cherry as she crossed the room to set her tray on an ornate sideboard against a wall. The dining room was in much better condition on this visit than on her initial tour of the house. The furniture was polished to a shine, as was the wooden floor. The portraits of Charles and Elizabeth hung appropriately at the far end of the room, while the portrait of the Woodfield children hung directly across, above Elizabeth's head. Evaline's stunning portrait was not among them. The high dining room windows allowed a clear view of the vast yard, unobstructed by the haphazard shutters of the 21st century.

"War, war, war." Elizabeth's voice broke through Summer's study of the room. "What fools the Yankees are. If they spent any time at all dealing with the darkies, they wouldn't be in such a hurry to set them free." She glared at Summer. "Don't just stand there, Evaline!"

Summer chastised herself for jumping at the bark. The woman was insufferable!

"I can't believe John is going away so soon after our marriage. It just isn't fair. I hate this war business!" The young, dark-haired woman dressed in a green and red plaid, sat alone on the near side of the table, her back to Summer.

"Now, now, Mary dear. Surely it won't go on long. I don't want him to go either. I don't want either of my boys to go."

Cherry handed Summer a large tureen and ladle. The aroma of soup filled her nostrils, causing her stomach to growl; she'd hadn't had a bite to eat this day. Cherry nodded toward the table. "Go," She whispered.

The scent of rose water on the women intermingled with the pea soup, as Summer ladled the thick green liquid into each of the women's bowls. She was hungry enough to sit herself down at the table and eat from the tureen.

"You don't know that, Mother. This war has been brewing a long time," a fair-haired woman replied.

"She's right, Mother. How long have we heard talk of it? Now it's really happening. Arthur will be leaving tomorrow, too."

The short exchange of conversation allowed Summer to place each of the younger women; weeping Mary, who sat alone on one side of the table, was the wife of John Woodfield. The two women on the far side would be fair-haired Susannah, in hunter green, and Margaret, the dark-haired wife of Arthur Ascot, dressed in a bright paisley.

A sudden loud commotion from the foyer turned heads at the dining table. Men's voices filled the house and, shortly, they filed into the dining room, a white haired man, followed by three younger men, all dressed in riding clothes.

"Sorry to keep you waiting, ladies." The white-haired man bellowed.

The hairs on the back of Summer's head stood on end in recognition of the hanging ghost, Charles Woodfield. Her heart beat loud and fast in her chest, and she could only stare at her ancestor. How cruel was this dream! She knew the fate of half of the people before her, and none was a sweet death! Charles, himself, was robust and full of life, and yet she had seen him in his most grotesque and personal moment.

As he sat, he winked at her. "Hello, Evaline." He called across the room.

Summer could not avoid the look of disgust on Elizabeth's face. *If looks could kill...*she now fully understood the impact of that expression. She moved immediately to the sideboard where Cherry stood. *This is only a dream,* she reminded herself, and again accepted the soup tureen that Cherry placed in her hands.

"Go." Cherry whispered, and Summer set about serving soup again, this time for the men.

"I don't know what we should do with Evaline, Charles. She tried to burn the house down today," Elizabeth said.

"Do tell!" a dark haired man exclaimed, taking a seat next to Margaret. Summer glanced to see the man smiling at her. He was nice looking, in a boyish way. His dark hair was combed away from his face, revealing dimpled cheeks. *Arthur Ascot,* she surmised. It was genetics at work; he was so like Blaine!

"Really," Elizabeth continued. "How can we tolerate this insolent tart? I could have been killed in the fire!" Elizabeth rolled her eyes and touched a handkerchief to her breast. "She needs to go to Mr. Mason. He may be able to beat some manners into her, but I doubt it."

"Oh come, Elizabeth. You know Charles won't let Mason lay a hand to her. Send her to Royal Palms for a few days. I'll straighten her out."

Summer glanced again at the man, and he winked.

"I'm sure you would, Arthur," Margaret added, coolly.

With the soup evenly distributed, Summer returned to the sideboard, where Cherry handed her a platter of the roast chicken. She was hungry... and fuming! Elizabeth was doing her best to infuriate her—talking as if she weren't even in the room! She bit her tongue to keep from blasting the woman.

"I'll see Evaline in my study later," Charles said.

"And nothing will come of it." Elizabeth snipped.

"Let's discuss it later my dear, and enjoy this night with our sons. Tomorrow they muster in Savannah."

Summer felt Arthur's eyes follow her every move. As she served the chicken, she was startled to feel his hand caress her buttocks through the homespun frock. With great restraint she controlled the platter, fighting the urge to pound the man with it. *How dare he!* She felt her face flush and gave a quick glance at Margaret, who seemed oblivious to her husband's indiscretion, even though she was just an elbow away. The other diners did not take notice, either. *What bravado!*

"Massah Ascot have his hand up yo' ass?" Cherry whispered, when she returned to the sideboard for another platter. "He's a bad one, dat one." Cherry seemed much attuned to the doings of Mr. Ascot, and Summer couldn't agree more. Poor Margaret. Did she know what a scoundrel she was married to?

"Stop your whispering!" Elizabeth yelled across the room, causing all conversation to come to an abrupt halt. "I'll have none of this insolence!"

Summer snapped to attention, then hated herself for it. *'Ears like a fox'*, Ruth had said just that morning. Having to answer to the woman was a detestable predicament. The woman purposely harassed her, with no regard to the ridiculousness of her behavior. Cherry sent her off with bowls of candied yams and steamed greens, and again she made rounds of the dinner table, steering clear of Mr. Ascot's groping hands.

Later, as she and Cherry stood at the sideboard waiting for the next barking order from their mistress, her feet began to ache. She prayed there was only one day of this; tomorrow she would surely wake in her own century! Having time to think, in this state of inertia, she realized she was bone tired. When she thought back on the day—from the moment Ruth woke her with the candle—it seemed an eternity had passed. She pressed her body against the wall hoping for relief from the weariness. The buzz of conversation from the table lulled her, caused her eyelids to become heavy. The voices soon wove themselves into an abstract dream in her head as she drifted off into a state of blissful semi-consciousness.

"We'll have them whipped in no time, Mother!"

Summer jerked awake, realizing she had fallen asleep—standing up!

Edmund, a glass of sherry in hand, stood from the chair. "Long live the South!" he proclaimed, the glass saluting the air before him.

Summer felt such a voyeur into their lives, knowing already that there would be neither wife nor child for poor Edmund. He would never return home alive. John, a handsome man in any century, would perish in the war and his marriage would produce no heirs. *Heirs.* All of the men in the room, aside from Arthur Ascot, were dead ends. How could she have inherited the plantation if she did not descend from any of these people?

Susannah sat across the table from Edmund. She was fair-haired and blue-eyed, a mousier version of her mother. Little did Susannah know that she would raise the child of Evaline, the slave girl who served her supper this day. Susannah smiled when she caught Summer staring. "Please bring the biscuits again, Evaline," she asked sweetly. Summer felt an immediate kinship—alas, a kind voice from her gene pool!

Margaret Woodfield Ascot was rounder, softer, darker and prettier than her sister. It was she whose line would ultimately produce the dimpled man next door, Blaine Ascot. How she wished she was in the presence of Blaine Ascot at this moment, and not stuck in a time warp!

At last, the supper was finished. The men retired to the study, where Summer supposed she would be called later for her personal chat with Charles Woodfield. She stood mesmerized when the women scurried—no, *floated*—to the parlor, their hooped skirts bobbing gently from side to side as they drifted across the floor in a sea of fabric. *If they could see us now,* were the words that crossed her mind when the last peek of hoop disappeared behind the door. What in the world would these women think to see her in her *real* world, her *real* century, wearing low-rise jeans, a tee-shirt and sandals?

Summer was dead tired and ready for bed, but Cherry systematically stacked the dishes, making her way around the cluttered table.

"No wonder Miz 'Lizbet always scolding you. Ain't you gonna help?"

"Do they eat like this every day?" Summer asked.

Cherry stopped, and loaded a tray with dirty dishes. "I don know what's got into you, Evaline, but you better get yo'self back t'gether, 'cause I's gonna be sendin' you to Massah Mason myself if you don' get yo' ass busy." She disappeared with her tray out the door from which they had entered.

Summer commenced stacking the remaining dishes onto one corner of the table. A mess it was, indeed; spilt wine, chicken bones, biscuit crumbs, all manner of debris littered the table. She remembered there was no kitchen attached to the house, so all of the dinnerware would require a trip down the dark servant's stairway. Just the thought of lugging the dishes clear across the yard brought tears to her eyes.

Tears turned to shock when she felt a hand on her newly acquired right breast. Before she could let out a scream, a hand covered her mouth from behind. His breath came hot in her ear, and she knew it was Arthur Ascot.

"When you gonna come see me, Evaline? I got something good for you." His hand moved from her breast to her crotch. He was not gentle—so deceiving from the charming, dimpled smile. While his left hand clenched her mouth, his right hand groped her privates.

Enough was enough! She jabbed him in the ribs, hard as she could in her restrained position.

"You bitch!" he whispered, letting go.

"Keep your hands off me! I'm not afraid to tell Mr. Woodfield what you're up to."

Arthur was obviously stunned. Summer wished she had a photo of his face—the surprise in his eyes!

"How dare you talk to me this way!"

"Don't touch me." She backed away with the sudden realization that in his world, she was way out of line.

Mr. Ascot's eyes narrowed into slits. "You listen to me girl..." he jabbed an index finger in her direction. "You're gonna get what's coming to you and it won't be pretty." With that remark, he left the dining room.

"Oh, you's in big trouble now, Evaline." Cherry peeked around the door. "He's a bad one, dat one."

'It won't be pretty'. She was vulnerable in this strange place, and those words shook her. She was glad to see Cherry. "Has he bothered you?" she asked.

"Oh, he done bother me but good! I don' know why you don' remember."

Summer sighed. Of course she couldn't remember. She wasn't even born yet, and here she was stuck in a time warp and everyone looking at her cross-eyed because she couldn't remember a thing they thought she should remember. "Let's get this mess cleaned up and get out of here."

If Summer was tired before, she was nearly at the point of collapse by the time the dining room was cleared and the dirty dishes lugged down the servant stairway and across the lawn to the kitchen. She was ready for bed and could scarce believe Lucy was cooking again.

"I can't do this again," she whined, hands on hips, watching Lucy stir a big pot of soup. "I'm about to fall over. I need sleep!"

"Well who don't, girl?"

The trek down the dark servant stairway carrying an overloaded tray of dishes did not hold a good memory and she was not eager for a replay "At least let me sit a while, okay?"

Lucy nodded to the dark room that led to the outside. "Lay yo'self down on da cot a while."

Summer gladly laid her weary body down on the cot in the small, dark room. It was nothing more than a plank of wood braced on bricks and covered with a tattered quilt, but she was grateful for the solitude and drifted off to sleep. It seemed that only moments had passed before she woke to Percy standing over her.

"Miz 'Lizbet say you be up to da study dis minute! Massa Woodfield waitin' to see you. She say you don't get der quick, she gonna take a stick to you."

Summer sat upright and swung her legs to the floor. Her hands, which had recovered nicely throughout the afternoon, now felt tender again. Her head pounded at the base of her skull, and her stomach was nauseatingly empty. *What misery!* A desperate loneliness filled her as tears rolled down her cheeks onto the homespun dress. When was she going home? That she had fallen asleep and still awakened in the same nightmare, pitched her into despair.

✳ ✳ ✳

Her stomach churned with nerves as she knocked on the door to Charles Woodfield's study. What would she say? What would he say? Would he catch on to her façade? Should she tell him the truth...tell him the dismal future that awaited him? It was a dreadful state of being, to know the man's fate and not be able to warn him. She was powerful, yet powerless in her knowledge.

"Come on in, Evaline."

Summer closed the door softly behind her and she approached Charles' desk, carrying the oil lamp. She stood a moment, waiting for him to finish his task of check writing. She looked around the room that she knew as the library. The books were still there, only in better condition than previously viewed on her initial tour—at least they looked that way by lamplight. The room was comfortable and warm, a contrast to the empty, dusty shell she first viewed.

"How are you, Evaline? Were you hurt in the fire?"

Her eyes returned to Charles, who was studying her with blue eyes that looked lovingly at his favorite child. "My hands, but they're better now." She wanted to run around the desk and throw herself onto his lap—cry onto his shoulder and beg to be returned to the 21st century. He had that effect on her, until she recalled Jesse's tale of Evaline's child perhaps being fathered by Charles, himself. She stepped backward so as not to be within arm's length of the man. He seemed kindly, but was he an incestuous molester in disguise?

"Tell me about the fire, and how you got the bruise on your cheek."

Summer touched her cheekbone, and winced. "Miss Elizabeth hit me with her hairbrush." *No sense letting the bitch get away with it.*

"I see." A flicker of anger flashed in his eyes. "How did the fire start?"

"When Miss Elizabeth hit me, I dropped the breakfast tray and the oil lamp caught her robe on fire."

"Ruth says you saved Miss Elizabeth's life. Is this true?"

"Yes."

"I cannot see any reason for Mr. Mick to punish you for saving Miss Elizabeth's life. Can you?"

"No sir."

"You don't sound like yourself, Evaline. Are you practicing your speaking voice?"

I'm not Evaline, she wanted to scream. She wanted out of this dream! *Should I tell him the truth?* Charles gazed at her with endearment, his white hair reflecting the golden glow of the lamp as he waited patiently for her answer.

"Yes, sir. I'm practicing." What good would it do to tell him the truth? How could he believe a crazy story like this nightmare? It *was* just a nightmare. She would wake up soon.

"Good girl. You can go now."

"Thank you, sir."

When she opened the study door to leave, Elizabeth stood on the other side.

Summer avoided eye contact and moved swiftly aside as Elizabeth swooshed into the study. She closed the door behind her, leaving Summer the perfect opportunity to eavesdrop.

"I knew nothing would come of it!" Elizabeth's voice penetrated the thick wood of the door.

"She did nothing wrong. If you hadn't beaten her with the hairbrush, there never would have been a fire. She saved your life, for God's sake."

"She never does anything wrong in your eyes."

"I got rid of Jamaica—that's what you wanted."

"It's not enough. I want that bastard child out of my home!"

"She belongs here, and that's the end of this conversation."

"Oh no, it's not. You've made me the laughing stock of Bluebell, the way you fawn over that girl—it isn't natural. This conversation isn't over until Evaline is out of my house!"

"Enough!" Charles yelled. Summer yanked her ear off the door. "Act like a lady, for God's sake!"

Elizabeth yelped and Summer ran for cover, opening the servant staircase door and closing it, but for a fraction of an inch. The crack gave her a clear shot at the study door, which opened wide, allowing Elizabeth to float past the servant stairway, her face fire red. It sent a chill up Summer's spine to see her in such a state. Bearing the full brunt of Elizabeth's wrath that morning, Summer was not eager to be on the receiving end again. The woman hated her—hated Evaline—and she shuddered to think what may come next. Guided by the lamplight, she followed the narrow stairway to the basement, and back to the kitchen.

"I'm practicing my speaking voice," she said to the tireless Lucy, still at the stove cooking. Why hadn't she thought of it before? A simple explanation for a complex set of circumstances.

"What fo'? So you's can be a high-talkin' slave gal? Ain't gonna git you nowheres, girl. You's nothin' but a niggah slave like da rest of us. Massah Woodfiel' ever drop dead, you's better high-tail it over to Miz Margaret. Maybe she can save you from Miz 'Lizbet.'"

"Master Ascot may be a worse fate."

"Uh huh, Cherry knows."

"What happened to Cherry?"

"Evaline, how can you fo'get po' Cherry and da baby? My lord, you done practice your way outta yo mind."

"Refresh my memory."

"You 'member po' Cherry get caught by Massah Ascot on the stairway. He was hidin' in der like a spidah. Po' Cherry girl, nobody to help her. When he done wid her, she had a eye black as tar and a baby in her belly."

"Where's the baby?"

"I 'bout had it wid you, Evaline. Percy. Percy da baby!"

Summer was shocked. "Percy? But he's at least 6 years old! How old is Cherry?"

"Cherry 'bout nineteen, like you don' know."

"Master Ascot raped her when she was thirteen years old?" Between the gnawing hunger and this bit of shocking news, Summer was gripped with nausea.

"Ain't nothin' new for us women folks," Lucy mumbled. "I had my first chil' when I was fifteen, and den had three mo' every year after dat tils I got sold to Massah Woodfiel'. Den I don' get no mo'. Had 4 chillun by da time I's Cherry age."

"Where are they now?"

"Don' I wish I knowed. Dat massah mine back den, he was a mean one. Dey was his babies, but he sol 'em off…sol dem off like hogs." Lucy caught a sob in her throat. "He sol dem off one after 'nother, cause he had debts to pay. He paid his debts with my babies, and now I don' know where dey is." Lucy brought an apron corner to her eyes.

"Oh, Lucy. I'm so sorry." Summer moved to the stove and stretched an arm around the large woman.

"Can't go thinkin' 'bout it no mo'." Lucy wiped a last tear away. "If I thinks 'bout it, I can't live." She shooed Summer away. "You go sit girl. I got supper for you."

Anger crept across Summer's heart as she stared at the soup and biscuits Lucy set before her. She was half starved, and yet so sickened by Lucy's story, she didn't know if she could eat. What kind of people were the Woodfield's and Ascots? How demeaning for Arthur Ascot to grope her the way he did in the dining room. How demeaning for poor Cherry to be raped at such a young age, with no one to defend her. How heartbreaking for Lucy to lose her children. She looked at the big woman stirring the large steaming pot, beads of sweat shining on her dark forehead. Night approached, and Lucy had been standing at the stove nearly the entire day.

"When will you rest, Lucy?"

"When da good Lord calls me home."

9

The memory of the soft bed of the previous night faded into reality as Summer made a futile attempt to fluff the tired, flat pillow on Evaline's lumpy cot. The pillow stubbornly returned to its former state after a brief promise of comfort. One good thing, her belly was full after a hard day of labor. Lucy made sure of it, feeding her the thick soup of peas and ham bits, along with biscuits and jam. She laid her head down, giving a brief thought to bedbugs and lice, but was too weary to care. This was hell, and she was stuck in it.

As bone-tired as she was, her eyes refused to close and she stared at the pale moonlight streaming through the window. A scratching sound caught her attention and she turned her head toward the attic door—the door that lead to the frightening mirror at the top of the stairs.

Scratch, scratch, scratch...

Surely a rodent was trying to get into the room! She hated rodents, and just the thought of one sharing the room with her prickled the hairs on the back of her neck. *Damn.* The room was spooky enough with the candle casting shadows. The scratching only deepened her anxiety, and she wanted to scream—scream until she woke up as Summer Woodfield again!

Hold it together. She was disgusted at her weakening spirit. *I made it through today, and I'll make it through tonight.*

Scratch, scratch, scratch...

"Alright," she replied to the invisible intruder. Throwing the thin covers off, she took the candle from the wooden box that served as a nightstand and stepped to the attic door. Her own shadow loomed large and dark on the wall and sent shivers up her spine.

"Go away," she whispered to the unseen creature on the other side. She tapped lightly on the door. "Shoo!"

Scratch, scratch, scratch...

"Bold devil, aren't you?" She gingerly placed her hand on the latch, daring herself to open it.

Scratch, scratch, scratch...

She wished she had a weapon…a stick…a hammer…anything to give her a little courage. "Damn" she whispered, and quickly unlatched the door. Not losing momentum, she swung the door open and thrust the candle into the opened passage.

"Go away", she said, her eyes fighting to focus in the stairwell.

Scratch, scratch, scratch…

The sound was clearer now, and came from above. Gooseflesh crept like a rash over her trembling flesh. She raised the candle over her head, illuminating the stairwell until it stopped at a curious sight—hovering toes! Summer jerked the candle, feeling the hot wax burn her wrist. *Toes?* Not solid toes, but faded, transparent toes! Her entire body trembled now, as she forced the shaking candlelight higher, bringing into view a ghostly apparition; only one word came to mind…*Evaline!* In this terrified state of being, Summer stood transfixed,

*Scratch, scratch, scratch…*One hand strummed the wall like a guitar, while the other pointed weakly to the bottom of the stairs. Her mind raced to make sense of the floating apparition before her, but there was no sense to it; only that the figure was trying to communicate.

*Scratch, scratch, scratch…*The face did not emit expression of any kind; the lips did not smile or frown, the eyes stared—or seemed to stare—*through* her. Then, the unthinkable; the figure began to descend the stairs! With all control lost, Summer let out a shriek and slammed the attic door. Her feet flew across the room, the candle spewing hot wax before its final flicker into darkness.

"Ruth!" she screamed, reaching for the moonlit latch of Ruth's door, terrified to look behind.

The door blessedly opened, throwing Summer into Ruth's arms.

"What is it, chile?"

"Close the door—quick!" she screamed, clinging tightly to poor Ruth, whose balance was seriously threatened in this act of panic.

"Git off me Evaline, I can't hardly breathe. Can't see nuthin', neither."

"I'm *not* Evaline! Evaline is on the attic stairs—I *saw* her, I saw her ghost!"

"Shhh…hush yo' mouth, girl. You's gonna wake da devil, you keep dis up. *You's* Evaline, and you's havin' a bad dream."

"I can't go back in there, Ruth!"

"Well I ain't got room 'nuf in my bed for da two of us!"

"Come with me, Ruth. I'll get my blanket…I'll lay on the floor by your bed, but I'm not sleeping in there!"

"Oh Lordy, girl," Ruth mumbled as they shuffled their way through the pale moonlight of Evaline's room to the cot, Summer clinging like a shadow.

Later, as she lay on the floor wrapped in the thin quilt, her head on the flat pillow, Summer's fears no longer fell to the rodents, bedbugs, and lice, but to the terror of the woman hovering in the stairwell. It was Evaline—it was surely Evaline—trying to communicate, trying to tell her something, but what? What was she pointing at? Tomorrow, she would muster her courage and open the attic door.

✻ ✻ ✻

Free will—a luxury unknown to the hapless slaves of Magnolia. Sadly, Summer had to include herself in the lot. Ruth stood over the makeshift bed on the floor and welcomed her by candlelight to another grueling day of survival. When the memory of Evaline's visit came to focus, Summer realized that her investigation into the incident would have to wait, as much more important matters awaited her—Miss Elizabeth's breakfast tray, for one. She shuddered at the thought. What was in store for her today? She was at her mistress's beck and call, and any plans she had made for herself, such as investigating the apparition of the previous night, would have to be put aside. After all, she was without free will.

Lucy may as well have been a fixed statue, standing at the stove stirring large and steaming pots of whatever concoctions were called for this day. It occurred to Summer that she hadn't seen Lucy in any other position since her first introduction.

She plunked herself down at the worn table. "Any chance of coffee this morning?"

"Sweet Jesus, girl. You think you's one of da whitefolks. "

"It's too much to ask, huh?" she groaned. "I need coffee to get myself going. It's not even daylight outside."

"Miz 'Lizbet seen me givin' you her precious coffee, she'd have me at da whippin' post," Lucy grumbled, but shuffled to the table with a small cup in her hands. "Don' let nobody see I give dis to you. Don' even Pompeii git no coffee dis mornin'. "

"Bless you, Lucy," Summer said, and winced when Lucy touched her wounded cheek.

"Dat woman done got you good."

Summer had not seen a mirror since viewing her reflection in Elizabeth's bedroom yesterday morning. She didn't want to see one. It frightened her to view herself in this present state—a stranger—and yet feel so much herself inside. She took a sip of the coffee, nearly gagging. *Not Starbucks.* She hid her grimace. She was trouble enough, and Lucy was kind to pilfer a few ounces for her. "Is Miss Elizabeth's breakfast ready?"

"Sho' 'nuff".

Summer did not need guidance nor direction from Ruth today. She took the tray with the lit oil lamp and trudged across the grass and through the basement door. "Good morning, Percy," she said to the small figure sitting in the darkness against the whitewashed wall. Percy ran to open the stairwell door for her, and she rested the tray on his head long enough to lift her skirt, stationing it between her hand and the tray. "What will we do when you grow too tall, Percy?"

He grinned his toothless grin, and she saw that the telltale Ascot dimples graced his cheeks. *Do the women of the house not realize that Arthur Ascot fathered this child?*

As she ascended the stairs she was grateful that she knew what to expect on the other side of Elizabeth's bedroom door. Her nerves were calm as she knocked and turned the latch. Elizabeth sat at the dressing table brushing her golden hair.

"It's about time, Evaline."

The icy stare from Elizabeth did not unsettle her. How could it, after coming face to face with the transparent figure of Evaline in the stairwell? How could it, after the hanging ghost of Charles Woodfield, after the vision of a young Evaline dressed in a ball gown? How could this petit, vile creature rattle her? She had to keep it in perspective.

"Good morning, Miss Elizabeth." She threw in a curtsey for good measure and set the tray on the table by the window.

"You must have something up your sleeve this morning." Elizabeth viewed her suspiciously. "I'll keep my eye on you today. Better yet, I'll send you to Mr. Mick for instruction on how to behave properly toward the mistress of the house."

"Yes'm". Summer curtsied again.

"Little witch," Elizabeth murmered. "Oh, and Evaline, the Master and the boys will be leaving for the mustering this morning. Mr. Mick will visit for his instructions this afternoon. Please inform me when he arrives."

"Yes'm."

"Get out of my sight."

"Yes'm."

"Now!"

Summer left Elizabeth alone to her breakfast, pleased with herself and relieved that the drama of the previous day was not revisited.

A bell tolled as she crossed the yard to the kitchen, and through the mist of morning she heard a hum and then a melancholy chorus of voices in the distance. When she questioned Lucy, she was informed that it was the paddie hands, doing their own mustering for a day's work in the rice paddies.

"And, is Jamaica there?" she inquired.

Lucy's shoulders slumped. "Jamaica, she out der in da paddies'. She weren't raised no fiel' hand, but dat Miz 'Lizbet make da massah send her out da house...make her be a fiel'han. It's a sorry life for Jamaica. Your own mama, and der she is."

The morning passed in a flurry of work, while thoughts of Jamaica nestled in the back of Summer's mind. Ruth instructed her to shake the bedding—all the bedding of the Woodfield clan—which took a few good hours. She watched from an upstairs window as Miss Elizabeth, Mary, Margaret and Susannah bid the men goodbye. Summer watched forlornly, as she knew this was the last ride for the Woodfield boys. They would not return, except for Mr. Woodfield, who would return after seeing his sons off to war at the muster in Savannah.

In the afternoon, after dinner, Miss Elizabeth became ill with a headache and removed herself to her room with instructions to announce Mr. Mason when he arrived. Summer and Cherry cleared the mess in the dining room and lugged the dishes clear across the yard to the kitchen. Just as Summer sat at the worn table for a rest, Percy flew into the kitchen.

"Massah Mason is heah! He ride up on da horse."

Summer raised her weary body off the bench and trudged across the yard, through the basement, up the steps and opened the front door. He was a black shadow against the afternoon light, a tall and sturdy figure filling the doorway. Summer sensed the fear he evoked in others, just in his stance.

"I've come for my instructions," he said, his voice deep and dark.

Summer stood silent, awed by his presence. His demeanor sent a shiver through her and she couldn't help but visualize the agony the man had caused through his time as overseer. He stepped past her, into the doorway and removed his hat.

So like Robert...like Guy. His hair lay thickly settled on his head, molded by the hat he had removed. The dust of the road was painted on his face, moistened with sweat. The stubble of his beard bristled and reflected the light from the open doorway.

"Git with it girl," he barked. "I ain't got all day for you to gawk." With that he reached a large hand out and pinched the nipple of her left breast, not releasing it. "Do you need a lesson from ol' Mick?"

Summer winced with pain as he continued to apply pressure to the nipple. "Leave go and I'll announce you!" she exclaimed, trying in vain to wriggle free before he completely ripped it off her breast. *Perhaps, he would find pleasure in that,* she thought.

He laughed, and let her go. She didn't waste time making her way to the servant stairway. Elizabeth was primping in front of the mirror when she entered.

"Send Mr. Mason up," the mistress ordered.

"Up here?"

"Don't question me, Evaline! Send Mr. Mason up. I have a wicked headache, and I must give him his instructions!"

Odd, she thought, traversing the narrow stairway to the landing. When she relayed the message to Mr. Mason, he climbed the stairs, not seeming to need direction. Summer returned to the kitchen, and asked Lucy and Cherry if Mr. Mason always visited Miss Elizabeth in her bedroom.

Cherry grinned and Lucy raised her eyebrows.

"When da cats away..."Lucy said under her breath.

"Come wid me," Cherry commanded, and Summer followed, bewildered.

"Don't say nothin'," Cherry ordered, as Summer followed her up the narrow servant stairway to the third landing. When the door opened on the third floor, she followed suit as Cherry tiptoed into the nursery room and knelt to remove a small rug, revealing a split in the floorboards. Cherry knelt and pointed to the hole in the floor, indicating Summer to peek.

The creaking of the bed frame reached her ears before she set her eye to the hole. With great difficulty she muffled the gasp from her lips as she focused in on the vision below her—the prim and righteous Miss Elizabeth was giving Mr. Mason quite a ride! She sat atop him, her golden hair flying over her bare shoulders. Her corset lay on the floor beside the bed as she straddled him, still wearing the pantaloons that split at the crotch for relieving oneself...and obviously for allowing access to overseers!

Red-faced, she looked at Cherry who grinned from ear to ear. Cherry peeked through the hole in the floorboard, and put a hand over her mouth to keep from giggling aloud. This was obviously great entertainment for the girl. Summer was ashamed to admit that the sight *was* intriguing. When she looked again, Mr. Mason was groaning with extreme pleasure, his large hands on Miss Elizabeth's hips, as she hastened her actions, rising and falling fast on his torso, and moaning in pleasure herself. At last, the show ended as both apparently climaxed in unison and groaned loud enough to bring the servants running—except the servants *didn't* come running. They apparently knew to stay away when Mr. Mason was visiting.

Summer sat on the floor, and stared at Cherry, her mouth open in amazement. Cherry held a finger to her lips, a signal to hush. They sat in silence a few moments listening to the conversation below.

"...a good thing he went off today." Mr. Mick said.

"Not often enough," Miss Elizabeth replied.

Summer and Cherry crept downstairs and back to the kitchen.

"I can't believe what I just saw."

"Not that you ain't seen it before." Cherry said.

"I don't remember."

"Da massah ever find out, der be big trouble," Lucy said, stirring one of the endless cycle of pots.

✳ ✳ ✳

Later, in the kitchen, the women jumped when the door swung open revealing Mick Mason, blocking the doorway with his large frame.

"Come with me, Evaline," he commanded.

The mirth of the afternoon dissipated in a flash. Summer's heart crashed in her chest and then pounded in her ears. Did he know that she had witnessed his interlude with Elizabeth?

"Why?" she asked, and then remembered she had no free will and should not have asked the question. Too late.

"Don't sass me girl," he said, and jerked her off the bench by the neck of her frock. She stumbled, trying to keep from falling in the dirt, as he dragged her out the kitchen door. His hold on her garment remained tight and he didn't stop his pace until they reached the back of the smokehouse, at which time he slammed her against the outside brick wall. Summer fought the trembling of her limbs, but Mr. Mason had that effect on her; he was a frightening figure, the square set of his jaw, the bristled stubble of beard and the eyes—like a viper—staring her down as she cringed against the bricks. She cursed herself for remaining silent. She didn't belong here in this century, with this monster!

"Miss Elizabeth tells me you've been a naughty girl, puttin' on airs, talkin' funny. She says you set her afire."

Taking the blame for the ridiculous fire event got her dander up. "Miss Elizabeth set herself afire when she knocked the oil lamp off the breakfast tray." She was glad to feel a rush of courage, but kept her eye on the curled bullwhip.

"I can hurt you bad, girl," he said, waving the whip in front of her face. "Just keep sassin' me like that and you'll find out in a hurry."

Those words, coming from the fearful Mr. Mason, were unnerving, but she had an ace up her sleeve and hoped it would turn the tide. Did she dare use it? It was a gamble.

"You're not going to hurt me—not unless you want the master to catch wind of your 'instruction meeting' with the mistress."

Mr. Mason's chiseled face went limp, but only for a moment. He crossed his arms over his barrel chest and grinned. "Ain't you the smart little yella wench."

"Ain't I though," she replied, crossing her arms defiantly over her own chest, hoping to disguise her fear. "You don't touch me, and I won't tell."

"Ain't you never heard of accidents, gal? I could get rid of you in a hurry."

"But you won't, will you. My daddy sure would miss me, and he'd know who to look for, too." A double whammy.

Mr. Mason straightened his broad-brimmed hat and cocked his head to squint at her. "You show your mistress some respect...and stop puttin' on airs and talkin' funny," he ordered.

"I'm not talking funny. You just don't know proper English when you hear it." With that, she turned and walked toward the kitchen, feeling his eyes bore into her.

"Keep sassin', girl! I can still turn that pretty face ugly," he yelled, and cracked the whip so close to her head that she felt her hair blow with the breeze of it.

10

Supper was light, as the men were off to mustering in Savannah. Cold ham, soup, leftover from the midday meal, and fresh biscuits sufficed for the mistresses of Magnolia Plantation. Summer couldn't help but eye Miss Elizabeth during the serving of the meal, conjuring up the vision of her riding the sturdy Mr. Mason as if he were a treasured stallion. Summer snickered, thinking that Miss Elizabeth was quite a stallion in her own right, and one would never know to look at her, sitting daintily at her end of the table.

The younger women, Mary and Susannah, seemed restless and preoccupied, and especially Mary, whose love for the handsome John Woodfield shone brightly not only in her heart, but on her exterior as well. She periodically dabbed at her eyes with a lace hankie, while Elizabeth patted her hand and reassured her that the men would return in one piece.

"They are Woodfield men, dear Mary. Our men are strong and undefeatable, as is the South!"

Arthur Ascot had mustered along with the Woodfield men that morning, but Margaret had stayed at Royal Palms, tending to her own household duties in her husband's absence. Susannah was to join her at Royal Palms after supper.

"War is war, mother," Susannah said.

"I suggest you have more faith in our boys," Elizabeth snipped. "Your attitude will not help poor Mary here."

"My brother's lives are at stake and I fear for them."

"And I don't?"

"Of course you do. I didn't suggest that you were without trepidation. I just feel that we must prepare to face the consequences of war."

Susannah appeared to be the only Woodfield with any sense. As the conversation changed to dresses and parties, Summer's thoughts returned to Miss Elizabeth's secret life. How devious was Elizabeth to toss out Jamaica from the only comforts in her life, and in turn deceive Charles Woodfield with an affair of her own. Life was unfair, and for Evaline and the others, *without free will*. It was a difficult state of being for Summer to grasp. Jamaica certainly had no choice in her future, and Summer had no choice but to stand wearily at the sideboard waiting for the women to finish their supper, and for this nightmare to end.

With the meal finished, Elizabeth instructed Summer and Cherry to share the leftovers among the house slaves. In the kitchen, the remaining portions of soup, ham & biscuits, were divided equally. Summer, Lucy, Ruth, Cherry, Pompeii and Percy sat at the worn table in the kitchen and shared what food was left. As demeaning as it felt—eating Elizabeth's leftovers— Summer joined the others in gobbling the food like a Thanksgiving feast. Food was rationed out at Elizabeth's mercy and whatever they got was savored and eaten. It seemed to Summer that Lucy, in her position as cook, should be able to hoard plenty, but Summer learned differently. Elizabeth kept most foods locked in a room in the basement, along with cured hams, flour, rice, sugar and basically everything needed to sustain life. The key to that room was kept hidden from all eyes.

"I can't help but think on what po' Jamiaca is eating." Ruth said. We don't hardly see her no mo'. Juba say she jes' barely git 'round dees days, all worn out from da paddies. She weren't born no paddie han'. Don't know nothin' bout dat way."

"If Juba don't come to see Cherry, we don' know nothin' 'bout her." Lucy added.

"Der's goin' be big trouble if Mis 'Lizbet know Juba comin' here," Pompeii warned.

It was the first time Summer heard Pompeii speak. It was hard to guess his age. The only other time she'd seen him was that first morning, eating his porridge. He was wiry, withered, his eyes rheumy; he appeared to be quite frail. She wondered if he was married to one of the women, but knew the stares of incredibility she'd get if she asked.

"Don't nobody tell, and there won't be no trouble." Cherry replied.

The talk of Jamaica at supper brought a strange feeling of intrigue to Summer. She knew the paddie hands had returned from their day's labor at last light, and she had an urge to find Jamaica.

"Which cabin is Jamaica's? she asked, when the last supper dish was dried and put away in the cupboard.

"What's you thinkin'? Lucy's black eyes narrowed into slits behind her chubby cheeks.

"I'm going to visit my...my mother."

"Mis 'Lizbet ain't gonna like dat one bit."

"Miss Elizabeth doesn't have to know. I want to see Jamaica. Which cabin is hers?"

Lucy stared at her.

"You're thinking I should know which cabin, aren't you? Well, I don't know and I can't explain why so you'd understand. I just don't know which cabin it is. Help me, would you? I think there are nine cabins, so which one is hers?"

"You sho *don't* know! You think Miss 'Lizbet let Jamaica have one o'dem cabins by da big house? No ma'am. Mis 'Lizbet send po' Jamaica to da River Row. Paddie han's live der."

Summer opened the door into the night. The air was heavy and damp, pregnant with the sounds of summer. "Well, I'll need a lantern then," she said, staring into the darkness and fighting the gooseflesh that prickled her arm. She never did like wandering around outside in the dark. Thoughts of Bruno loomed in recent memory, and she wondered how far down to the river she had to go. Blaine hadn't mentioned cabins by the river. "You'll have to tell me where it is. Is there any food I can take her?"

"One ol' biscuit," Lucy said, removing a brick from the fireplace wall and retrieving a biscuit from the hidden spot. She wrapped it in a rag. "I'll go wid you part way, or you won't never find it, since you done lost yo' mind." She lit two oil lamps, handing one to Summer.

Summer followed Lucy toward the river, and they cut off onto a pathway to the right before they reached the riverbank. Either side of the path was thick with azalea bushes in dire need of a trim before they closed the path off entirely. Lucy stopped, and ahead in the lantern light a small footbridge was visible.

"Follow dat to de other side. Stay on de path and you come to da Row." Lucy turned and headed back to the kitchen, leaving her alone with the night. She shuddered against the creepiness of the situation, but crossed the bridge and followed the path to the left. Before long, she caught a glimmer of campfires through the brush and heard voices in the distance. Coming out into the clearing, she was astounded at the settlement that lay before her; the small cabins were made of wood, not tabby like the others, and lined a dusty and narrow road. Nearly each shanty had a campfire in front, and by the firelight, she could see the cabins were thinly whitewashed, the wash having worn through. Porches were non-existent, with doorways only a few inches off the ground. The cabins stood close together—ten feet apart, perhaps—as if the builder wanted to cram as many dwellings as he could into the given area. She reminded herself that she didn't need to be afraid, these were *her* people—Evaline's people—and Evaline had come to see her mother.

It occurred to her that she should probably know the names of the men and women who stared at her as she approached River Row. Nobody called out to her. Men and women, both, either sat on a crudely hewn chair or barrel, or stood alongside their campfire and watched her pass. The settlement was a dismal and shabby disgrace. Even in her potato sack garment, she felt well dressed compared to the inhabitants of the Row.

"I've come to see Jamaica," she called to a couple who stood by the first cabin. They were unresponsive, their impassive and watery eyes emitting neither recognition nor interest as she passed.

"I've come to see Jamaica!" she called louder, hoping that Evaline's mother would hear the call. A woman at the second house pointed to the end of the row.

"She down der," the woman said, stirring a pot suspended over her fire.

Summer continued down the road, catching glimpses of small children peeking from the doorways. Larger children filed in behind her, as she made her way to the end of the row. "Shouldn't you children be in bed?" she asked.

"Ain't had supper yet." The reply came from a barefoot boy, close to Summer's height. "You lookin' for Jamaica?"

"Yes I am. Do you know where she is?"

"You don't talk like no niggah."

"I'm sorry," she replied.

"Wha'd you want wid Jamaica?"

"Don't you know me? I'm Evaline. Jamaica is my mother."

"No, she ain't. She ain't got no chile' talks like you."

"What's your name?"

"Moses."

Summer stopped on the dusty road. "Well, Moses, I'm Evaline. Pleased to meet you."

Moses smiled.

"Where will I find Jamaica?"

"Right der." He pointed to the last shanty on the right.

"Thanks, Moses. You go on home now. Go have your supper."

Summer thought it odd that a small group of people were gathered around Jamaica's doorway.

"Your Mama's dead, Evaline." Summer turned to see a woman standing in the road. The boy, Moses, stood next to her.

"What?"

The woman shrugged. "She dead, jus' today. We's gettin' ready to bury her. I'm sorry, girl."

Even though she had never met the deceased, tears filled her eyes. Her own mother, in the 21st century was dead, too. This was an opportunity to have another mother here, in this strange new world of hers. Now, that chance was gone.

"What happened?"

"Dis ain't no big-house-life here on da row. She weren't born no paddie' han. She talk 'bout you all da time, but don' see you none. I reckon' it done broke her heart." With that, the woman and Moses walked across the narrow road and disappeared into a shanty.

Summer turned to face the eyes of the strangers gathered by the doorway. She wanted to shrink back, out of sight. Did they blame Evaline? Why didn't Evaline come to see her mother?

The group parted, making way for Summer to enter the tiny shack. Inside, a turbaned woman leaned over a cot on the left. Shadows from the lantern danced against the plank walls, while faint embers burned in a fireplace. Above those, a cast-iron pot hung on a bracket.

"What's you doin' here, girl?" The turbaned woman stood, groaning as she straightened her spine.

"I came to see my mother."

"It's too late, girl. Da good Lord come to take her home."

"I didn't know she was sick…"

"Da spirit left her. She didn't want dis life no more. You tell her sister, Ruth, dat Jamaica is gone to rest."

"May I see her, please?"

The woman moved from the cot allowing Summer to lower herself to her knees. She studied the face of Evaline's mother, Ruth's sister, and Charles Woodfield's hapless concubine. How kind could he have been to her if he allowed her to be banished to a life of thankless toil in the rice paddies? She was probably Elizabeth's age, but worn, wrinkled from too many years in the hot Georgia sun, long days standing in the waters of the rice paddies, surviving the threat of malaria, surviving the deadly cottonmouths that weaved through the rice stalks. She was years gone from the big house, banished by Elizabeth, used and abused by Charles Woodfield. Her only child (*am I her only child?*) stolen from her. Is that why Evaline didn't come to see her? Evaline was a small child when her mother was banished, and most likely didn't even know her mother at all.

"Goodbye, Jamaica." She whispered. "Rest in peace." The crowd at the door had squeezed in to witness the scene. She rested her forehead on the cot. With everyone watching, she wanted to make a good impression—the daughter who never came to see her mother. *What a pathetic and sad life; all of Jamaica's precious years on earth slaving for others.* It was so shameful.

"You don't sound like no niggah slave," the woman said.

"I...I'm practicing my speaking voice," she replied, and stood to wipe her eyes.

"It ain't gonna git you nowhere, girl. Dat ol' hant, Miz 'Lizbet, she ain't gonna let you do nothin' but clean da piss pots. You's da Massah's chile and she ain't never gonna forgive dat man...and she ain't never gonna let you live no fancy life."

"The master left today with his boys. The war has begun, and the boys are mustering in Savannah."

"Da war?"

"President Lincoln wants to free the slaves. We're at war now."

The woman laughed. "I be long dead fore' us is free."

"Don't say that. You *will* see it. I promise."

"Evaline, chile', I ain't got da spirit no more, neither. Dey done yanked it outta me; dat Mason man, da paddies. I ain't got nothin' left but da good Lord to call me home along wid Jamaica here."

"Don't give up hope. I'm telling you, it *will happen.*"

The moment was pierced by a shrill voice calling for Evaline; a stark and frantic sound breaking the moment. She was angry at its intrusion.

"Evaline!" The voice grew louder.

Summer left Jamaica's side and the crowd opened again, creating an exit path for her. Percy ran to the shack door, panting and glistening with sweat.

"Evaline...you gots to come. Miz 'Lizbet done lost her head. She callin' for you...and she don' sound happy."

Summer glanced at the turbaned woman. "I've got to go now, but I'll be back."

"Don' come back. Yo mama's gone and you don' belong here on da row."

Summer left the death scene behind and trotted the dusty road after Percy, who was a good fifteen feet ahead of her.

"Come on," he called, "we gots to go fast!"

When they reached the riverbank, Summer called a halt to the foot race. "Stop, Percy! Miss Elizabeth will have to wait like any other normal human being."

"Huh?"

She realized she had forgotten the lantern, but the moon had risen casting a silvery shimmer on the river and on the boy.

"Stay put," she ordered, as she approached him. "Now, what's got her majesty's nose out of joint?"

"Can't you talk like you used to, Evaline? I don' understand nothin' you's sayin'."

"Of course I can," she said, rustling his curly head, and he smiled in the moonlight. "Now, what is Miss Elizabeth freaking out over now?"

"Huh?"

"What has Miss Elizabeth so upset?"

"I don' know, but hers hollerin' in her room and Auntie Ruth say you better get yo'self over der right dis minute."

✴ ✴ ✴

Her hand quivered slightly, allowing hot wax to drip and harden on her mocha skin. Candles were dangerous in the stairway and she didn't like to use them. She would have to remember to retrieve the lantern at the next opportunity, or send Percy for it.

"Come in." Elizabeth commanded from the other side of the closed door. Summer turned the doorknob. She had to admit she was nervous about this encounter. She took a breath and pushed the door open.

"Yes Ma'am. You called for me?"

Elizabeth glared at her and paced the length of the room. "Close the door."

Summer obliged and stood erect, waiting silently.

At last, Elizabeth approached, her eyes disappearing into a foreboding squint. "You bitch," she hissed. "Now you spy on me!"

The candle flickered in the heat of Elizabeth's breath. Summer prayed there would not be a fire mishap.

"It's not enough that you have ruined my life—you and your whore mother—but now you spy!"

"I beg your pardon?"

"*I beg your pardon*," Elizabeth mimicked. "Stop the nonsense! Stop speaking like that!" Her eyes exploded from the hateful squint into a burst of blue ice, wide, cold and condemning. Summer expected at any moment for Elizabeth to take a punch at her, and she was ready. The woman was *not* going to strike her again—not if she could help it.

Elizabeth paced the room, the tail of her white robe flowing behind her on the floor, her anger heating the atmosphere. Summer suspected this was about the romp with Mick Mason, and waited, having not moved from the closed doorway. Her mind raced for a response. She could not—would not—let this woman get the best of her.

Elizabeth stopped at the dark window of her room, and turned. "I swear, Evaline...I swear that if you ever breath a word to the master about what you saw—what you saw between Mr. Mason and myself—I will personally see to it that you do not live to take another breath. Not one word, do you hear me?"

Tongue-tied, Summer shuffled her feet as if to fill the empty silence. The dual identities of Elizabeth Woodfield were to the extreme; the demure plantation mistress was the polar opposite of the seething creature who stood before her at this moment.

"Answer me!"

"I'll promise if you promise me that you will let up on Cherry and Juba."

Elizabeth was taken aback by the remark, but only momentarily. She marched toward Summer with a face scarlet in anger. "What's this? The whore's daughter is telling me what to do?"

Summer determined that if she could stand up to the intimidating Mr. Mason, then surely she could handle this stressful moment! She straightened her back and looked the crazed woman in the eye.

"Jama...my mother is dead and I'll thank you not to speak badly of her!"

Elizabeth broke out into an exaggerated laugh. "Dead? At last!"

"She was worth more than you any day. My father thought so."

Elizabeth's arms shot to her sides like steel rods. In the flash of a second her face bunched into a ball of wrinkled flesh, swallowing her eyes into the fold. Her small feet pounded the floor in a frenzied staccato while guttural rumblings escalated to a piercing scream. The fine hairs on the back of Summer's neck prickled. *Like a horror movie*, she thought, and tried to push that thought out of her head before it set off an internal panic button. Then, like magic, the scream ended, the scrunched ball of a face unfolded and Elizabeth returned to her more earthly appearance, much to Summer's relief. It was far easier to contend with her in this natural state.

"Get out!" Elizabeth screamed, and Summer complied.

The candle shook in her hand as she made her way down the treacherous stairway. Instead of heading to her room on the third floor, she needed to talk with Lucy or Cherry about the incident...especially Cherry. Heaven forbid Mick Mason should learn of her as an accomplice to the bedroom scene! Summer questioned whether she was triumphant in the encounter with the Elizabeth or not. She didn't have the answer, but she was proud that she did not collapse or buckle under due to Elizabeth's extreme behavior. She hoped Lucy and Cherry were still in the kitchen. It then dawned on her that she didn't know where they slept. Ruth was probably snug in her cot on the third floor of the big house, but where did the others sleep?

As she entered the kitchen she was relieved to see Lucy's backside leaning over the table...but something was wrong. Sobs came from the other side of Lucy's form, as she rounded the large woman, she realized it was Cherry, sobbing. Summer gasped at the sight of Cherry's pretty face, her left eye purple and swollen against her dark skin, with blood leaking from a cut on her bottom lip.

"My God! What's happened?" The thought crossed her mind that Mick Mason had discovered Cherry's part in the spying incident...but how?

"I want to kill dat man," Lucy growled.

"What man? What's happened?" Summer was terrified that she had somehow implicated Cherry.

"Massah Mason," Cherry howled through her bleeding lip. "He done caught me 'n Juba by da smokehouse. Oh Juba!" she wailed, laying her head on the table.

"Where's Juba? What's happened to Juba?"

Lucy looked ready to kill, and she shuddered against the hate brewing from beneath the dark brow. *This is how Elizabeth looks at me.* The look could not be shrugged off, and Summer realized with great clarity that Elizabeth could and would have her killed—make it look like an accident—and no one the wiser except for the slaves. She shook herself back to the moment as Cherry began to speak between the sobs.

"Massah Mason, he come on us at da smokehouse. He take dat bullwhip and lash at us like da devil himself! He crack dat whip and get poor Juba in de back. Po' Juba, he run off and Massah Mason turn on me with dat whip and look what he done!" Cherry turned on the bench, exposing her backside to Summer. She opened her torn and bloody blouse to reveal a deep slash running across her right shoulder blade.

"Jesus", Summer swore under her breath and felt herself go faint. She sat across the table from Cherry to keep from hitting the floor. Blood and battering were not something she was familiar with.

"Leave dat down," Lucy said and went to her cabinet returning with a wet rag and the brown bottle that had relieved Summer's pain from the burned hands. She gave Cherry a spoonful of the amber liquid and then dabbed at the slice across her shoulder with the wet rag. Cherry winced and the sobs began again.

"Where is Mr. Mason now? Where is Juba?"

"We don' know," Lucy said. "It ain't gon' be good for po' Juba if he get caught."

Lucy's remark sparked a howl from Cherry's swollen lips.

"What is Mr. Mason's objection to you and Juba being together?"

"Can't nobody be wid nobody less Miz 'Lisbet say so. She don' want me to have no man...leastways not Juba," Cherry moaned. "You *knows* dis, Evaline. She wants you 'n Juba be together. It be like a splinter for da Massa knowin' his pretty Evaline wid dat black boy."

"Po' Juba! Po' sweet Juba!" Lucy wailed.

11

Summer blew the candle out and pulled the thin quilt up to her chin, while Ruth snored softly above on her cot. She couldn't bring herself to sleep in her own room; she couldn't deal with ghosts tonight. The day was exhausting, as were the days before and, she assumed (should she remain in this time warp), would be tomorrow and the days to follow.

Earlier, in the kitchen, Lucy answered the question of where she and Cherry slept; Lucy slept on the hard cot that sat on bricks in the back room of the kitchen, while Cherry and Percy slept beside her on the floor. Pompeii was in charge of the horses and slept in the barn. The years of listening to her parents brag of the grand plantation took on a darker side in this, her new life. In reality, the grand plantation was built on the misery of others. Surely her parents had ignored the fact, but she was trapped in the nightmare of living with those faces of misery. *They* had names. *They* had lives (miserable as those lives were), and oh, how *they* suffered!

※ ※ ※

Morning came abruptly, with Ruth accidently stepping on her while getting out of bed on her way to the chamber pot, a stinky and unpleasant reality of life in a house without modern convenience.

"Evaline!" she scolded. "You gots to go to yo' own bed tonight. You scared da devil outta me!"

My own bed. Her own bed was now occupied by the evil Miss Elizabeth, and she had no clue as to how she would get it back—*if* she got it back. With those bothersome thoughts she lifted herself off the floor, the memory of the previous night trickling in to dim any optimism that should come with a new dawn. She sighed heavily and trudged to her turn at the chamber pot. *Oh for a flush toilet!* She wondered if it was her turn to empty the darn thing.

Summer kept mum about the incident with Cherry and Juba. Best to let Lucy tell Ruth. She was anxious to get to the kitchen to see what shape Cherry was in today. Primp time was drastically cut short in her 19th century life. There was no makeup to fuss with, no eye drops to wake her sleepy eyeballs, no deodorant to ward off the day's body odor. Her hair required the most care, as her 21st century hair was stick straight and cut short. Evaline's hair was thick, coarse, long, and had a definite curl to it. Summer wasn't used to curls of any kind. *My kingdom for a hair band!* "Ha!" she laughed aloud as she tied a bandana around the unruly mop. "I have no kingdom!"

"What's you sayin', Evaline?"

"I have no kingdom, Ruth. I have a King and Queen, but I am a lowly slave trapped in a nightmare."

"You's getting crazier by da day." Ruth shook her head and began the descent into the dark stairwell with Summer following close behind.

When the women entered the kitchen, Lucy was at her station at the stove, and Cherry slumped over the table. She raised her tear stained, battered face, which sent Ruth into a ranting.

"What's wrong wid you? Oh Lordy, what dat wicket Miz 'Lisbet do now? Po' Cherry girl!" Ruth sat at the bench and pulled the sobbing Cherry to her great bosom. When Lucy explained the situation, Ruth wiped a tear or two away from her own eyes. "A sorry life, dis one. Po' chile'. What happen to Juba? Dat po' boy ain't gonna see another day if dey find him. Dey always find da run'ways."

Nerve-racking as it was, Juba's perilous predicament could not stop the day from happening. Elizabeth needed her breakfast, and Summer trudged the dark stairway guided by Lucy's lantern. She paused to collect her wits before knocking. She was in no mood to tangle with the woman. When she entered the room, Elizabeth sat brushing her hair. The women glared at one another in the mirror. Summer found it hard to believe that she stemmed from these people, and especially from the evil woman eyeing her with such hatred.

"Poor Juba," Elizabeth sighed, continuing to brush her hair. "If you had taken him like I wished, he could have been spared."

Summer's ears perked. "Where is he?"

"On the run, but no one escapes Mr. Mason. He'll be found by sunset and whipped to a bloody pulp." She turned to face Summer. "I can promise you that," she smiled. "Of course, he may be spared if you promise to take him. Only ten lashes if you say you'll take him and leave my house. I'll give you your own cabin."

What a predicament. Juba's fate was now in *her* hands, but Elizabeth was ready to barter.

"Spare Cherry. She's already been beaten."

"Oh, no, Evaline. She'll get the whip, too. 100 lashes for him, 100 for her—if you don't take him."

How casually the woman determined the brutal fate of others!

"*No* lashes for Juba *or* Cherry."

Elizabeth flashed red and slammed the brush onto the dressing table. "Enough! Do not forget who is the master and who is the slave!" she barked.

"Don't forget what I saw...*you*, riding Mr. Mason like a stallion!" Oh the satisfaction in those words; the satisfaction of watching Elizabeth's red face turn white!

Elizabeth rose from the stool and steamed toward her. Summer stood steadfast, the tray between them. "Remember the fire..." she warned.

Elizabeth checked herself, stared at the lantern a moment and backed off. "You take Juba and get out of the big house before the master returns."

"And?"

"And, what?"

"What about the lashes?"

The bartering was broken by a great ruckus in the yard below. Elizabeth and Summer, both, ran to the open window to see much activity with the slaves in the yard. Dogs howled in the distance, coming closer with each passing second. Chills ran up Summer's spine. She could guess the occasion; Juba had been found.

"Ha! There he goes—in the trees." Elizabeth smirked as she pointed to Juba's desperate figure darting in and out between the oaks, past the front gate and then disappearing behind the big house. "I told you he wouldn't get away! There's nowhere to go."

The howling dogs suddenly appeared into view with Mr. Mason quickly behind. Slaves scattered to save themselves, and the children, from the erratic path of his horse. It was a frightening scene filling Summer with sudden apprehension as to Juba's fate. It truly was in *her* hands.

"Save him!" she yelled. "I'll take him...hurry!"

"If you want him, you'd best run before Mick gets a hold of him. Tell Mr. Mason to see me before he takes action."

Summer set the tray down, grabbed the lantern and scurried down the stairs. She set the lantern on the floor of the basement and, seeing Juba in the distance running toward the river, she followed suit. Mr. Mason passed her on his horse, which grunted in labored snorts with each pounding of a hoof.

The howling dogs followed, sending a rod of panic through her. *This is how it feels to be tracked like an animal.*

"Stop!" she yelled to Mason's backside, but her voice was drowned out by the howling dogs and thumping hooves—or was it the pounding of her heart?

Juba ran ahead, falling, and then rising. Mason kicked his horse and was close enough to Juba to lash out. The whip caught him on the back and he stumbled, but rose again, running the path to the river.

A shriek from behind caught Summer's attention and she stopped momentarily to see Cherry racing behind her. Even in the distance Summer could see the purple bruises on her face. She ran like the wind, her skirts hiked up, and her breasts bouncing under the power of her strides.

Summer hastened her pace. "Stop!" she yelled again, but Mason galloped forward in pursuit. Juba disappeared from sight and as she approached she saw that Mason was off his horse, his shirt drenched in sweat. He cracked his whip, the tip stinging the air with a loud 'snap'. She skirted around him to avoid being lashed.

"Stop!" she yelled. "Miss Elizabeth says to see her first!"

"You're a lyin' bitch," he said, cracking the whip over her head.

"No! Listen! She said to talk to her first before you do anything. I swear!"

"Well, look where the boy is now." He nodded toward the river and laughed.

Juba stood up to his waist in water, gasping for breath, the dogs snapping and snarling on the river bank. Apprehensive of the dogs, she put her fear aside and stepped in up to her ankles. "Get out, Juba, it's okay! Miss Elizabeth says so." She motioned him forward but he held his place, his eyes darting between Summer, Mason, and the vicious dogs.

"Get out Juba!" Cherry was beside her now. "Evaline say it's okay. Come on out now!" She turned to Summer and whispered. "You ain't lyin' now, is you?"

"No, but I'll explain later."

"I ain't comin' out. Dem dogs is gonna get me, and he's gonna whup me."

"Call off the dogs!" she yelled to Mason, who stood grinning and much too cocky for Summer's liking. "He can't get out with the dogs here!"

Mason relented and pursed his lips into a shrill whistle. The dogs retreated and, much to Summer's surprise, seemed to forget about Juba entirely as they set their noses to the ground pursuing other adventures.

She was about to tread in after Juba when Mr. Mason's voice boomed from behind.

"You'd better get out, boy, or that gator's gonna get you." The exclusion of alarm in Mason's voice delayed the reaction to the warning. The message didn't sink in until Mason nodded to the right of Juba where, to Summer's horror, was a sight that would haunt her forever; an alligator—a monster of an alligator—sailed smoothly toward Juba, his great tail a thick rudder, his eyes peering calmly above the water line.

"Run!" Summer yelled.

"The gator!" Cherry screamed, pointing to the alligator which was only a few feet away from its target.

When Juba realized the danger, he frantically tread forward, but the river at waist deep was an enemy, holding him too long from safety. The gator disappeared beneath the waterline as did Juba, his arms thrashing as he went under. The women screamed and begged Mr. Mason to help, but he stood fast, his arms crossed over his chest, watching, as Juba surfaced long enough to let out a garbled wail—a wail to chill the bones of the women on shore. He surfaced again amidst the splashes of the reddening river, hapless victim to the alligator's death roll, and then there was stillness, a few faint ripples where once a man stood.

Cherry collapsed to the ground, shrieking. Summer looked at Mr. Mason with genuine loathing, a living reminder that she had not yet met a worthy human in this strange world besides Ruth, Lucy, Cherry, Percy and Pompeii...and poor Juba, now gone. *Nightmare...a dream*, she reminded herself. With that thought in mind, she let her fury loose. She flew at Mr. Mason, pounding his chest as hard as she could, her fists tiny weapons against his stocky form.

"Beast!" she yelled. "*You* are the beast!"

He pushed her hard and she landed painfully in the dirt.

"You let him die!" she cried.

"He had it coming," Mason snarled, and went for his horse, which had moseyed back to the yard and was grazing on the grass. He turned and looked at Cherry, still slumped on the bank of the river. "You ain't out of the woods yet, Cherry girl," he warned, mounting his steed. He cracked his whip in the air, kicked the horse, and off he galloped across the field, the dogs following behind.

Summer helped the sobbing Cherry to her feet. *Please God, let me wake up!* It tore her heart apart to see Cherry like this—to remember poor Juba's failed attempt to reach the bank. She could barely control her own tears.

What a miserable life, what a miserable end for Juba. Not even a burial...just the bottom of a river. A life forgotten, barely lived. The thought brought more tears as the women walked across the field, arm in arm, each holding the other up. It was not yet even noon.

12

Oh cursèd time! Morale was low as the days dragged on at a sluggish pace. Cherry fell into a deep depression and couldn't see her way out of it. No matter how hard Lucy, Ruth and Summer tried, Cherry could barely get herself off her floor mat in the mornings. Percy tried to cheer his mother with childish silliness, but to no avail. Cherry ate little and completed her duties in a trance-like state. Elizabeth was on edge and snapped at everyone. She was downright merciless toward Cherry. At least Cherry was spared a whipping, thanks to Summer's bartering. She was quite pleased that she now had leverage with which to fight for her rights and those of the others. It didn't matter that it was blackmail. This was a wicked place that required a wicked defense in order to survive.

On the eighth day after Juba's horrific death, Mr. Mason came for another instruction meeting. Summer thought it odd that Elizabeth would chance a meeting with Mason now, considering Charles was due back from Savannah at any time. She took it upon herself to visit the hole in the nursery floor, but surely Elizabeth had rectified the situation by now. Still, on the slim chance the hole was still there, perhaps she could learn what tricks Elizabeth and Mason had up their sleeves. When she lifted the corner of the rug off the floor she was disappointed to find the hole had been nailed over with a patch of wood.

"Darn," she whispered. "I guess the show is over."

Backtracking down the servant stairway, she stopped at Elizabeth's bedroom landing and listened by the door.

"...and you're a damned fool. You should have tried to save Juba, at least. He was a fine buck and Charles won't be happy about losing him. He paid good money for that boy."

"Wasn't nothin' I could do, Liz. That gator was on him in no time. My job ain't to wrestle no gators, my job is to keep the darkies in line."

"Don't' call me 'Liz'. You might make a mistake one of these days in front of Charles."

"What do I call you then, whore? Tart? Or, how about bitch?"

Summer felt the sting of the slap Elizabeth presumably planted on Mason's cheek. A short scuffle followed.

"That's my girl," Mason said. "Bitch is the right word."

"Bastard," she spat. "I'm beside myself and you call me names! What will I do about Evaline? She was set to go off with Juba. Now I'll never get her out of here!"

"There's always accidents."

Accidents? A chill ran through Summer. She had lost count of the days she was stuck in this dream. Was it Ten? Twenty? Thirty? The longer it went on, the more she feared she'd never see the 21st century again. Mr. Mason could bring that fear to reality. Summer had the power of blackmail, but Mason had the strength and motive to do her in.

"Think of a *good* accident, would you, Mick?" Elizabeth's malicious voice had turned sultry. "You have another job, too, besides controlling the darkies," she purred.

"And what's that?" Mason's tone had also changed from the usual gruff to a deep and sexy low.

"To do your mistress's bidding, and keep her happy."

That woman is shameless! Summer pressed her ear harder to the door, and cursed the patch on the floorboard overhead.

"Wait," Elizabeth said.

Summer's heart skipped a beat when she heard the patter of footsteps. She attempted to blend into the wall should Elizabeth open the servant stairway door, even though the lantern light would give her away.

"Hurry up, you hussy," Mason called.

Again, she heard the footsteps cross the floor, and held her breath.

"Be patient. I just want to make sure Charles isn't riding up the road while his overseer is riding his wife." She giggled. "We don't want to get caught now, do we?"

"And ruin all this fun? Hell no!"

Summer pressed her ear to the door again, but heard only the creaking of the bed and the escalating moans of the shameless couple. She crept down the stairs fearful of her fate after hearing the casual way in which they considered her demise. She would have to remain alerted to danger at every waking moment. *If this is a dream and they kill me, will I really be dead?* A time traveler had many unanswered questions.

She jumped when the servant stairway door opened as she reached the main floor landing. Susannah stood in the doorway, afloat in yards of plaid taffeta. Summer did not know she had returned from Royal Palms today, and wondered if Elizabeth knew she was in the house.

"Good day, Evaline," she said, beckoning Summer to join her. "I wish to speak with you."

She followed the sway of the hoop to the parlor, frantically summoning up a reason for Mason's horse to be tied to the hitching post, should she be asked. Susannah motioned to an armchair. In the 21st century Summer wouldn't hesitate to sit, but in this time-frame she felt very outclassed and out of place sitting in the big-house parlor like a mistress of the manor. She reminded herself that she truly *was* the one and only mistress of Tanglewood Plantation, but Susannah certainly wasn't aware of it.

"I see Mr. Mason's horse is tied outside. Is he in the house?"

Oh my.

"Well?"

"Uh…I believe he is."

Susannah sighed. "Is he in mother's room?"

Summer shuffled in her seat.

"You can tell me, Evaline. We've been friends long enough, haven't we?"

Have we? Oh the things she didn't know about Evaline! Her eyes wandered the room and then back to Susannah, her new-found friend. "Yes," she said quietly.

Susannah sighed once more as she paced the room. "You mustn't say a word to father about this. I believe there would be bloodshed if he knew."

"I would never…"

"No, I know you wouldn't." She paced again, the hooped skirt gently swaying with each step. Summer wondered if she would look so graceful, had she a hoop to wear.

"Such a disgrace," Susannah muttered. She stopped her pacing in front of Summer's chair. "I heard about Juba. I'm sorry, Evaline. It must have been terrible."

"Mr. Mason didn't help him."

"Could he have?"

"Maybe, but he didn't even try."

"Father will not be happy." She glanced at the ceiling to the rooms above. "Father would not be happy about many things."

"No Ma'am."

Susannah looked at her quizzically. "You don't seem like yourself, Eva-line. You seem different...speak differently. I cannot quite place your accent."

"I...I'm practicing my speaking voice." *I'm stuck in a nightmare—I'm from the 21st century. You are dead, Susannah. Everyone in this house has been dead a long, long time!* Oh how she wanted to tell the truth!

"Well, it's quite remarkable, but it will probably get you into trouble."

"Yes ma'am." It wasn't a lie.

"All right, you may go about your duties. Remember our secret."

"Yes ma'am," Summer replied and scooted out of the parlor to the servant stairway. She was sweating. This was practically the only conversation she'd had with the hierarchy that wasn't a direct peril to her existence; but still, it felt so awkward. *Susannah knows.* What a strange predicament, her mother fornicating with the overseer! She couldn't recall a soap opera that was better than this story. If only it hadn't jeopardized her own life!

✳ ✳ ✳

Charles sat at the head of the supper table. Summer didn't know him well enough to read his every mood, but it was obvious he was angry over the death of Juba. Elizabeth sat demurely, the Southern wife, quiet, compla-cent—everything she was not, in her true self. Mr. Mason had left in the nick of time, earlier. No sooner had he untied his horse from the hitching post, when Charles trotted up the road, home from Savannah.

Now, Charles sat with Elizabeth, Susannah, and Mary at the table— the nearly empty table, with the boys gone.

"If you had not so vehemently denied Juba and Cherry a union, he would be alive today. He was a good boy, Elizabeth. I had plans for that one."

"I thought he was better suited for Evaline."

Charles laid his fork down and leaned forward. "Let's clear up one issue, my dear. *You* do not determine Evaline's future."

Summer wondered if this conversation was as uncomfortable a situ-ation for Susannah, Mary, and Cherry, as it was for her. She glanced at Su-sannah and Mary, their heads bowed over their soup bowls. Cherry leaned catatonically against the wall by the sideboard, her eyes half-closed, lost in her thoughts, or memories.

"Why was Mason here today?" Charles asked.

Susannah shuffled uncomfortably in her seat and glanced at Summer.

"A trivial matter. It is now settled." Elizabeth stared calmly across the table at her husband

"Tell us about the mustering, father." Susannah interjected.

Relief! Susannah had thought quickly enough to divert attention from Mr. Mason's visit!

Charles looked at his daughter, his eyes taking on a sudden keen alertness. "So many men—even boys—mustered for the cause. It was a sight to behold with pride; a hundred gallant and brave men off to fight the demons of the North. Why we'll have those Yankees running home with their tails between their legs!"

"And *our* boys, Charles? How were *our* boys."

"They're not boys any longer, mother, they're men, fighting for our rightful way of life."

"Fighting to keep the darkies in bondage, you mean."

Susannah's remarked surprised Summer. There was more beneath that white skin and hooped skirt than met the eye. A thinker, perhaps?

"I'll not have you speak that way, young lady. This is our tradition and has been ever since I can remember. My daddy owned slaves, his daddy owned slaves, and his daddy before him. This is the way of the South and no Yankee president has the right to tell us how to live or how to run our business." Charles spoke passionately, the veins in his neck standing out.

"I'm sorry father, but I cannot bear the thought of my brothers dying so that you may work the darkies to death."

"Susannah! Do not speak to your father in that tone!" Elizabeth held a hankie to her nose looking truly upset.

Quiet Mary stood out of her chair, her face flushed a bright red. "No! Do not speak of John and Edmund in such a way. They *must* come home… John *must* come home! Oh, I cannot bear to think it!" Mary ran off, the hooped skirt gliding as if she were on roller skates.

"See what you have done!" Charles slammed a fist to the table. "You may be excused!"

The sudden thump of the fist brought Cherry back to attention. Summer had no clue what to do at this point. Susannah followed Mary out of the dining room leaving Charles and Elizabeth the only patrons of the grand supper that still awaited them.

✳ ✳ ✳

Later that night, as Summer laid in her cot, the thin quilt tucked beneath her chin, she thought of John and Edmund and their final venture in life, a war that would bring so much death and suffering, one that would be lost in the end. A sudden guilt struck her; she was the only one who knew the outcome, and yet she had not given warning. She had not warned Charles that he would hang himself from the fountain. She had not warned Elizabeth that she would meet her death on the staircase. She had not warned Mary that her husband would not return. She had not warned John or Edmund that their lives were about to end. She had warned no one. Would they believe her if she had?

Just as she drifted off to sleep, she jerked awake. *Scratch...scratch... scratch.* She shivered beneath the quilt. She had forgotten about Evaline! Indeed the ghosts had left her for a while, or perhaps she had become too entangled in other events in this, her new life, to notice. *Scratch...scratch...scratch.* She was grateful she had dozed off with the candle lit. The light, though creepily casting shadows, was all that saved her from panic. She sat up on the cot and stared at the attic door. *Scratch...scratch...scratch.* Evaline was calling to her, but why? What did she want? Summer stood and took the candle off the table. Slowly, she approached the attic door, all the while fighting the urge to run to the safety of Ruth's arms. Gooseflesh prickled her body. The hairs on the back of her neck stood out, and yet she continued toward the door. *Scratch...scratch...scratch.* She wanted to cry. Why was she trapped in this world? Her hand shook as she reached for the latch.

She paused in an attempt to gain composure. The memory of the translucent figure at the top of the stairs was one that she wanted to forget. Yet, here she was, poised to relive the moment. Her heart pounded in her chest; the candle flickered in her breath. The trembling of her hand soon became the trembling of her body as her fingers lifted the latch. She counted to three, swung the door open and found herself looking into the eyes of the ghost of

Evaline. She opened her mouth to a silent scream and stood in horror as Evaline motioned to the lower stairs. Then, there was darkness. When she awoke, she was lying on the floor with her head in Ruth's lap.

"Po chile! Good thing I hear dat big clunk o' yo' body goin' down. What's you doin'?"

"I'm okay, Ruth." What was the point of telling her otherwise? Everyone thought she was nuts. Even *she* was beginning to believe it. Was she really Evaline? Did she time travel, or is this really her life? Did she dream the 21st century? On the other hand, if she *were* Evaline, then who was the figure on the stairs?

Ruth helped her to her feet, closed the attic door and guided her to the cot. The candle had fallen from its holder when she fainted and Ruth stuck it down again with hot wax from her own candle and relit it. "Der you is. Get to sleep, Evaline. Be'fo you knows it, Miss 'Lizbet be ringin' dat bell for her breakfas'."

"Goodnight, Ruth. Thanks."

"G'nite, chile'."

She was alone again, the candle flickering its ominous shadows. She was surprised the horror of the encounter hadn't killed her. It *was* Evaline… but what was she trying to tell her? If only she could get over her fear long enough to think…to figure it out; the scratching, the pointing…the pointing…pointing at what?

She sat again on the edge of the cot. *Evaline is gone or she'd be scratching,* she reasoned. Summer took the candle and approached the door. *I'm a glutton for punishment.* This time she didn't pause. She turned the latch and opened it to the empty darkness. "Down", she whispered. "Evaline is always pointing at something…something downward." She kneeled on the landing, holding the candle with one hand, while the other attempted to lift the tread of the first stair. It held tight. She tried the tread of the second stair, and it, too, held tight. She tugged at the third tread and to her surprise, it lifted slightly upward. Setting the candle down she used both hands and a bit of elbow grease to lift the tread the rest of the way. She shone the candlelight into the hollow darkness, and there lay a book. Her heartbeat quickened. "She *was* trying to tell me something!" Summer set the candle on the fourth stair and lifted the dust-covered book from its secret home. The horror of the dark attic above her was forgotten. After sneezing several times, she opened the cover to find a journal. The handwriting on the first page was faint, but legible.

May 5, 1861

My heart is so heavy I can barely write. Poor Cherry girl. Our hearts are broken and I wonder if they will ever mend. Mr. Mason—that evil man—him and the hounding dogs chased Juba into the river today. Miss Elizabeth told me she would spare Juba the whip if I would take him for my man. She wanted I should leave the house with him, that she would give me a cabin of my own. I knew it would break Cherry's heart, but it would be far better than the grief she bears now, for Juba is dead and so cruelly killed! If only I could wipe the memory from my mind! Mr. Mason stood as a still as a scarecrow as the gator grabbed Juba and pulled him under. The water filled with blood, and Mr. Mason did not move a muscle to help....

Summer turned the page only to discover that the next page was blank. *All* the pages were blank after the one entry.

13

The summer passed in a sweltering, steamy stretch that Summer thought would never end. The lack of deodorant was a constant consternation to her. She was well aware of the box beneath her cot that held Evaline's meager toiletries: a crude toothbrush, charcoal powder to use as toothpaste, a bit of rosewater and a tin of smelly cold cream. She made do with what she had but was embarrassed to serve at mealtimes knowing how badly she smelled. They *all* smelled, even the white folks (as she now referred to them), but considering the household slaves did all of the physical labor required to run the house smoothly, they smelled worst of all.

Autumn did not come boldly, as an autumn in Chicago. It crept slowly into November, teasing with a cool breeze now and then to lift the oppressive body odor that permeated the household. When, alas, the hot weather was truly gone, then came the cold. Summer was in charge of the fireplaces, and work she did to keep them going. It was a good thing that heat rises, that she was on the third floor, and that one of the chimneys ran through her room with vents to force the heat upstairs. Otherwise, she would be doubly miserable.

She often wondered if she were missed in the 21st century, and then at times she wondered if she had ever existed there at all. Time seemed to have passed, judging by Percy's growth. Wasn't it just yesterday that Juba had been killed?

Each day was a struggle. Each day she hung on with the hope that her true name was Summer Woodfield, and not Evaline. Since the discovery of the journal, the pages still empty, Evaline had remained quiet. All the ghosts were quiet, leading Summer again to believe that perhaps she had imagined it all.

✳ ✳ ✳

"…And by virtue of the power, and for the purpose aforesaid, I do order and declare that all persons held as slaves within said designated States, and parts of States, are, and henceforward shall be free; and that the Executive government of the United States, including the military and naval authorities thereof, will recognize and maintain the freedom of said persons."

The soldier stood at the top of the veranda reading the Emancipation Proclamation to the slaves of Magnolia Plantation.

Lucy jammed a finger into her ear, and shook her hand, as if to dislodge a foreign object. "Wha'd dat man say?"

"He says you...*we* are free!" Summer exclaimed. The word 'free' passed through the crowd at the speed of light, followed by a stretch of silence.

"This document, issued by the President of the United States, January 1, 1863, declares that you folks are free to go," the soldier said.

January 1863? Summer was shocked. Just yesterday it was 1861—or was it 2011? She was dizzy from the time changes.

"You are free to go," the soldier reiterated.

Summer surmised he was wondering why the crowd was standing like pillars of salt around the fountain and not high-tailing it for freedom road.

"We's free!" a voice yelled from behind. The silence was broken by a great calamity of screams, alleluias, tears, dancing and cries of joy. The Woodfield family stood glumly on the veranda viewing the rejoicing crowd before them. Charles stepped to the forefront to stand beside the soldier and raised his hands in a futile attempt to quiet the group. With the crowd wild in jubilation before them, the soldier shot his pistol high over the heads of the celebrating mass, bringing a restless quiet.

"Mr. Woodfield has something to say. Please listen," he shouted.

"We don' gots to listen no mo'!" someone yelled, stirring up the crowd again.

The soldier poised his pistol over the heads of the group, and they hushed once more.

"You have all served me faithfully," Charles began. "You are free, but consider that you have no place to go. You are welcome to stay here, as before, and work the fields and paddies as hired hands."

"Dat mean pay?" someone asked.

"That means pay—when this war is over. If you choose to go, I cannot stop you, and I wish you well, but in the meantime, you have a place to stay if you're willing to work and wait out the war." Charles stepped back in line with his family.

"You may go," the soldier said, and many in the crowd took off like buckshot, whooping and hollering their way across the lawn, some toward the tabby cabins along the approach road, some to the left outside the gates, and some around the back toward River Row. A few, Summer noticed, headed straight down the approach road, beneath the live oaks, and just kept on going. All that remained around the fountain were her own particular group; Ruth, Lucy, Cherry, Percy, and Pompeii.

"What we gonna do now?" Lucy asked.

"I ain't goin' nowheres. Dis is my home til I think of sometin' else." Ruth said.

"I'se goin' to Savannah," Cherry said.

"No you ain't," Ruth scolded. "You ain't taken' dat lil' boy and goin' nowheres."

"I'se too old." Pompeii moaned.

"Under the circumstance of nobody knowing where to go, I think it's best we all stay here," Summer said.

"Amen," Lucy agreed.

✳ ✳ ✳

The war news was not good; so many men had died, old and young. Mid-January of 1863 Arthur Ascot returned home, wounded in the thigh by a Yankee bullet. After him, came Robert Mason, a bullet through his shoulder. Elizabeth assigned Summer to care for Robert at his residence—the house of the overseer, Mick Mason, which sat behind the stable.

Vengeful...sadistic...dangerous. Summer's head filled with adjectives to define Elizabeth, as she made her way from the warmth of the big house, across the vast lawn to Mason's cabin. The wind blew wickedly, passing through her homespun dress like a sharp knife. The sweater Ruth had knit her from scraps of yarn was a small buffer against the frigid air. None of the remaining servants had sufficient warm clothing or coats to take them through the winter, and no means with which to buy them.

Shaking from the cold—and the thought of running into Mick Mason—she noticed a water pump on the approach to the front door of the overseer's cabin. Keeping in mind that she would probably need to haul water shortly, she wondered how it kept from freezing, unprotected as it was from the wind. The one-story cabin was decent enough from the outside, whitewashed, with a small porch. She knocked on the door and waited, but hearing no reply from the interior, she knocked louder.

Hearing a faint 'come in', she opened the door wide enough to peek in. Seeing no one, she entered. "Hello," she called to the emptiness. It was only a hair warmer in the cabin, and she shivered, wrapping her arms tightly around her body.

"In here," came a weak reply.

"Where?" She was suddenly gripped by the thought that this was to be the 'accident' Elizabeth and Mick Mason had planned for her. Even though it didn't make sense that they should do her in with Robert in the house, she couldn't shake off the possibility. *Maybe it isn't Robert in the house?*

"In...here."

She felt a fluttering within when she recognized the deep voice as the same that had awakened her from the drugged sleep her first day at the plantation, the day Elizabeth hit her with the hairbrush. She passed through a sparsely furnished room. A small dining table with two chairs sat on one side of the room, while a sofa sat on the other. A wooden box sat between the sofa and chair topped by an oil lamp. Obviously, a woman did not live here, for there were no comforting corners to telltale a feminine touch.

"Miss Elizabeth has sent me to help," she said, standing in the doorway of a room. It was dark but for a stream of light filtering through an opening in the drapes, and she couldn't get a good look at the figure on the bed. Moving forward, she grew alarmed as she approached Robert Mason, her eyes focusing on the white bandages covering his chest and shoulder at a diagonal angle. "I guess you're hurt badly," she said.

"Bad enough...." His breath fogged in the cold air.

"Tell me what I can do for you."

"Change...bandage." He pointed to the pile of muslin on a dresser against a wall.

She set to work, helping him to lean forward, which allowed her to undo the bandage from the back. His broad and naked shoulders bulged from the muscle beneath as she gently unwound the soiled and bloody muslin. With her eyes now adjusted to the level of light in the room, she couldn't help but gasp at the sight of the exit wound, the red and purple tender skin surrounding the blackened hole. *Stop,* she told herself, afraid that she would alarm him. The wound required a medical doctor, but its fate was in the hands of Summer Wodfield, aka Evaline, both trapped in a nightmarish time that hadn't an inkling of the miracles of modern medicine.

"Oh, my god, Mr. Mason, I...I need something...something powerful to treat this." *Not even a drugstore here!* Frustrated, she put a hand to her forehead and massaged her temples. Elizabeth sent her to nurse Robert Mason, but didn't arm her with nursing supplies. "Wait! Alcohol! Do you have any whiskey? Rum?" She had seen it done in a movie once, where a bullet wound was cleaned with whiskey.

"Out there." He pointed weakly toward the living area.

She covered his shoulders with a wool blanket, then searched the sparse outer room. She spotted a dark brown bottle sitting on a shelf in a kitchen area and popped the cork, taking a whiff. "Phew!" *Bingo.*

Every little thing was an inconvenience in the 19th century. Running water, for example; if only she could grab a pot, turn the knob on a stove for fire, and run water from a sink! She fought back the urge to cry; a man's life depended on her and she was such a stranger in this time zone—and a useless one at that! At least she was proficient at starting up the woodstove, and lying in a freezing house couldn't be doing Robert Mason any good. She took the one cooking pot that sat on a hand-hewn counter top and ran outside through the frigid air to the water pump she had noticed on her way in. She whispered a prayer of thanks as the water poured forth on the third pump of the handle. Filling the pot three-quarters full, she hurried back into the house, the icy water sloshing down the front of her thin dress. An arctic chill ran up her legs. *I'll be the next one sick,* she thought, and then wondered if she could even survive a bout with pneumonia here, in this cruel and impassionate world.

Inside, she stoked the stove with the sufficient supply of wood that sat beside it, thankful that Mason had managed to hang onto a small supply of stick matches. She prayed for the cabin and the water to heat quickly. Every moment counted in saving Robert from serious infection—if it were not too late already. She peeked into the bedroom to see him still slumped over, his hair falling heavily in front of his face. He needed a shave and a haircut. "Please," she called, "just a moment more. I've started a fire and I'm waiting for the water to boil. I found some alcohol. We have to clean your wound before I can wrap it again." *A watched pot never boils.* She remembered her mother saying those words once, and averted her eyes from the woodstove and returned to the bedroom. She had to keep him sitting while they waited for the water.

"How did you make it back here?" she asked, reentering the dark room. Indeed, it was remarkable that he should be sitting here at all.

"Hm?" His voice was weak and made her anxious.

"How could you make it back here, wounded as you are?"

"I left...."

"But, where were you?"

"In northern Georgia," he mumbled, clearly fading.

Boiling or not, here I come. Realizing she'd have more of a problem if she kept him sitting in such an uncomfortable position, she scavenged the house for a cloth with which to grip the now steaming pot; another reminder of the inconvenience of her predicament. Finding a towel next to a washbowl in what she assumed was Mick Mason's bedroom, she stretched it to reach both handles of the pot. *Better than nothing.* The trick was getting the water to the bedroom without scalding herself. Moving slowly, it seemed an hour had passed before she set the pot of water onto the nightstand. The heat of it felt good, and the house was just beginning to warm up nicely. The towel sufficed as a washcloth and, when she felt the wound was sufficiently cleansed, she doused the entrance and exit wounds with the putrid contents of the brown bottle. Robert groaned at the burning of the alcohol, but remained in his slumped state as she finished the task of wrapping his shoulder.

At last, she gently pushed him back until his head met the pillow, and brushed the hair from his eyes. "Please rest. I'll return in a while. I'm sorry if I hurt you."

As she turned to leave, her hands full with wet and bloody muslin rags, she was surprised at the sudden grasp of his hand on her arm.

'Thank you, Evaline," he whispered, his dark eyes glimmering in the stream of light that traveled through the drapes. His hand lingered a moment more, and then released itself to fall onto the bed.

It was then, at that precise moment, Summer Woodfield fell hopelessly in love with a man she could never have.

❈ ❈ ❈

"January 19, 1863

What has happened to me? I was sent to Mr. Mason's cabin to dress his son Robert's wounds today and I have returned transformed! I did not know that love could pierce the heart with the mere touch of a hand. What now? What now? My heart is lost forever."

Summer shuddered against the chill erupting over her flesh. On her return from the cabin, she was compelled to retrieve the journal from the stairs to chronicle the amazing feelings that overcame her today when she left Robert Mason—but it was already written! She sat on the second stair and stared at the faint but flowing curves of the script. Her hand was not trained to produce letters with such flourish, and yet, here were her very thoughts in print! Evaline was speaking again, but what was the message, the reasoning? Why were events written *after* the fact?

"You could at least tell me beforehand what's going to happen," she said to the empty darkness of the room above. *I'm in love with a ghost. They're all ghosts, aren't they? And what am I?* Her stay in the 19th century was becoming much too complicated.

✳ ✳ ✳

Miraculously, Summer's novice and primitive nursing skills were working wonders on Robert Mason. Each day, she made the trek across the frigid lawn to the overseer's cabin to dress his wounds. Elizabeth had no choice but to replenish the bottles of alcohol and whatever other medical supplies she could salvage from the dwindling stash. After all, the mistress was enjoying the attributes of Mick Mason; the least she could do was to help his son return to good health

Summer's cracked and bleeding hands did not deter her from the daily washing of the bandages with the lye soap. She was in love and determined to do whatever it took to make Robert well. He appeared to enjoy her company as much as she enjoyed his. Indeed it was a pleasure to escape the ever watchful eye of the mistress, for company that did not treat her with such contempt.

This February day was particularly cold and windy as she reached the cabin. She had the routine down pat, and immediately set about lighting the woodstove and retrieving the water from the pump; not a favorite task in this weather.

"You're too good to me, Evaline," Robert said, finally well enough to sit in a chair by the woodstove for a haircut. The wound was healing nicely, and she was secretly sad that these times would soon end.

"It's my pleasure. I've enjoyed helping you heal."

"And I have enjoyed your company."

She stood before him now with the razor in hand, shortening the shock of dark hair that fell across his eyes so many times during the bandage changes of the past month. His eyes…they were mesmerizing. For a month those eyes had followed her movements around the room, as certainly as her own eyes watched his stationary figure from every angle as she went about her duties. For this short time, he was hers, exclusively.

"You're a beautiful girl, Evaline, if I may say so."

The world slowed, and her heartbeat with it. *Would he think Summer Woodfield beautiful?* She was an imposter, a pale-skinned blond from the 21st century, mysteriously inhabiting the supple body of a beautiful 19th century mulatto girl.

"Yes, you may say so," she said, after a moment's hesitation, reminding herself that his compliment was for Evaline; *she* was beautiful, not Summer Woodfield.

"I wish..." he began, and sat mute, his dark eyes penetrating her own.

"You wish what?"

"I wish this didn't have to end."

"Does it?" The razor fell from her hands, floating to the floor—or so it seemed—as time came to a halt. A dazzling heat infused her body. She did not have to lean far to embrace his chiseled jaw between her trembling hands and place her lips on his. She was surprised at the strength with which he pulled her to his lap, their lips never losing their precious contact. The dazzling infusion within became a searing flame, diminishing the memory of his injury and the world around them. Their passion was so heated and intense that they did not hear the door of the cabin open.

"What are you doing with that wench, boy?"

Startled, Summer jumped to her feet at the sound of Mason's voice. Her hands, which moments ago trembled in passion, now trembled in fear, and she cursed herself for her reaction to him. *He is a ghost, a mere ghost!*

"That girl ain't nothing but trouble. Get out of here, Evaline." Mason said, jerking his head toward the door.

She was happy to comply, having no desire for confrontation after the loveliest moment of her life, but Robert grasped her arm as she hastened to leave.

"Stay, Evaline," he commanded glaring at the large form of his father in the doorway.

Summer often wondered how a wonderful and educated man such as Robert, sprang from the loins of such a cruel and insensitive being, but the standoff between father and son told the story of their relationship; the hostility was obvious.

"Suit yourself," Mason said, 'but Charles Woodfield ain't gonna like you manhandling his precious bastard nigger wench."

"For God's sake—have some respect for once, father!"

"I got no respect for them black whores."

Just the white ones, Summer wanted to add.

Mason's comment brought Robert to his feet, and she quickly stood between them.

"Really, I must go," she said. "I have to get back, and you need to rest." She tried to guide Robert toward the bedroom, but he stood fast, his eyes cold and hard on his father.

"Good riddance," Mason said, the sound of his boots heavy on the wood floor as he made his way to the back of the house. "Bitch," he said, as he passed.

"He's a cruel man, Evaline. I'm sorry for the things he said." Robert spoke the words none too quietly, and Summer prayed Mason would not return to retaliate.

As soon as she closed the door of the cabin behind her, the tears came, icy and bitter down her cheeks. She had never been treated in such a way by any man, or called such names in her other life! *'Bitch'...'whore'.* She wanted to kill Mason, but he was already dead!

※ ※ ※

She was ever grateful when the Woodfield family evening meal was finished, the kitchen cleaned, and the fires stoked for the night. She wondered if perhaps the mistress had heard about the confrontation at the cabin, but her mistress seemed oblivious as Summer stoked her fire. If she knew, she did not mention it.

Summer fled Elizabeth's room quickly and traveled the narrow stairs by candlelight to her room on the third floor. She was anxious to retrieve the journal, to see if the day's events had been written. She checked the journal every day now, to see if Evaline had written, but the pages remained empty... until now.

"February 22, 1863

Tonight I am both happy, and in great despair. Robert Mason kissed me on this day! In truth, I kissed him first. A great passion overcame me and I was helpless against its spell. But he must have felt it too, for he pulled me onto his lap and we engaged in a most shameful embrace until we were interrupted by the arrival of Mr. Mason. Imagine my fear, having been caught in such a posture by that evil man! He is a beast, but he dare not harm me as he did Cherry when she was caught with Juba. The master loves me, and his love protects me. Mason harmed me in a deeper way. I am ashamed that I should be called a whore and a bitch before the man I love. I believe Robert was ready to battle his own father in my defense, but I hope he did not after I left. His wound is not quite healed. I could barely hold back my tears until I closed the cabin door behind me..."

❊❊❊

Respite from Elizabeth's wrath did not last. Summer was summoned to Elizabeth's room at noon the following day.

"You are a whore like your mother, Evaline. It's disgraceful, lusting after a white man."

"I could say the same for you, Ma'am."

Elizabeth glared. "You had better pray that no evil ever befalls Master Woodfield. He is all that stands between you and hell. Need I say more?"

"No Ma'am."

"You are released of your duties to Robert Mason. You may not see him again."

"But..."

But *nothing*. And..." she added, "you will not complain to the Master either, because I can assure you he will *not* approve of your bawdy behavior yesterday in Mr. Mason's cabin."

He wouldn't approve of your bawdy behavior with Mick Mason either, she thought, but remained silent.

"I know what you're thinking Evaline. Leave it where it stands. Robert will be returning to the war soon anyway. He told his father so."

Her shoulders slumped in despair as she trekked the dark stairway to the basement. Her heart was heavy as tears welled behind her eyes. *Leaving? Returning to war?* She tried in vain to remember the exact duration of the Civil War, but her lack of interest in American history during her school years revealed its consequence by blocking any retention of the ending date. One thing was certain; if Robert returned to war then the chances were high that he would not return to her. Oh the confusion! She knew for a fact that Robert and Evaline never had the opportunity to nurture their love for one another. *But wait...the baby! Surely he returns, and the baby Evaline has belongs to him!* The thought of that union sent a thrilling current through her body. *Perhaps there is hope after all....*

14

Summer prayed the lantern light was not visible from the upstairs windows as she made her away across the great lawn to the river. Earlier, Lucy had conveyed the message for her to meet Robert there when her duties were finished. It was ten o'clock by the time she stoked Elizabeth's fire. Her mistress was in bed attire and hopefully sleeping by this time.

Here it was, mid-March, and Summer hadn't seen Robert since their passionate few moments in his father's cottage. Butterflies flew haywire in her stomach at the thought of being with him, touching him again. She pulled her sweater tightly around her, as the night air still retained winter's chill. The time without him had passed in such slow and painful drudgery and she wondered if he had experienced the same sadness at their distance. Surely he felt something, for he had sent her the message to meet him.

She wondered if Elizabeth missed Mason in the same way. Charles had not travelled at all since his return from the mustering in Savannah; therefore, there was no chance for the 'instruction' meetings the illicit lovers had enjoyed so well. With Elizabeth's hot temperament, it was difficult to tell whether her sharp tongue of late was due to her own personality, or the fact that she was unable to share her body with the burly overseer. Surely it was simply lust and not love that drove her!

Summer's approach to the river raised gooseflesh. There was something ominous about the dark water that snaked its way through the saw grass, hiding that which could do great harm. She had seen it with her own eyes, Juba's arms flailing in terror as he disappeared beneath its murky surface. Her memory of Bruno in her other life—the life that included Jesse Williams and Blaine Ascot—also sent chills up her spine. The vision of the large alligator waiting and watching in both worlds, transcended time and brought caution to the forefront, even blocking the anticipation of meeting Robert. She approached the river slowly, stopping a distance away from its bank. The night was black except for the yellow glow of lantern light that illuminated the ground before her.

"Robert," she whispered. "Are you here?" A great wave of disappointed ran through her when she did not hear a reply. *I'm too late!*

She stretched the lantern out in front of her, to the left, to the right. "Robert!" she called again, only louder. She jumped at the sound of branches breaking and swung around to see him step out from between the azalea bushes that grew so thick and lush along the river, happily shaded by the spruce pines and sassafras.

"I'm here," he assured her, and she ran to him, bold 21ˢᵗ century thoughts racing through Evaline's 19ᵗʰ century body. She *wanted* him—wanted him desperately! "I thought I was too late!"

"I could never leave you without saying goodbye."

He stood tall in the soft glow of the lantern. "Don't leave," she begged. Certainly the only pleasant thing in this, her new life, was her love for Robert Mason. She put a hand on his chest. "Please, don't leave me here," she whispered. He could not know the depth of her words.

He took the lantern from her hand and set it on the ground. Pulling her to him, she found her head snuggled against his chest, his voice vibrating directly from his lungs to her ear, heavy, deep, sweet, a voice she would remember forever...*is this the last time we will be together?*

"I must leave, Evaline. I'll no longer fight for the cause. I'm heading north to take the pledge and join with the Federals."

At this point, Summer didn't care *who* he was fighting for; the war was *over*, the North had won. She just *wanted* him, here, and *now*.

"This way of life will be finished forever. The times are changing, and I will help finish it."

She gently pushed him away and focused on the dark eyes she knew so well. This was most difficult, saying what she wanted to say without him thinking her a brazen hussy. "I want you, Robert."

She wasn't certain whether he was confused by the statement or if the light and shadows of the lantern caused the puzzled look on his face.

"I mean it, Robert, I want you *now*, before you leave. What more do I have to hold on to?"

The meaning of her words took hold. He pulled her to him, his lips on hers. The sassafras bark bit into her back as he pressed her against a tree, the heat index of the moment rising. The kiss deepened as his hands slid over her breasts to her waist, to her hips, to her buttocks. He pressed his body into hers and she felt the swell of him through the thin fabric of her garment.

At last, he is mine! She wanted him desperately. She would lie on the bank of the river—forgetting the crushing jaws of the alligator—she would do whatever he wanted. *Just let him ask!*

The moment broke; the chill of the night sliced between them as he stood back. He grasped both her arms and looked into her eyes. "No!"

No? She was not only shocked by his answer, but at the force with which he said the word.

His grip tightened. "That is not the way it will happen for us, Evaline. That is the way of my father, your master, and all the other white men who take advantage of the women trapped in their keeping. It is not *my* way. So help me, when I return, we will not need to hide in the dark of night to see each other, and we will have each other honorably, without shame."

She was glad he could not see the blush that fired up her cheeks in the lantern light. *This would not have happened at home—I would not have been refused!* The division of time that separated their worlds was never more apparent in their short love relationship than it was now. Despite the homespun dress down to her ankles (and one she wouldn't be caught dead in anywhere else except in this place), despite the lack of beauty aids, modern conveniences, modern medicines, and all comforts of the modern world, despite all that had befallen her since she touched the fingerprint on the old letter, it was Robert's respect for her that presented, with full force, the difference between the past and the future. She was embarrassed and ashamed. She would not feel such in her own time, but here, with Robert, she had overstepped the boundary of decency.

"You're right," she sighed. I'm so sorry. I've made a fool of myself."

"No...no, you haven't Evaline. I'm honored that you feel this way about me." He pulled her to him and this time they kissed, long and hungrily, without interruption.

When their lips parted, Summer's heart fell to her knees. *This is it. I'll never see him again!*

"I love you, Evaline. I will return for you, I promise." He tipped his hat and she watched as he walked along the riverbank until he became a shadow that blended into all the other shadows of the night, and was gone.

* * *

She tiptoed up the servant stairway, ever so careful to not make the slightest noise and wake Elizabeth. *'She has ears like a fox...'* Ruth had warned that first day. The stairs did not always comply, and she cringed with every random creak. The very last thing she needed in this, her sorrowful moment of despair, would be to deal with Elizabeth.

Safely snug in her room, she opened the attic door and removed the third step board. She knew, of course, that Evaline would have written the event of her and Robert's meeting.

'I love you Evaline. I will return for you, I promise.'

He said these words to me and oh, blessed God in heaven, please do not let these be the last words I hear from Robert's lips!

* * *

It was perplexing to Summer, as she looked back on her infatuation with Robert Mason, how easily she had stepped out of her 21st century life— how easily she would have given it up to be with him, how easily she would have succumbed to her desires had he been willing. The reality of her present situation sunk in as the days passed in a constant parade of tedious servitude. Why couldn't she escape this nightmare? To what purpose had she been tossed to the wolves, so to speak? And again, the sneaky suspicion that perhaps this wasn't a dream, that her life as Summer Woodfield was the dream for which she had traveled forward in time, and then, by some miraculous twist, returned to her real self, as Evaline, the mulatto child of Charles Woodfield.

15

The tedious, repetitive drudgery of her every day chores strangled her. No parties, no dates, no movies, no restaurants, no shopping sprees. No pampering when her period came upon her; no tampons, no Midol to relieve the pain; no Robert, no fun. What few spare moments there were in a day to interact with the kitchen crew were spent in expressions of fear. The world was crashing around them.

The Woodfield men's exclamations of victory at their last supper together—the last before the mustering in Savannah in April of 1861—proved to be false. The Southern gentlemen who left for war, vowing to whip the Yankees and return home in a week's time, would return crippled, maimed, or not at all. Of course, Summer knew the outcome already, but could not share with the others. She had blended into life at Magnolia. Cherry, Ruth, Lucy, Pompeii and Percy accepted her change of speaking, her lack of memory; to them, she was simply Evaline.

"Where we goin' when we leave here, Evaline?" Lucy stood stoically at her station stirring a large pot of soup for the afternoon meal at the big house. "I don' know nothin' 'bout out der."

The August heat mingled with the simmering soup, creating an oppressive sauna atmosphere in the kitchen. Kinky hair pulled tighter to the scalp. The dreaded body odor again permeated the household, dulled only somewhat by the talcum powder reserved only for the revered white hierarchy. It seemed odd to Summer that Elizabeth wouldn't dole out tins of the stuff to the servants, as it might have made mealtimes more pleasant to the olfactory senses. Summer could suggest it (risking an argument), but store-bought supplies in Savannah had dwindled to nearly nothing. The ravages of war were taking hold.

"I just don't know, Lucy." Indeed she didn't know. Where would they go if she were still stuck in this nightmare when the war ended? She could go home to Chicago, but would it be the Chicago of the 21st century, or the Chicago of the 19th Century?

"I'm leaving dis place," Cherry said. "I'm goin' to Savannah and work in a big fancy house. I'm gonna buy me some pretty dresses and hoop petticoats, and a bonnet with flowers and feathers." She sashayed around the kitchen, her hands framing her tiny waist. "I'm gonna meet me a rich man and he's gonna take good care o' dis girl."

"Ha! Hoop petticoats and bonnets...you's gonna git yo'self in a hoop full o' trouble, is what," Lucy replied. The kitchen filled with laughter—a welcomed respite in trying times—until Percy burst through the door.

"Come quick, Evaline! Massah hollerin' an' Miz 'Lizbet, she screaming like she on fire! Miz Susannah say you come quick!"

Without a moment's hesitation, Summer ran out of the door behind Percy, breathing hard to keep up the pace of his quick and youthful strides across the lawn to the basement. Leaving Percy behind, she ran up the servant stairs, stumbling on the hem of her skirt and cursing the fact of having forgotten a lantern to light her way. Even from the dismal stairway she could hear Elizabeth's wails. Her heart beat in thunderous thuds inside her chest. She followed the wails to the parlor and was greeted by Susannah, obviously in great distress.

"Help me, Evaline!" Susannah floated between her parents, Charles on the sofa, Elizabeth collapsed on a side-chair flanking the fireplace, her hanky pressed against her nose, her eyes red and bright with tears.

"It's Edmund—he's dead!" Susannah looked at Summer as if she held the power to change history. Could she have? She knew this moment was coming, and here was the result of her secret knowledge: hysteria and mayhem.

Mary sat on a chair beside Elizabeth, her shoulders shaking with sobs. "It will be John, next. I just know it!"

"Damn Yankees! I'll kill them myself!" Charles bellowed, leaping off the sofa. "I will join the cause this minute. Fetch Pompeii, Evaline!"

"You'll do no such thing, Father! Evaline, get the laudanum, quickly now, upstairs in mother's room!"

Summer flew to the servant stairway and hesitated, remembering that she had no lantern to guide her. She quickly advanced to the foyer and viewed the double grand stairway for one moment before leaping upward, two steps at a time. She was out of breath by the time she reached the second floor and swung open the double doors that faced her at the landing, only to remember that this was presently the ballroom and not Elizabeth's bedroom. She stood confused, trying to place Elizabeth's room in the rambling house. After all, she reached it on a daily basis through the treacherous servant stairway and not the grand staircase. Things looked different from this angle.

The screaming below did not lessen. "Hurry!" Susannah yelled, from the inner cavity of the parlor. Her voice was somewhat muffled from the distance it had to travel in order to reach Summer's ears, but there was no mistaking its hysterical tone.

Finding the correct room at last, Summer headed directly to Elizabeth's dressing table. Perfume bottles, cold cream jars, hair trims and the infamous brush that had so badly bruised her cheek on that first day, all sat in neat display on the table top. She opened a drawer and then another in search of the laudanum, until she found the brown, corked bottle lying on its side. It was a duplicate of the brown bottle Lucy kept for nervous emergencies. Lifting it out of the drawer, she gasped; her heart skipped a beat. There, beneath the bottle, lay an envelope—an envelope addressed to *Miss Evaline Woodfield, Magnolia Plantation, Bluebell, Georgia.* She took it in her hand and, turning it over, her heart leapt with joy to see *'Robert Mason'* written on the back flap. She sighed in relief to discover that it was unopened. *How unlike Elizabeth,* she thought, wondering how the woman was able to contain her curiosity.

"Hurry, Evaline!" Susannah's shrill plea reached her ears. "I need you!"

Evaline tucked the letter under her arm and hurried to the door. *It's my letter. She has no right to keep it from me.* Not until she reached the bottom stair and attempted to hide the letter in a pocket, did she realize she had lost her most precious discovery; it had slipped away!

Elizabeth was a mess. Summer couldn't believe this was the same wanton woman who, in those moments of illicit passion, had ridden the overseer like a wild stallion, her golden hair cascading over white shoulders, her corset tossed to the wayside like garbage. Hysteria transformed her to the wizened creature who sat before her now, whose body trembled in grief. For one brief moment Summer felt great compassion for the woman whom she considered her ancestor, but that moment quickly dissipated as Elizabeth swung out at her as she offered the laudanum.

"Get away from me you bitch—whore! Get out of my house!"

'Bitch' and 'whore' to you, too, Summer wanted to say. *Keeping my letter from me like the witch you are.*

Susannah retrieved the laudanum from Summer's hand. "You must take some, mother—please!" She pulled the cork out of the bottle and offered it to Elizabeth who took a sip, and then another.

"All is lost," Elizabeth whimpered. "My Edmund…gone." She took another sip before Susannah removed the bottle. Charles helped himself to a glass of sherry, and stared blankly at the empty fireplace. A hush fell over the group, broken only by the sudden sobs of Susannah, who was finally allowed to cry for her lost brother.

✳ ✳ ✳

At the first opportunity, Summer sneaked into Elizabeth's room to search for the lost letter, but to no avail. She opened the drawers of the dressing table, searched under the bed and under all the furniture in the room. *Elizabeth has it—I know she does!* Regardless of the realization that the union of Evaline and Robert was not to be, she so desperately wanted to read his words…to feel close to him again.

✳ ✳ ✳

Six weeks had passed since news of Edmund's death. Elizabeth's challenging temperament became even more so, while Charles alienated himself from her in his study, in Savannah, or simply overseeing the overseer throughout the plantation. Rice farming had become nil with so little help, and he and Mason busied themselves with repairs, or directing the few freed slaves who remained on River Row. On this night, he would have to succumb to propriety, as Arthur Ascot and Margaret were joining the family for the evening meal.

Summer and Cherry carried the heavy trays of food, in the still oppressive heat, across the yard into the coolness of the basement and then up the stifling, airless stairway.

"Whew!" Summer whispered before entering the dining room. "I smell like the pigs!"

Cherry giggled. "Dey smell better n' you, gal."

The young women set the heavy trays on the sideboard and proceeded to fill the family soup bowls with the steaming pea and bacon concoction. The vision of the family gathered in the dining room never failed to amaze Summer; Charles and Arthur dressed in their black coats and bow ties, and the women afloat in enough black fabric to sink a steamer; the entire household was in mourning for the loss of Edmund. All four women wore their hair parted in the middle and formed into a roll at the nape of the neck, neatly contained by nets. Charles's white sideburns and mustache were prominent features on his round face, while Arthur's sleeker and shorter style brought attention to the dimples that gave him a playful and cheerful appearance. They appeared a proper group, maintaining dignity despite the crumbling world around them.

A *deceiving group,* Summer thought, as Arthur's hand caressed her left buttocks as she ladled the soup into his bowl. She jerked her leg, giving a signal (she hoped) for him to refrain from his lecherous behavior. It was consternation to her that no one ever noticed Arthur's advances. Beneath those dimpled cheeks, he was no better than Mason himself.

"I don't know about Magnolia, Charles, but what darkies remain at Royal Palms are getting quite feisty and insubordinate. I hear talk of downright rebellion from other planters." Arthur stopped to sip a spoonful of soup and wipe his mouth with the linen napkin.

"Later, Arthur!" Charles' face reddened as he shouted across the table. "You'll upset the ladies!"

"It truly astonishes me that you would expect otherwise," Susannah said, and sipped her wine as if she'd just wished them nothing more than a 'good evening'. "That's what happens when you keep people in bondage and treat them worse than dogs, then free them and *still* treat them worse than dogs!"

"Daughter, I love you, but have you not learned anything of the art of womanhood?" Charles turned to Elizabeth. "Did you not teach this child anything?"

"Enough said, Susannah," Elizabeth snipped.

"We will continue this conversation in the library, Arthur." Charles dipped his spoon into the bowl of soup Cherry set before him.

After supper, Arthur sent Margaret home alone in the carriage, while he remained behind, sequestered in the library with Charles. Arthur had set the stage with his talk of rebellious behavior. Summer, the evening chores complete, put an ear to the library door. All was quiet, and she assumed Arthur had left. It was late. It was *always* late before she was allowed to put her head to the pathetic, flat pillow on her cot. Exhaustion consumed her. She would have liked to listen in on the conversation in the study, but kitchen duties had demanded her time. She wearily opened the stairway door and closed it behind her, the lantern bobbing gently in her hand.

"Put the lantern down, Evaline." A chill as sharp a knife ran through her at the sound of Arthur's voice. She turned quickly to see him standing behind her on the dark landing.

"What are you doing here? Get out—go home!"

"You insolent, girl. Put the lantern down, I said.'

"I will not." Her neck hairs bristled as she turned her back to him. A grave mistake, she soon realized. He had his arm around her neck in the flash of a second, gripping her tightly against his chest, and cutting off her oxygen supply. With his free hand he took the lantern from her and relaxed his hold long enough to set it aside in what small area was available. She tried to elbow him, but he was too quick. She gasped for air as he whipped her around to face him. This time he grabbed the hair at the back of her skull and put a hand over her mouth.

"You scream and I'll break your neck, girl." He said, forcing her onto the stairs. The treads bit into her back, but she was helpless against his strength. Thoughts of poor Cherry, a young girl of thirteen in the grips of this monster, ran through her head.

"I've been waiting for this, you spoiled bitch. It's about time you got what's coming to you—put you in your place. This is all you're good for. Do you understand?" He tightened the grip on the handful of hair at the base of her skull, as his nails dug into the tender skin around her mouth. She smelled the brandy and the cigar on his breath. He briefly let go of her hair to fumble with his pants, but she was literally pinned, and painfully so, against the stairs—a nightmare within a nightmare. Nausea swept her. She wanted desperately to scream and tried to bite his palm. At last, with tireless effort, her mouth was free, and she screamed long and loud, filling the dark stairwell....

✳ ✳ ✳

"Summer! Wake up! Wake up!"

She woke up swinging. Jesse ducked to avoid being smacked in the face. "Stop, girl! You trying to kill me?"

"Jesse!" Oh my God, it's you! Is it *really* you?" Summer jumped out of bed and wrapped her arms around Jesse, nearly knocking them both over. "Am I really here?" she asked, leaving Jesse to open the great doors of the veranda and step out into the morning light. "I'm here—and I'm free!" She took a deep breath before the trembling began. Shrinking back into the bedroom she wrapped her arms around herself. "Unless...unless this is the dream and the other is my real life." Tears raged down her cheeks. "It was horrible."

"What's happened to you? All I know is you were screaming your bloody head off—scared the you-know-what out of me."

"What day is this? I was gone so long..."

"Gone? Where? You went to bed last night and now it's morning. You had a nightmare, my friend."

"I...I don't know, it was so real. I was Evaline, the slave girl. Miss Elizabeth hated me and she was so evil. She was sleeping with Mick Mason, the overseer. And then there was a pretty girl named Cherry, and her boyfriend, Juba. Poor Juba was killed by an alligator....and then that lecher Arthur Ascot, he raped Cherry when she was only thirteen and she had a baby by him, and then he had me in the servant stairway and was about to rape me when...when you saved me!"

"Slow down, girl, I didn't think you had *that* much to drink last night."

"I'm not joking, Jesse. Your Ruth was there too. She took care of me when Elizabeth beat me with the hairbrush and started her bedroom on fire."

"Fire?"

"I swear, it was *so real*. And the journal, Jesse, the journal—come with me!"

"You have really lost it, girl. What journal?"

"Evaline's journal. Let's see if it's there."

"Where?"

"In the attic stairwell."

"Summer, maybe you'd better have some coffee and relax a while."

"No, come with me. I have to find out."

Jesse followed her up the stairway to the third floor, through the nursery, through Ruth's old room to Evaline's room. Summer rested her hand warily on the attic latch. It was the same as the latch in her dream.

"Open the door, I gotta go to work," Jesse said impatiently.

Summer was half expecting to see Evaline staring back at her, but the stairwell was empty aside from floating dust particles. She sneezed.

"The third step," She mumbled to herself, and bent to pull on the tread.

"What in the world are you doing?"

"There's a journal in there—or I think there is. I hope it isn't. I don't want the dream to be true."

At one pull, the tread remained sturdily fixed. At two pulls it creaked. At three pulls it lifted completely into Summer's hands and sent her flying backward into Jesse.

Balance regained, they leaned together, peering into the dark pocket of the stair.

"Can't see a thing," Jesse said.

Summer reached her hand into the hollow darkness. 'Oh, no." she whispered, pulling out a dusty, worn book. "No, no, no. This can't be."

"Let me see that."

Summer leaned against the stairwell wall and handed the book to Jesse. "I can tell you what's in it."

"You're creeping me out again, girl," Jesse said, taking the book.

"Go to the first entry."

Jesse opened the book.

"It goes something like this... Poor Cherry Girl. Our hearts are broken..."

"Oh, my God! This is incredible."

"This is when the alligator killed Juba. Mr. Mason did nothing. He just stood there and let it happen."

"I don't understand this at all, Summer."

"And you think I do? I didn't ask for this! I was friggin' *there!* What now? What happens now?"

16

It was mystifying to Summer, that lying again in the comfy four-poster would feel strange. She dreamed of this moment for what seemed an eternity while living as Evaline, yet, here she was, tossing and turning the night away, wondering what was happening in the kitchen with Lucy. What was Cherry up to? Did Ruth miss her? Most of all, what happened to Evaline during the scuffle in the stairway between she and Arthur Ascot? Did she escape? These thoughts occupied her mind until the morning sun sent streams of light through the slits of the drapes. Thus began her second day back in the 21st century as Summer Woodfield.

"May as well get the heck up," she said, tossing aside the fluffy comforter. She leaned her hands on the sink in the bathroom and took inventory of her face; puffy eyes from lack of sleep, hair straight as uncooked spaghetti. She was so white, so flat chested, so...*dull. Gosh, I'm boring to look at.*

After a hot bath, she slid a pair of shorts over her deflated fanny and pulled on a t-shirt, half expecting Ruth to burst through the door to inform her that 'Miz 'Lisbet' was 'ringing dat bell.' It did not happen. It was quiet at Tanglewood Plantation.

Things livened up mid-morning when she noticed Guy's truck in the driveway. Her heart leapt! It seemed forever since she had seen him, and so much had happened since then. He said he would return on Wednesday to begin the reconstruction. Could it be that she had seen him only two days ago?

"Good morning, Guy," she said, resting her hands on a dilapidated picket of the old fence. "Whew, it's a hot one today, isn't it?" Already beads of sweat burned her eyes.

"It always is, in August," he replied. He stood perusing the overgrown and tangled vegetation in what was once Aunt Ada's show-worthy flower garden. "I'm just getting my bearings before I dig in."

"Uh, Guy, I thought of a couple other projects that perhaps you could help me with."

"Sure. Shoot."

"As you know, I have to live here for a year, and I'd sure like to hang the shutters on the house straight. They look so...so spooky as they are."

"I was going to suggest that. What else?"

"Blaine is trying to find me a live-in lady so I don't have to be here alone. Jesse needs to get back to her place in Savannah—guess she can't baby-sit me forever. The only decent bedroom is Aunt Ada's, and it's mine, now. I'd like to fix one of the other rooms up and make it livable. Most of the house is in pretty bad condition."

"No problem. Let me finish my other jobs this week and we can start on the weekend. Okay with you?"

"Sure. Oh, and...uh...if you have a moment later, come in for iced tea. I want to show you something...something very strange."

"Is everything okay?"

"I wish I knew. In fact, just come in around noon and I'll fix you lunch."

"After that cryptic statement, you bet I'll be there."

✳ ✳ ✳

"You sure have my curiosity up, Summer." Guy vigorously washed his hands at the kitchen sink.

She handed him a towel and again marveled that the smell of a man working in the sweltering heat of Georgia could be an aphrodisiac. "Love the bandana," she said, of the blue bandana that wrapped tightly around his forehead to keep the sweat from his eyes. "You are definitely geared for this climate."

"Years of experience."

She told him to take a seat at the table, and glanced at the journal that sat in the middle, where once the small chest from the attic sat between them at their first tea together.

"Is this what you want to show me?" he tapped a large, tanned finger on the book.

"Let me explain first—if I can. I...I had a nightmare Monday night, after our dinner party, only it seemed so real. Now, don't laugh at me, I'm very upset over this."

"I'm not laughing." He took a gulp of tea and watched her intently, his dark eyes—Robert's eyes—staring beneath the brow.

It rattled her a moment, that he and Robert should resemble each other in such a way, but she continued. "I dreamed I woke up and it was 1861, and I…I was Evaline! I was still myself, but I was a slave here and couldn't get back to my time. The people in the paintings in the dining room—they were here, too; Charles and Elizabeth Woodfield, Margaret, and her husband, Arthur Ascot. Susannah, and…and Mick Mason too. He was terrible, Guy, so cruel! And there were the slaves, Ruth, Lucy, Cherry, Pompeii, Juba—he was killed by an alligator—and Percy, a little boy. But Guy, Robert Mason was here too, and I was Evaline and I fell in love with him!"

"Well, that's quite a dream, Summer."

"Then, Evaline's ghost kept coming to me. She was trying to tell me something. She wanted me to find her journal, and I did. It was hidden in the third step from the bottom in the attic stairway."

"A very well defined dream, I'd say."

"The only thing is…I don't think it was a dream."

He raised his eyebrows. "Why not?"

"At the end of the dream, Arthur Ascot was trying to rape me—or Evaline, rather—in the servant stairway, and I screamed and screamed. That's when I woke up and was myself again."

"And?"

Darn. She could see the disbelief in his eyes. She really liked this guy and now he knew for sure she was nuts.

"And when I woke up, I told Jesse about the journal hidden in the stairs, and we went to look and…." She nodded to the book on the table.

Guy's eyes widened. "You mean *this* is the journal?"

"Jesse is my witness. And I told her, without looking, what was on the first page."

They both sat silently staring at the journal.

"Not too much is written in there. Go ahead and look."

Summer busied herself around the kitchen preparing lunch while Guy read the few pages in Evaline's journal.

"Well," he said, finally. "This sure answers the paternity question of Evaline's child."

"What do you mean?" Summer asked, placing a tuna sandwich and chips in front of him.

"Didn't you read this part?"

"Let me see that." Summer wiped her hands on a towel and took the book from him.

"October 8, 1863
What did I do to deserve this misfortune? What will I say to Miss Elizabeth—to my father? And what will I say to Robert if he returns to see my belly big with child? Oh mercy, he will think I have deceived him! God, strike me dead and curse Arthur Ascot!"

"Oh, my god, this wasn't here yesterday!" Summer plopped herself onto her chair.

"I don't know what to say, Summer."

"Just don't tell me I'm nuts. I'm telling you, I was there! I *was* Evaline. I don't understand what's happening to me. Ever since I came here, strange things have happened; Charles Woodfield hanging from the fountain—did you know that really happened? He hung himself out there on the fountain. Then there's the horrible sound the fountain makes, and...the mirror in the attic."

"The mirror?"

"Oh never mind. It's too hard to believe anyway."

"Try me."

Summer weighed the pros and cons of confessing all the supernatural events that had befallen her, and decided to take a gamble. "When Jesse and I found the trunk in the attic, we also found a larger trunk full of period clothes. Jesse talked me into trying on a dress—a fancy dress. She helped me put it on and when I looked in the mirror, it wasn't me! I didn't know it then, but it was Evaline I saw in the mirror—wearing the same dress that's in the tintype I showed you. Then, the man, your Robert, he was in the mirror too, staring at me."

Guy was silent. She handed the book back to him. "I don't blame you for not saying anything. What's to say? Maybe I *am* going crazy, that's all. But, be my witness, look at the following page. Is anything written there?"

Guy turned the page. "Nothing."

"Take it with you. I can't duplicate the handwriting in case you think I wrote that stuff. Take it with you, put it in a safe place and if anything new is written, bring it back to me."

"It's not that I disbelieve you, Summer. It's a hard story to swallow."

"It's hard for me to swallow, too."

Summer picked at her sandwich, while Guy appeared to consume his in two bites. He stood, securing the journal gently under his arm. "Back to the garden. Thanks for a delicious lunch. Don't get yourself into a slump, now. I don't think you're crazy, if that's what you're thinking. Let's put the book away and forget it for a while. Meantime, I'll be back on Saturday and we'll get started on the house."

Some impression I'm making. She wouldn't blame him if he thought up an excuse to stay away. On the other hand, she couldn't keep this all to herself, and would have to take her chances.

* * *

"Good news," Jesse said, plunking her purse and a bag of groceries on the kitchen table. "Blaine may have found you a housekeeper. He'd like to drive her out tomorrow for an interview. Okay with you?"

So soon? She was accustomed to Jesse at this point. At least Jesse was in on the oddities of the place. "Well, okay. I'm sure you're looking forward to getting back to your life."

"I love ya, Summer, but it's a haul driving back and forth to Savannah every day. I won't leave until we have someone permanent, though. This house gives me the creeps once in a while, too."

"I told Guy about the diary today, and you won't believe what happened...there was another entry."

"Ano...you're joking."

Summer shook her head. "Nope. I can tell you who fathered Evaline's child, Arthur Ascot, Blaine's ancestor. It was written in the journal today."

"What?"

"It was so sad, what he did to Evaline. I gave the journal to Guy to keep for a while. He must think I'm nuts or that I wrote the entries, but you know I didn't, don't you?"

'It looked too old for you to have written it, and why would you, anyway?"

"Exactly. What crazy reason could I have to make up a story like that? To tell you the truth, I don't think I have the imagination to make it up. I gave Guy the book to keep for me, and told him if there was another new entry, to bring it back and show me."

"This place gets creepier and creepier," Jesse said, unpacking the brown grocery bag. "I don't blame you one bit for not wanting to stay alone. Wait till Blaine hears what a bad boy Arthur Ascot was. Oh, and I almost forgot. I brought copies of the deeds, from the first to the last."

Summer's heart skipped a beat. "Well, let's see them, for Pete's sake!"

"Okay, hold your horses."

Sitting at the table, Jesse removed a large envelope from her briefcase. "I didn't read them completely, I just copied. Okay, here we go. Let's see...in 1803 the land was purchased by Edmond James Woodfield. Land was deeded in...1843 to son Charles Woodfield. In 1864, the land went to Susannah as her brothers were both dead, and Charles was dead, too. In 1890, Susannah dies and the property is deeded to...oh!"

"Oh, what?"

"Oh my god, Summer, you won't believe this!"

"What? Tell me!"

"Susannah leaves the property to Evaline's son, James!"

Silence was never so silent.

"Go on," Summer whispered.

"Okay...okay." Jesse took a breath. "In 1922 James died, and the property was deeded to his son, George. In 1962 the property went to George's son, David and George's daughter—I can't believe this—Ada Woodfield!"

"I'm glad I'm already sitting down." Summer said.

"When David died, Ada maintained the house. Your father, son of David, died, and therefore the property went to you...the last Woodfield."

Summer laid her head on the table. "I can't believe this. No wonder I couldn't find a connection at the courthouse. Did Aunt Ada know? Did she know about Jamaica?" She sat up, the realization of the discovery taking full effect. "This means Evaline is my...my what? My great-great-great-great grandmother?"

"Good grief, girl!" Jesse jumped out of her chair. "You and I are cousins, since Jamaica and Ruth were sisters!"

"I don't know how we missed the family resemblance." Summer mumbled.

"And you know what else? You and Blaine are cousins, too!"

17

On Saturday morning, as promised, Guy stood at the front door, a pile of tools stacked beside him on the porch.

"Come in for coffee, Guy. I have something very interesting to tell you."

"You can always be counted on for a surprise, Summer."

"You must be getting tired of those surprises. I gather I am appearing more and more like the Woodfield lunatic. Evaline has avoided the journal, I suppose."

"I haven't checked since Thursday."

Guy followed her to the kitchen, where again, an object of interest sat as a centerpiece. "Is this the interesting thing you have to tell me?" he asked, tapping a large, tanned finger on the stack of deeds.

"It is," she replied, setting a mug of coffee in front of him. "Oh, cream & sugar?"

"Black."

"Taken like a real man," she said, and sat across from him.

"I'll get straight to the point. Jesse brought home copies of the entire set of plantation deeds this week. Here they are, from 1803 to the present." She tapped the pile between them. "It appears that the reason I couldn't find a link between myself and the Woodfield boys, is because I don't descend from either of them."

"Are you sure?"

"According to this stack of papers, legal and proper, I descend from Evaline Woodfield, the child of Charles Woodfield and the slave woman, Jamaica, and Arthur Ascot, owner of Royal Palms Plantation and husband to Margaret Woodfield. Talk about soap operas…."

"Whoa! Let me catch my breath. You never cease to amaze me, Summer Woodfield!"

"I find it pretty amazing myself. Aunt Ada must have known this all along."

"Well, don't worry yourself over it," he said after a long silence. It's not really of any consequence. It's just an unusual circumstance, and a pretty interesting one at that. You were worried about not being a Woodfield, and now you can be assured that you are."

"I'm stunned."

"In a way, Tanglewood is more yours than anyone else's."

"What do you mean?"

"Look at it this way, you descend not only from the plantation owner, but from the slaves as well, the people who made it the success it was."

"Are you placating me?"

"No. I can understand what a shock this is, but, on the other hand, I think it's an honor for you to be standing here, in this place, the final product of such an amazing history."

"The painting of Evaline in the dining room takes on a whole new meaning now, as does the journal, the tintype and the dream—if it were a dream. And, you're right, Tanglewood is exclusively mine."

"So, Mistress of the Great Plantation, shall we get to work?"

✷ ✷ ✷

Guy proved as thorough a worker inside as he was outside. Together, they scraped the windows in the room that once was Elizabeth's. That particular room was not Summer's first choice. It gave her the creeps, but it was the only bedroom without damage to the glass in the windows. She had chosen paint colors in town earlier that week; pale yellow for the walls and white for the window sills and trim. By mid-afternoon, the scraped and painted windows were a recognizable measure of improvement.

"I love immediate gratification," she said, standing back to admire the freshly painted sills. The room should be light and cheery by the time we're done."

"I'll rent a sander in town and we can get this floor back into beautiful condition, perhaps even get that burn spot out." He pointed to a blackened spot in the center of the room.

Summer had been eyeing it for hours, and could hold back its origin no longer. "I can tell you exactly how that happened, but you'll think I'm crazier than you think I am already."

"I'm all ears. Your surprises are growing on me."

"On my first day as Evaline, I was sent to Miss Elizabeth's room with her breakfast tray. Being a total idiot in the art of slavery, I didn't present the breakfast tray to her properly. Of course I had no clue at that time how much she hated me—or Evaline, rather. She was brushing her hair when I came through the door. The next thing I knew, she stormed at me like the lunatic she is…was…and hit me in the face full force with the hairbrush she had in her hand. It hurt like the devil, too. I dropped the breakfast tray, and the oil lantern that I carried to light the servant stairway, fell to the floor and the oil spilled, which started her robe on fire. I saved the day, of course, but she never said a thank-you for saving her life." Summer crossed her arms over her chest. "And that is why there is a burn mark in the middle of this floor."

They stood looking at each other, the burn mark between them.

"I know you think I'm nuts, but let me carry this a step further. Let's see…." She paced the room, looking up at the ceiling. "There it is," she said, pointing upward. "Come with me, I have a treat for you." She lifted a small flashlight that arrived with his pile of tools and opened the servant stairway door. "Watch your step, these are very narrow treads."

"I'll say," Guy said, hunched over behind her. "This wasn't built for tall folks! My feet don't fit, either."

"Bear with it. If you were a Magnolia house slave, you'd have no choice but to use this stairway. You're too big, though. They'd have you outside using your muscle."

"A natural born plantation mistress, you are. You instinctively know where to put me."

Summer opened the door to the nursery, and marched straight ahead to where she remembered the old peeping hole. "I hope it's still here…let's see…aha! This must be it!" She kneeled down on all fours and gestured Guy to join her. "Oops. Do you have a screwdriver or penknife on you?"

"I come prepared for all emergencies," he said, and whipped a small knife out of his back pocket.

"See if you can lift this piece of wood here." She pointed to a thin slice of wood the size of a house shingle, nailed to the floor.

Guy pried the wood up and uncovered a hole in the floor. "What's this?"

"You might say this was Cherry's television set. Cherry was a slave here, too. When Mick Mason came for his 'instruction meeting'—which he only came for when the master was away—this is where the meetings were held. Take a peek."

Guy put his eye to the floor. "It's a room."

"It's Elizabeth's bedroom."

"Are you telling me that Elizabeth and Mick Mason were...*you know?*" She swore Guy blushed.

"Yes, indeed, they were '*you know*'. Elizabeth's bed was beneath this peephole, and Cherry and I came up here and watched." She flushed with the memory.

"You voyeurs, you!"

"Now tell me truthfully, how long do you think that piece of wood has been nailed there?"

Guy lifted the peephole cover, complete with the four nails that tacked it down still protruding through the wood. "I'd say these aren't any nails I could buy at Home Depot. And, I'd say that piece of wood was there for quite a while."

"Strange, don't you think? Strange that Summer Woodfield, screwball from Chicago, would know exactly where to look for a teensy peephole in a floor in a house that's a couple centuries old?"

"I have to admit it's a mystery."

"Come on, one more visit."

Guy followed her to Evaline's room, where she paused at the attic door. She never knew what she'd find on the other side and it always caused her a moment of trepidation. Opening the door, she realized she had neglected to replace the tread back over the third step when she and Cherry retrieved the journal.

"This is where I found the journal. Odd I would know that, don't you think?"

"Odd." He agreed and laid the tread back in place.

"And that," she said, once at the top of the stairs, "is the mirror."

She removed the black dress that Jesse had thrown over the mirror under her instruction that day, and stepped to view her reflection. She felt brave with Guy nearby. The mirror did not disappoint, for there stood Evaline, full breasts, small waist, mocha skin, black curls framing her beautiful face. Robert appeared behind her, standing tall and handsome, the dark shock of hair touching his brow, his eyes intent on her, his love. She melted when she felt his hands on her arms turning her, turning her to face him, lifting her face, and then touching her lips lightly with his—then passionately. It was a treasured moment, one that she would cherish.

"You have such an effect on me, Summer." Guy said, releasing her

Summer opened her eyes from the rapture. "I guess you didn't see them in the mirror."

"See who?"

She paused. "Evaline, and Robert."

I saw you and me, Summer Woodfield and Guy Mason."

"Were we kissing?" she asked.

"You don't remember?"

"I…I just wasn't quite sure it really happened, but it was wonderful."

❋ ❋ ❋

Blaine arrived mid-afternoon with Emma Jenkins, short, stout and eager for the position of housekeeper. She was robust and cheery, which were very welcomed attributes considering the ominous atmosphere of Tanglewood Plantation. Summer was delighted and hired her immediately.

"I'll see you next week," she said, as Blaine and Emma walked across the grand portico to the steps. "The room will be ready when you return!" she called, as they stepped into Blaine's limo.

Summer was surprised to see Guy's truck approaching as Blaine's limo pulled away. He had left shortly after the strange episode in the attic that afternoon and hadn't planned on returning until the following day. She waited in the doorway and felt a wave of alarm run through her as he stepped out of the truck with the journal in hand.

"Evaline has spoken again?"

"After your vision in the attic, I decided to take a look, and here it is," he said, tapping the cover of the aged book.

"Time for coffee, I guess."

Guy followed her to the kitchen where they once again sat at the worn table.

"Maybe you believe me now?"

"I do. I don't understand any of this, but I certainly do believe you."

✳ ✳ ✳

The Journal of Evaline Woodfield

March 16, 1863

I think the baby will come in May—if I live so long. Miss Elizabeth does not stop badgering me and would work me to death if she could get away with it...

✳ ✳ ✳

"I think I should like you to clean the fireplace this morning, Evaline."

"Beg your pardon, Ma'am, but I don't think I can." Evaline rubbed her swollen belly, indicating her reason for the objection.

"I'm not asking, Evaline, I'm *telling* you. I want my fireplace cleaned, and I want it cleaned *now!* Do you understand, or must Mr. Mason convince you?"

"I understand," she mumbled, eyeing the mess of ash and burnt wood.

"It's not my fault you are such a brazen whore, sleeping with Robert Mason and getting with child. The master is very disappointed in you. You should have thought of the consequences."

Elizabeth Woodfield sat at the dressing table brushing her hair. Not once did she take her eyes off of Evaline's reflection in the mirror during their verbal exchange. Not once did she smile, or show a glimmer of concern for the very pregnant, young mulatto girl who now lowered herself with difficulty to the hardwood floor.

With a hand shovel, Evaline scooped the ash and wood bits into the pail that always sat next to the firewood stacked neatly to the side of the fireplace. Each shovel-full brought pain and anguish to her back forcing her to stop between scoops and rest a moment. In the mirror, her mistress watched, her lips curled in a smile.

"That should teach you to lay with a white man. He doesn't care a hoot for you. You're just another nigger wench—one of many."

The words hurt, but what could she do to stop them? The master was already angry, thinking Robert was responsible for her pregnancy, but she feared the repercussions should she tell her father the truth of the matter, that Arthur Ascot had raped her. Mr. Ascot would deny it, and she would be punished severely if the mistress had her way. She could even end up *dead*. She thought of leaving a note with Ruth to give to her father, should anything happen to her. She couldn't bear the thought of dying with her father thinking she had willingly brought the situation upon herself, and with the overseer's son at that! It had to be known, should she die as a result of wrongdoing, that it was Arthur Ascot's child she carried, and not Robert Mason's.

"My father thinks me a whore, Ruth," she confided later that night.

"Po' chile'", Ruth said, rubbing Evaline's back and shoulders as she lay on her cot. "Dat woman workin' you to da death on purpose."

"She hates me."

"She hates you, 'cause you's yo' daddy's favorite chile'.

"Sometimes I wish I wouldn't wake up in the morning."

"Don' say dat, Evaline. We's gonna leave here one day and on dat day, you's gonna be glad you's alive! You an' yo' little baby gonna live free from dis misery!"

✳ ✳ ✳

...Ruth believes we will be able to leave here one day. What will Miss Elizabeth do then, when she has no one to do her bidding?"

✳ ✳ ✳

"Oh, poor Evaline," Summer said, laying the opened journal on the table."

"Why Summer Woodfield, I do believe that is a tear rolling down your cheek."

Summer wiped her eyes with a napkin and sighed. "It's hard reading Evaline's words, now that I know we're connected. I know what her life was like because I lived it, but these past two entries are hers—in her own words—and they're touching. Before, the pages in the journal appeared *after* I experienced an event, but this...this is different." Summer turned the page, wondering what the next installment would bring, and stopped short, her body shot with gooseflesh. "Guy! Quick!"

Guy leapt out of his chair in time to witness words appearing in bursts of pencil on the previously empty journal page.

"Good god, she's writing!"

Summer was just as shocked as Guy. Words formed sentences, and sentences, paragraphs, as they stared on in amazement.

April 25, 1864

Mr. Ascot rode up yesterday with terrible news, John is dead! Despite my feelings toward Miss Elizabeth, I feel a terrible sorrow for her and the master. So many are dead, and fear is rampant. The Yankees rode through and took most of the livestock with no thought to the rest of us. We have our freedom but we're afraid to leave and too afraid of the Yankees. And now...I can hardly bare to write this...Mr. Ascot and Miss Margaret were here tonight and...

✻ ✻ ✻

"...Ain't no chickens left," Pompeii announced. He set the hatchet down on the outside of the door as he stepped into the kitchen.

"Dem Yankees took everything when dey come through." Lucy stood at the stove stirring a large pot. "Got nothin' to put in the soup but a few greens, a potato and a sorry onion. Miz 'Lizbet ain't gonna like dis."

"Don' worry bout Miz 'Lizbet. She won't be wantin' no soup today," Cherry said.

"No, I s'pose she ain't," Lucy sighed. "I don' know what we's gonna eat tonight. Ain't enough even for da white folks."

It was a meager supper, indeed, compared to meals of yesterday's past. Instead of trays overloaded with chicken, ham, potatoes, greens and pies, Cherry carried a tray bearing a lone soup tureen while Evaline carried a basket of biscuits. It took extreme self control and fear of Mr. Mason, (who still taunted with a whip) to keep them from stealing a few biscuits, they were so hungry. It wouldn't be long before there was no flour in the bin for the making of biscuits, and what would they do then?

In an atmosphere heavy with grief, Cherry ladled the thin soup into the bowls of the Woodfield and Ascot families, while Evaline set a biscuit at each place setting.

"Is this all, Evaline?" her father asked.

"Yes, sir. There is nothing else."

"Damn Yankees. May they rot in hell—every last one of them." Charles Woodfield bore the brunt of the Yankee's passing with a purple bruise on his right cheek; his reward attempting to stop soldiers from stealing the last of the livestock.

The ravages of war were beginning to show in every aspect of the privileged family. The propriety of dress waned as an aging rose, barely noticeable at first, and then tinged and limp, the petals fell. As the remaining servant's anxieties rose, the usual competence with which they each worked their tasks, lessened. They were no longer slaves in word, but still bound by poverty and illiteracy. Despite Mr. Mason's presence, the plantation slowed from a bustling city within itself to a pool of sludge through which its inhabitants dragged their weary limbs.

"All is lost, Charles." Elizabeth's weak and defeated tone sounded strange to Evaline's ear. This was not the woman who spent every moment of her day contemplating Evaline's ruination; this was not the woman whose sharp tongue cut as deeply as Mason's whip.

After supper, the ladies retired to the parlor while Charles and Arthur took their brandy in the library. The after-dinner-brandy tradition would soon end at Magnolia, for there was only one bottle left. Evaline had caught a glimpse of it the day before when she helped Miss Elizabeth take inventory in the locked storage room in the basement, before the bad news arrived regarding John's death. It was frightening to see the empty shelves.

Cherry left the dining room carrying a tray loaded with empty dishes, while Evaline remained behind to wipe the table and set the chairs straight. Her back ached from the long day of labor, as well as her feet from carrying the extra weight of the baby.

"Soon as that baby's weaned, I'm taking it."

Arthur's voice sent prickles up her spine. She turned to see that he had closed the dining room door behind him, and she was trapped.

"Should be near white, and it's mine. God knows my wife hasn't given me any children."

"What if I tell the master it's yours?"

"You're not going to do that, Evaline. If you do, I'll break your neck, and you know I will."

"You can't have my baby."

He came close until he grasped her chin in his hand. "Oh, yes I can—and I will."

"Arthur!" Miss Margaret's voice pierced the moment. "What are you doing in here?" she asked, poking her head around the now opened door.

"Uh...I thought I dropped my watch at dinner, my dear. But here it is, far down in my pocket."

"Goodnight, Evaline," Margaret said. "Come, Arthur, it's late..."

❋ ❋ ❋

..."I wanted to tell Miss Margaret what an evil man her husband is. I wanted to tell her that he wants my child, the one he forced on me, but I kept silent. When will this misery end?"

❋ ❋ ❋

Summer and Guy stared at the journal page waiting to see if Evaline would continue writing, but she did not.

"Poor Evaline. What is she going to do?" Summer felt sick with this newest entry.

"Don't you mean 'what happened'? It's already been done—over a century ago."

"I know...but it seems like it's happening *now.* In a way, it *is* happening now, and I *know* Evaline—I *was* Evaline—and it's like it's happening to me, too."

Night had fallen by the time Summer walked Guy to his truck. Jesse was late, and she didn't relish walking back into the house alone. "She should be pulling up any minute now, really." She tried to sound nonchalant, but felt like a whiney woman—she *was* a whiney woman, scared of her own house.

"We can talk a while," Guy leaned against the truck door. "This whole thing is so strange; I can barely compute it in my head."

"It's been like that for me since the day I arrived. It's like these people—these ancestors of mine—are trying to tell me something, but I don't know what it is yet. I feel like they're depending on me to do something for them, but I don't know what."

"I'd like to kiss you again."

"What does that have to do with the price of tea in China?" she asked.

"Nothing, but I'd like to kiss you."

"I'd like that too," she said, and within a fraction of a second his lips were on hers, at first gently, then passionately, taking her back to the river bank the night Robert left, to the sensual kiss by his ghost; it was all the same deep longing pulling at her heart.

"Whew," she said, pulling away, the warm summer night between them.

"Just like magic, Summer. I'm so drawn to you."

"And I, to you," she said, while thinking all the while that the love Evaline felt for Robert had carried through a century and a half to this moment. At last, there was a glimmer of hope—the promise of fulfillment for the star-crossed lovers.

"Can we do it again?" Guy smiled.

"You bet."

"Hey, you two, cut it out!"

So lost were they in their joint attraction, that they did not notice Jesse's car approaching. Embarrassed, Summer bid goodnight to Guy and followed Jesse into the house.

"Looks like you got something hot cookin' there, girl."

"It's strange, Jesse, but when I'm with him, I feel like I'm Evaline again, and he's Robert."

"Look," Jesse said, setting her purse on the kitchen counter. "Evaline and Robert are dead...we think, anyway. Lots of crazy stuff going on here, granted, but *you* are Summer Woodfield, *he* is Guy Mason, and this is today. The Civil War is done and over with. You are back from your nightmare, so just enjoy the man!"

Later that night, her head settled in the pillows on Aunt Ada's four-poster, Summer read again the words of Robert Mason.

"I leave a thumbprint on this page. Press your thumb to mine, dear Evaline, and feel the love I send to you. When you are afraid and lonely, press your thumb to mine and I will be with you. Distance and time cannot separate us, for our love transcends the evil circumstance of our world. Wait for me, my dearest. I shall return."

She wondered what would happen if she touched the thumbprint. Would she return to Magnolia Plantation? She cried for Evaline's dilemma and horror at the thought of losing her child to Arthur Ascot. *How can I leave them like this?* How could she go on knowing that Evaline was suffering so? What happened to the others? There were so many unanswered questions!

18

I don't want to do this! Send me back!" Summer peeked over her knees to the top of Ruth's head, which was all she could see from this position. "I made a mistake! Send me back!" she screamed. Her great belly contracted, creating a shooting pain that wrapped around her torso like a steel vise.

"Evaline, da baby's head is here! Another push and you's gonna be okay!"

Another push? She had no control over her body—it had taken on a life of its own, trying to kill her with a terrifying vengeance. She screamed as the vise tightened, sending the pain ever sharper into her lower back.

"Push now, baby. Give it a push!"

From somewhere, Cherry told her to hold on tight, and took Summer's hands in her own. "Come on girl, you can do it."

The vise tightened again, the knife-like pain twisting, arching her back, squeezing the breath out of her. She could not endure another minute of this agony!

"Push, Evaline! One more push!"

Push! With whatever ounce of stamina that was left, she filled her lungs and pushed with all her might to end this misery—this nightmare she had brought upon herself. One touch of the thumbprint on Robert Mason's letter had brought her to this moment!

It was over. A baby wailed out of sight, over her knees.

"Thank God," she said, more for the end of pain than anything else.

A few seconds of rustling and Ruth's head popped into sight, white teeth wide in a smile. "Look Evaline, what a handsome boy!"

Ruth came around the cot, the small bundle wrapped in a knitted blanket; another gesture of kindness on Ruth's part with yarn scraps saved from the making of shawls and blankets for the manor house.

"Oh, Evaline!" Cherry was beside Ruth ogling over the creature Summer had not yet set eyes on, the creature Summer had just gone through hell for, the creature who was Percy's half brother, Cherry's cousin and her very own great-great-great-grandfather.

Much to her own surprise, her heart melted when she finally saw the bundle that was placed into her arms. She was surprised at the weight of him, the solid form that came from her body, the little mouth that yawned, the eyes that opened briefly to check that his mother was near. "I'm here," she said, sticking a finger into his tiny fist. "He's so white."

Ruth laughed. "Dey's all white at first."

She rested her cheek on the brown fuzz that covered the top of his head. The moment of splendor was short lived when she remembered Arthur Ascots words:

'Soon as that baby's weaned, I'm taking it.'

"Oh, no!" she said aloud. "Mr. Ascot said he's going to take him from me!"

She caught the look that passed between Cherry and Ruth. "Well, he can't have him. I won't let him!" Fear wrenched her gut, as strongly as the pains that had racked her body a few short moments ago. "He's mine, and he can't have him. I'll...I'll run away."

"Ain't no place to run to, chile'. Take what joy you can while you have dat sweet boy."

✳ ✳ ✳

By November of 1864, Lack of news from Robert was accepted by Summer with a bittersweet mixture of relief and remorse. She didn't know what to tell him about the baby for fear he would think she was agreeably ravished by Arthur Ascot. Of course, nothing could be further from the truth and she hardy believed he could even imagine it as being such. Still, recalling how Robert refused her sexual advances and, considering the century she was in, perhaps it *would* make a difference in his feelings for her now that she, or rather Evaline, was not the pristine virgin he left behind.

She was so desperate to hear from him that she sometimes forgot about his 19th century morals and just assumed things would pick up where left off, should he return. But then, she knew for a fact that the lovers—or would-be lovers—*never met again* and that all her silly dreaming was for naught.

Maybe I really am crazy. Here she was, stuck again in the 19th century and worrying about her relationship with a dead man! *It isn't me he loves, anyway,* she reminded herself. But then, the pain of love lost took hold and wrenched her heart. She just couldn't help it; when she lived as Evaline, resist as she may, she was totally consumed by Evaline's life. "Like dual citizenship," she said aloud.

"What's dat, Evaline?"

"You wouldn't understand, Cherry."

This was Summer's first experience with wash day on the plantation and from her observation it wasn't going to be an easy task. The slaves who were responsible for laundry washing were long gone, due to the Emancipation Proclamation.

Cherry had fires going beneath two four-foot-in-circumference iron pots behind the smokehouse and the heat certainly felt good in the brisk November air. Wooden paddles, or 'battling sticks', as Cherry called them, lay in the grass beside the pots. A ten foot tree log, which had been sawed and sanded to a flat surface on one side, lay a few feet away, flat side up.

Percy and Lucy arrived shortly, both overloaded with straw baskets full of dirty clothing. Lucy dumped the contents of both baskets into the pot with the steaming, soapy water.

"Now what," Summer asked hands on hips.

"Get da stick, Evaline, b'fo I bats you with it."

"From 'can see' to 'can't see'" she muttered, repeating an expression she heard the slaves use referring to their endless workdays. "Bah humbug to emancipation!"

Lucy didn't appear to be in a very good mood, and no wonder; coming up with food for the white folks several times a day was a challenge she could barely accomplish. The garden was picked to pieces, the livestock gone, the smokehouse empty, and the root cellar nearly depleted of root vegetables. The flour bin was down to a cup or two and full of mealy worms. Even the mealy worms looked good at this point, and Summer resigned herself to the fact that every time she was lucky enough to bite into a biscuit, she was ingesting her fair share of the critters.

Summer picked a battling stick off the ground and followed suit with Cherry who was stirring the pot full of clothing. With her battling stick, Cherry separated the laundry load into two sections, scooting Summer's half to the other side of the pot.

"Dat yours, and keep yo' stick over der."

Summer obeyed, sensing Lucy's dour mood had affected Cherry's general good nature. Baby James, six months old now, was upstairs in the nursery under Ruth's care, and soon, Summer knew her nipples would begin to tingle and she would be reprieved of wash duty in order to feed the baby.

It was the strangest sensation—having given birth to and nursing an infant, when in her real life in the 21st century, she had never even been pregnant! The fact that she was totally in love with the baby caused her some concern. More outrageous was the fact that the baby was her ancestor! It was a mindboggling concept which she chose to push out of her mind every time the thought arose. She assumed she would return eventually to the 21st century, leaving her child—Evaline's child—behind, but until then, she would take the very best care of James.

"Take da clothes out!" Cherry barked, waking Summer from her reflections on baby love and the anxieties of separation that were beginning to creep up on her. Following Cherry's orders, she found the weight of the wet clothes on the battling stick enough to bend her in half.

"Puts dem on dat log."

Summer watched as Cherry laid a steaming white shirt belonging to Charles, out on the flat side of the log. She then took her battling stick and whacked at the shirt with fearful strength. When she felt the shirt was sufficiently whacked, she placed it into the pot of clear, steaming water.

"I guess 'battling' is a good name for this thing," Summer mumbled, viewing with disgust the pile of hot, wet clothing she had removed from the pot. By the time she had finished whacking her pile, she knew she was in for a night of pain and agony having used every muscle in her body. Not even an aspirin! *This may be a good night for Lucy's brown bottle; visit the 19th century and become a drug addict!* Things hadn't changed so much after all, between the centuries.

"You have got to be kidding!" Summer stood in awe as Cherry hoisted a basket full of wet clothing onto her head. It balanced perfectly atop her red bandana, creating a colorful picture for which Summer wished she had a camera; Cherry in her plain homespun shirt and skirt, an apron cinched tightly around her small waist, the red bandana and straw basket vivid against a clear blue afternoon sky.

"Evaline," Cherry said, ignorant of the photogenic moment, "gits da basket and lets go. I been here long enough today."

Summer looked with dismay at her own basket full of wet clothing. "I wouldn't even know how to begin to get this thing on my head, Cherry."

Cherry tapped her foot in the grass. "You's useless since you lost yo' head."

"I'm useless when it comes to laundry acrobatics! Okay, okay. I'll try it." Emulating Cherry's basket swinging action, Summer aimed for the top of her head but instead, smacked herself in the face with the basket, falling backward onto the grass, the clothes spilling out into a wet lump beside her. Suffering the humility of Cherry's squeals of laughter, she rubbed the spot on her forehead where the basket made contact. "If at first you don't succeed...." She had all intentions of giving it another go, when Cherry's squeals of laughter turned to shrieks of fear, sending ripples of gooseflesh up Summer's spine.

"Yankees! Da Yankees! Run!"

Summer craned her neck to see three riders barreling across the field at a gallop. Reason and history told her that these were the good guys, but the speed at which they approached raised her hackles. Cherry had dropped her basket and dashed toward the safety of the compound.

"Damn." Summer struggled to her feet, but too late. One rider reined his horse to a stop in front of her, blocking her path. The other two riders rode circles around Cherry until she stopped in her tracks. Summer watched her bend over, gasping for air, her hands on her knees.

"What are you doing?" Summer asked the stranger, feeling somewhat comradely since they were both 'Yankees'. He had two chevrons on his sleeve so she assumed he was an officer of sorts.

"Move on," the soldier said, then clicked his tongue at the horse. Summer had no recourse but to move forward, the horse's breath hot on the back of her neck.

"You haven't answered my question."

"I don't answer questions, girl, I ask them."

As they approached the other riders, Cherry latched on tightly to Summer's arm.

"What do we have here, but two pretty darkies!" The youngest soldier spit a wad of tobacco into the grass.

"Looks like our lucky night, Zach!" said the second soldier.

They were a ragged looking bunch, and Summer shuddered against the instinctive fear growing inside. *Maybe we aren't comrades.* She reminded herself that she was smarter than these guys. After all, she came from the 21st century; she knew the war was over, she knew who won. She had computers, television, and modern medicine. She *had* to be smarter and had to prove herself unafraid.

"What do you want?" she asked again, a bit more boldly.

The second soldier and Zach laughed. "What do we want, Corp?"

"We have no food to share."

"Well...what *do* you have?"asked the Corporal..

"Nothing for Yankee bullies. I thought you were trying to help us."

"Shut up, Evaline. Yo's gonna get us in trouble!" Cherry whispered.

"You don't sound like no southern darkie." Zach cocked his head and squinted at Summer. "Where you from?"

"Chicago."

"Wha...? What's you talkin' 'bout, Evaline?" Cherry leaned close into her.

"I'm a city girl and I don't take any crap from anyone."

"Well, 'city girl'," said the Corporal, while lifting the loop of a rope off his saddle horn. He threw a furry bundle at her. "Cook these up for us. We're hungry."

Summer jumped at the site of the animal carcasses laying at her feet; one rabbit, two squirrels and one possum, blank eyes staring up at her. Cherry was quick to lift the line of carcasses off the ground.

"We'll cook it if you'll share it." Summer said, astounded that she would even consider eating a possum.

"And what else will you share?" Zach asked.

"Nothing with you, junior."

The men laughed, but the red flags of warning continued to fly. *These men can't be trusted.*

Summer and Cherry walked arm in arm as they headed for the kitchen, the trio of soldiers following behind on horseback.

"I'm scared, Evaline." Summer felt the slight tremble of Cherry's body.

"Me too, but we're together. We'll be okay. Just stay with me." For one brief moment, Mick Mason was visible in the stand of trees by the river's edge, and then was gone. She hoped they could depend on him for protection. Oh, the irony!

"D'you see somethin' in them trees?" the second soldier asked his cronies.

"Prob'ly just another darkie. Bet these women got no men around for protection. Right ladies? That works in our favor, don't you think, Corp?"

"Are your men folk here?" the corporal asked.

"Just old Pompeii and he won't hurt nobody," Cherry said.

"No white men?"

Silence.

"I'm asking you a question, girl." The corporal's horse nudged Summer and she tripped forward.

Make a stand, she told herself. She turned and grabbed the horse's reins tightly in her fist. "I told you, I don't take crap from anyone. No. There are no white men here," she lied. She prayed Mason would come forward if they needed him. She let go of the reins and crossed her arms over her chest to hide her trembling. She certainly didn't learn anything about dealing with Yankee soldiers at secretarial school.

"No white men. Fancy that, Billy. You know what they say, 'While the cat's away....' We'll see how much these wenches like to play, later."

She'd have to keep an eye on Zach.

✳ ✳ ✳

"I ain't playing with dem no how, Evaline." Cherry loaded her tray with what few dishes of food Lucy was able to conjure up. The rabbit, squirrels and possum were fried to a golden brown. Even Summer had to admit that Lucy made them look and smell quite appetizing. She had dusted them in a tiny bit of mealy worm flour before frying them in bacon fat she saved from the last pig that was slaughtered before the soldiers took it all. She managed to make one dozen small biscuits with the mealy flour. That was the end of that. Charles and Arthur left the day before for Savannah. Food supplies were nearly nonexistent at Magnolia and Royal Palms. They were hoping to find at least a few staples in the city. If not, starvation would claim them.

Lucy foraged the food cellar and found four yams which she cut into small pieces and boiled. It would have to feed six; Elizabeth, Mary, Susannah and the three Yankee soldiers who had barged into the manor house as if they were long-time residents.

With the trays ready, Lucy set her large body down on a chair at the table. "Ain't nothing left fo' us. We got nothin' to feed ourselves. Got nothin' to feed Percy cept' dis." She pulled a small biscuit out of her apron pocket. "Lord knows what dey's eatin' over at da Row."

✳ ✳ ✳

Bone chilling fear permeated the atmosphere in the dining room. Elizabeth, Mary and Susannah sat still as stones at the long table. Time was taking its toll on their wardrobes. There had been no new dresses for quite a spell, but Summer noted that they had dressed themselves the best they could, in their worn and stained taffetas, just to sit with the enemy. *Belles to the end.*

The men filled the empty chairs; unshaven, unwashed, and unkempt, their presence made obvious the effect on the women—*southern* women of some stature—unaccustomed to the brusque and rowdy temperament of the Northern invaders.

"Nice of you ladies to join us!" the Corporal said to his dinner companions while removing his dusty cap. He placed it on the floor beside him and cleared his throat, a signal for the other two men to follow suit.

Summer rolled her eyeballs at the sight of the filthy hat-hair of the soldiers. They obviously had not shampooed or bathed for quite a while. The body odor permeated the dining room as it only did during the hot and humid days of summer. She could only imagine what Elizabeth was thinking.

"Well come on, girls. Let's get the food rolling here! You have three starving men to feed." Billy shouted.

"And three beautiful women, I might add," said the Corporal nodding to Elizabeth.

"Where are the men folk?" he asked as Summer and Cherry began to serve.

"Savannah," Elizabeth answered curtly. "Looking for food, since you Yankees have decided to starve us."

"It's a tragedy of war, that civilians need to suffer," answered the corporal. "We're hungry too."

"It's a tragedy created by the North, that they should think to force upon us their ideals when we have been productive and profitable and *civilized* for two centuries."

Go Susannah! Summer thought. Not that she was in agreement with slavery—and especially considering the fact that she practically *was* one a short time ago—but she had to admire Susannah's spirit in the face of the enemy.

"You have been productive and profitable on the backs of slaves, might I remind you, young lady."

"Our slaves are no longer, if you will recall. We take good care of our people, Mr....Corporal.... do we not, Cherry?"

Cherry's jaw dropped at being addressed by Elizabeth and she stared blankly at her mistress.

"Do we not treat you well, Cherry?" Elizabeth repeated, needling Cherry with an icy stare.

"Oh...yes ma'am, yes, Miz Lizbet," Cherry replied and nervously passed the tray of fried meats.

"And, how about you?" Billy asked Summer as she placed a hard and very small biscuit on his plate. "Are you treated well?" His hand on the back of her thigh caused her to jerk the tray. She swore later that she hadn't intended to harm him—that she hadn't intended to jerk the tray square into his temple.

"Ouch!" he yelled. "Idiot! Dumb darkies!"

Summer smiled. It was surprising how quickly she changed sides. This afternoon she was a Yankee; this evening she was a *Southerner.*

While Summer and Cherry took their stations next to the sideboard, the men ravenously attacked the fried critters. Elizabeth, Mary and Susannah picked at their food like the ladies they were. They had taken small portions, which was all that was left after the men had piled their plates with small bony legs, ribbed breasts and thighs. Lucy cut the meat into as many pieces as she could manage before frying. Summer knew the temptation was great to steal a few pieces in the kitchen, but Lucy refrained. Nobody knew what the Yankees would do if they had caught her stealing their food; nobody wanted to find out.

The feast was small and over quickly. Lucy prepared coffee from chicory, as coffee from coffee beans was unattainable. No brandy. No dessert. Summer prayed the men did not plan on sleeping in the house. She knew none of the women, including herself, would catch a wink of sleep if that were the case.

"You got a baby somewhere?" the Corporal asked.

"Why do you ask?" Elizabeth eyed him coolly.

"Because that wench over there has a wet shirt."

It was definitely one of the more embarrassing moments of her life. Summer looked down to see the entire front of her bodice drenched in breast milk.

"You may be excused, Evaline."

"Go with her, Zach," the corporal ordered.

Oh, great.

"You may take the grand stairway, Evaline."

Thank God for small favors. The thought of being in the dark and narrow servant stairway with Zach, sent chills up her spine.

Ruth nearly turned white when Summer entered the nursery with the young soldier in tow. James was stirring in his crib.

"It's okay, Ruth. The corporal sent him."

"You git, lady." Zach nodded to the door.

"She will not."

"I say she will, girlie, and she *will.*"

Poor Ruth looked totally confused.

"There's no reason for her to leave."

"It ain't up to you. Now git!"

"It's okay, Ruth. Go help Cherry clear the table." Surely Cherry was a wreck, having been left with the men.

Ruth exited, but not before twice indiscreetly nodding toward her bedroom door. Summer wasn't sure what it meant, but had no time to figure it out. James was crying now, and she had to feed him.

"Go on. Feed the kid." Zach said.

She took the baby in her arms and sat in the rocker. Normally, this was a pleasant and relaxing time—of which there were not many in her life as a former slave, and now servant—but tonight it was terrifying to have Zach gawking at her as she unbuttoned her shirt. She was afraid her fear would transfer to James, and tried to remain calm.

The sky had darkened dramatically. The only light was the lantern and she didn't like the way it shone in Zach's eyes—the lewd way in which he watched her. She knew what was coming, and dragged out the feeding process until James was obviously asleep.

Zach nodded toward the crib. She laid the baby in his bed and immediately Zach was behind her with hand on her breast, still exposed from the feeding.

"Don't touch me," she said.

"Come on, girl. The baby's sleepin'. We can have some fun."

Summer tried to break free, but he held tight with both arms and pushed her toward Ruth's door.

"What's in there?"

"Nothing for you. Let me go!"

He reached a hand out and turned the latch, pushing the door in.

"Ain't that nice." Ruth's cot was faintly outlined in the nursery lantern light. "A bed for us."

"Get your hands off me, you low-life."

"Come on, girl. Be nice to me and I'll be nice to you." He pushed her toward the cot.

"Never!"

"I got ya, girl. Give up the fight. Just relax."

"Bastard." This was not going to happen!

"You want me to be rough, bitch?" He pushed her hard onto the cot. She landed face down, the cot banging against the wall.

"You're not touching me!" She attempted to stand, but he pushed her down again.

"Who's to say?"

"I'm to say!" A large, black shadow outlined in lantern light appeared behind Zach. After a brief scuffle, a loud 'crack' sent the unfortunate soldier to the floor in a lifeless heap.

The relief was overwhelming. "Mason! Oh, my God, Mason! There are two more downstairs!"

"I know, Yankee devils; they ain't leaving here alive."

Summer stood and buttoned her shirt. Never in a million years would she have thought that she'd be glad to see Mick Mason. "Thank you, Mr. Mason." It killed her to say it. After all, the man wanted to do her in, but he saved her life...*for another time*, she supposed.

"See if you can get another one of them bastards up to Miss Elizabeth's room."

Get another one up here? Now I'm an accomplice to murder! She didn't dare disobey, considering Mason saved her from a very demeaning act. *Think, think, think.* "Oh, I know," she said aloud and took the third floor stairway to the second floor and stood at the top of the grand stairway.

"Miss Susannah! Miss Susannah!" she called.

Shortly, Susannah appeared at the bottom of the stairway with the soldier, Billy, at her side.

"What do you want, girl?" Billy asked.

"I need Miss Susannah a moment, if you don't mind."

"I do mind. I'm comin' with her."

Please do. She watched them climb the stairs.

"What in the world is it, Evaline?" Susannah asked, winded and befuddled.

"I need another blanket for James. It's very cool upstairs in the nursery. Mr. Zach is minding James a moment."

Susannah looked startled by the request but blessedly played along with Summer, following her to Elizabeth's bedroom.

"Ha! Zach minding a baby?" Billy snickered and followed behind.

"You know how Miss Elizabeth doesn't want me touching her things." Summer opened the door to the bedroom while the entrance hall chandelier, which hung over the grand staircase in a cascade of crystal and three sputtering candles, cast a sudden splash of dim light into Elizabeth's dark room.

"I must light the lantern," Susannah said, looking quizzically at Summer. With no response, she entered first when Summer indicated her to do so. Billy followed behind, and before he took three steps into the room he was ambushed by Mick Mason. Summer remained in the hallway, closing the door quickly, hoping to block any sounds of a scuffle. *Don't scream, Susannah,* she prayed, having neither the time nor opportunity to warn her that Mason was waiting.

It was disturbing to her that she felt so blasé about leading a man to his murder, not to mention that she was now an accomplice to the deed. *Tough times demand tough actions.* She had to justify it somehow.

When the door opened, Susannah stood by her mother's bed, the lit lantern in her hand. She was visibly shaken. "What shall we do now?" she asked. Her voice quivered as she spoke.

"We need to get the other one up here," Mason whispered to Summer, his large frame blocking the doorway. "If we give him some time, he should come on his own—looking for his buddies."

Shortly, the sound of boots on the grand stairway struck a chord of intense apprehension. She had a feeling that the corporal wasn't going down as easily as the others.

"Zack, Billy, get down here—now!" the corporal hollered.

"Get on out there, Evaline. Bring him in here." Mason had a firm grip on her upper arm.

"Jesus," she whispered. *This can't be happening.* She regretted touching the thumbprint the second time; she was in over her head.

Mason pushed her out into the hallway and closed the door quietly. The corporal was standing at the top of the stairway, his pistol drawn. His shadow loomed twice his size against the wall.

"Don't shoot!" Summer exclaimed, borrowing the words from the many crime movies of her life. "It's me, Evaline."

"Where are my men?"

"Uh...Zach is watching the baby a moment and...and the other one came upstairs with Miss Susannah."

"I know that. I don't have times for games, girl. Get them out here right now."

Now what? She stood frozen, her mind racing for an idea. He came closer.

"Mr. Billy! Mr. Zack! The corporal wants you!" She was scared down to her toenails.

"What are you up to?" His eyes squinted as he cocked the gun. She took a step backward.

"You'd better get them out here right now, missy. I don't want to hurt you."

With every step he took forward, she took one backward until she was pressed against the second floor railing. The corporal gripped her by the arm and held the pistol to her neck.

"Where are they, girl?" She could see his stubble of beard growth in the candlelight.

"Don't make me hurt you," he warned.

Where's Mason? The corporal's back was conveniently exposed to the bedroom door as he held her prisoner against the railing.

"I told you...."

Alas, the door flew open. Hearing the creak of the hinge the corporal swung around, but too late; Mason was on him.

Summer shrieked and jumped aside as the men punched and shoved, grunting as they scuffled down the hallway. With the corporal's pistol drawn and cocked, it was the main focus of the battle.

What if Mason loses? Jesse and Blaine hadn't told her anything about this incident! Summer gathered her courage and stayed ready to go for the weapon if necessary. *Maybe I'll laugh about this later*—she hoped.

A loud 'thump' caught her attention. The pistol slid quickly across the floor in her direction and she stepped on it, stopping its action.

"Get it!" Mason called. "Shoot him!" Mason was now straddling the corporal on the floor, battering his face.

She was paralyzed. *Shoot him?* She couldn't! Besides, what if she shot Mason instead? She hated to admit it, but he was their only protector now.

"Damn it, shoot him!"

She lifted the pistol off the floor with two hands, as its weight demanded. Standing now beside Mason, she witnessed the surreal scene below her; the corporal a bloody pulp, his face unrecognizable. Mason was atop him, vicious and obviously victorious in this small, private battle, a mere fraction of the major battle occurring around them in the countryside. He grabbed the pistol from her hand and did not hesitate to fire; the shot exploded in her ears. She shrieked and stepped backward into Susannah, who was now standing in the hallway.

"What's happening?" Elizabeth called from below. "Susannah! Are you alright?"

Mason staggered to his feet, the pistol gripped in his hand. "Stupid girl." He growled.

Some thanks. "Without me, you wouldn't have had the gun."

"Don't back-talk me, gal. Get something to wrap him in."

Mason was covered in blood, and later, as she and Susannah gathered yet another blanket for the dead trio, she was appalled to find that the corporal's blood and flesh had splattered the entire front of her blouse and skirt.

Summer, Susannah, Elizabeth and even Mary, helped Mick Mason roll the bodies into the blankets. Evaline, being a servant girl, was called upon to help Mason haul the bodies down the grand stairway. The men were heavy, and she was exhausted by the time all three were lined neatly before the front door. Ruth was instructed to remain with James, and therefore was spared the gruesome scene. Lucy and Cherry were without knowledge of the horrific events—until the word passed through the quarters at dawn, as surely it would. Mason left and returned with one of the soldier's horses hitched to a wagon. The other two horses were tied behind. Pompeii sat next to Mason on the driver's seat.

Again, Summer was instructed to help lift the bodies into the wagon, not a small task for someone of her size.

"What about the horses?" she asked Mason. "Where are you taking them?" Surely there would be hell to pay should any other Federals show up looking for the missing soldiers.

"Don't worry about it." he answered. "They won't look like this when you see them next. "Get go!" he said to the horse, slapping the reins on his rump.

The women watched the wagon and horses trot down the entrance roadway, turning left at the road to the old slave quarters.

19

The scrubbing of the hallway floorboards was a grim reminder to Summer and Susannah of the horror they had witnessed this night. With pails of water and torn muslin from already fragmented petticoats, and under Elizabeth's instruction, the two women mopped the pools of blood from the hallway; a testimonial to the fact that head wounds 'bled like a stuck pig'. The candlelight was not sufficient to show the true aftermath of the altercation. Summer imagined the floor would look quite unsettling in the morning light, as muslin rags without a strong household cleaner could never remove the evidence.

"Not a word of this to your father, Susannah," Elizabeth warned. "He has enough troubles as it is without worrying about us here alone. Mr. Mason took care of the situation satisfactorily."

"Mr. Mason killed three men." Susannah replied. "I think father may notice the stains on the floor."

"Mr. Mason killed three Federal soldiers who were here to do us harm. Whose side are you on?"

The bloody rags were wrapped in a sheet and sent with Summer to the flower garden where she met with Mr. Mason and Pompeii who were digging graves by lantern light.

"Miss Elizabeth says for you to bury these rags with the bodies." The words sounded strange coming from her mouth. Never, in her other life, had she been involved in anything so horrendous as a triple murder, or any murder, for that matter. Yet, here she was in 1864, an accomplice to a triple murder *and* the cover up! She would never look at Aunt Ada's garden again in the same way—providing she even returned to the 21st century. *Please, God, let me go home.* Her visit to the 19th century was becoming much too complicated.

✳ ✳ ✳

Mason was right. The horses did not return to the big house in the same form as they left; they returned as haunches to be hefted to the hooks in the smoke house.

"Dey's eatin' good at da Row tonight!" Lucy was elated. "And we's eatin' good tonight, too!"

"Have you ever eaten horse, Lucy?"

"No, missy, but my belly's callin' out for it just the same."

Mine too, she had to admit. She had to feed James and couldn't make milk on nothing. She had to eat, and if it was horse she had to eat, then so be it. Her stomach growled at the aroma of Lucy's concoction of horse meat chunks and mysterious root vegetables.

Leaving the kitchen, she walked around the side of the big house to the garden, which now hid the tale of their horrid deed. The afternoon was crisp, the sky a deep blue with not even a hint of the horror of the night of the soldiers. *You have now done murder, Summer Woodfield.* She scolded herself for her lack of remorse. Could she have done this in real time, and feel as detached as she did now? The dirt was fresh over the three graves. *They belonged to someone...someone waits for them at home.* She wondered if they should camouflage the graves with cut weeds and branches. General Sherman was in Georgia, and surely more soldiers would pass their way.

Leaving the garden she returned to the house and nursery. Susannah, who ogled incessantly over little James, had given Summer a rocking chair from her own room. Elizabeth objected vehemently upon the discovery, but with Susannah and Charles, both, to battle, she gave up. It was another burr under the saddle—another reminder that she had no control over Charles' affection for Evaline.

Summer was ever grateful to rest her aching body into the rocker with James snug in her arms. She took inventory of his fine features as he suckled her breast; the soft brown hair, the tender skin shaded with a hint of mocha, eyes favoring blue, staring up at her. Who could not love this child? Shadowing that thought were the words of Arthur Ascot: *"Soon as that baby's weaned, I'm taking it."*

Never! Even though she knew Arthur Ascot never followed through, it was a terrifying thought!

As she drifted off in the fading afternoon light, James asleep in her arm, she was bolted out of her semi-conscious state by a tremendous ruckus below—*a gunshot?* Setting James in his crib in the nursery, she stood still, trying to make out the loud but muffled words coming from beneath the floorboards. She did not hesitate to lift the rug—the one that hid the peephole—only to be reminded that the peephole was covered. "Damn!"

The voice was that of Charles, which surprised her, since he and Arthur Ascot should be in Savannah. She laid her head to the floor in hopes of hearing better.

"...appalled and shocked! Not even a year since your own son died!"

"Charles...I..."

"Shut up! You are a whore—nothing but a whore!"

"No, Charles...no!"

"I should have known!"

Terror filled Summer like nothing she had ever felt before—not even the three soldiers whose deaths she had partaken in. Something was very wrong! She ran to the servant stairway and traveled slowly downward in the darkness, listening. She heard Elizabeth scream and then a gunshot. *Oh God, no!*

Her heart thumped in her chest. When she reached the first floor she opened the door a crack to view the grand staircase, but saw nothing.

"Father!" Susannah shrieked from above.

Good lord! Summer was in a panic. Had Charles gone mad? Did he kill Elizabeth? Was he going to kill Susannah? She ran to the bottom of the grand staircase. Surely it didn't matter that she was a servant using the staircase at this point; Charles had obviously lost his mind and perhaps Susannah needed help. Before she reached the third step, Elizabeth came into view, walking backwards, clutching a sheet to her chest with not a stitch of clothing on underneath.

"Don't Charles...please don't!"

Charles came next with Susannah pulling on his coattail with all her might. He held a pistol in his hand, his face red and grimaced.

"Stop!" Susannah shrieked. "Father, stop!"

Charles did not appear to be the least bit conscious of Susannah's presence. He continued his advance on Elizabeth, slowly, deliberately. Summer wondered if he was debating whether or not he should shoot. There had been enough death in the house already; she had to stop him!

"Don't!" she yelled from the bottom of the stairway.

"Help me, Evaline!" Elizabeth called, but before Summer could even digest the request, a shot rang out.

Later, Summer would recall the scene in slow motion, for surely that is how she saw it; Elizabeth jerking backward against the banister on the second floor, toppling over the railing, the sheet, still grasped in her hand, sailing behind her as she fell ever so gracefully, like a golden haired angel floating from heaven.

The impact of her body hitting the floor was not heavenly in the least. Summer shrieked to see the woman, pale as the ghost she surely was now, spread in unnatural disarray on the wooden floor of the foyer, her golden hair spread about her face like the flames of a bonfire. Her body had never seen a ray of sunshine; the skin so soft and white it was nearly as pure as baby James. The sheet was kinder to her in death than she had been kind in life, for it gracefully landed on her body, covering her private parts to all who were present.

Susannah fell to her knees, white knuckles grasping the spindles of the railing. "Mother," she rasped, her agony obvious. "Mother," she sobbed.

Summer felt faint, for the sheet now began to soak like a sponge, the blood from the gunshot wound. She was the nearest one to the body and had no clue what to do. She recalled, at this moment, Blaine telling her that Elizabeth had fallen to her death. *He certainly doesn't know the whole story.*

Standing paralyzed on the spot, Summer watched as Charles descended the stairs. He passed her without acknowledgement, the pistol at his side, and disappeared into the library closing the door behind him.

Now what?

"Evaline," Susannah moaned. "Mr. Mason...Mr. Mason is dead too—in mother's bed. What shall we do?"

Summer sat on the third stair from the bottom and rested her head in her hands. *This truly is a nightmare; two more corpses, and a man with a gun!*

"What about father? He killed mother *and* Mr. Mason. What shall become of him?"

'Call 911!' She wanted to yell, for that is exactly what she would have done had she been home in the 21st century. Here, there was nothing—nobody to call for help. She was terrified.

"What will we do, Evaline?" Susannah whimpered overhead, still white-knuckling the spindles of the railing.

Before Summer could even lift her head off her palms, the front door opened and within seconds a chilling shriek filled the foyer. Mary collapsed into the circle of her hooped skirt, her bonnet peaking at the center of yards of mourning black.

"Susannah, help!" Summer called. "Get down here!"

Mary's head bobbled as if it were teetering on a pinhead. On viewing the blood-soaked sheet covering Elizabeth's body, another shriek escaped her lips.

"Shut up!" Summer yelled. Don't let the others hear!" Summer had no clue where the gumption came from, but something spurred her into motion. Mary had instructed Pompeii to take her to Margaret at Royal Palms that morning, saying she needed to get away from the nightmare of the previous night. Something certainly changed, or Charles would not have returned, Elizabeth would not be lying naked on the floor, Mick Mason would not be dead in her bed, and Mary would not be a flounce of fabric collapsed on the floor.

Summer helped Mary to her feet, quickly closed the door and guided her to the parlor where she plunked her on a chair by the fireplace.

"Oh, my god, what has happened? What have you done, Evaline?"

"There's...there's been an accident....hurry, Susannah!"

When at last Susannah appeared in the parlor doorway she, too, looked as if she would collapse. "Pull yourself together, girl," Summer whispered in her ear. "I need your help. You have to be strong—you can't leave this all to me."

"What's happened, Susannah? There so much blood!"

Susannah stood mute as a tree stump while Mary fanned her face frantically with a fan she pulled from her handbag.

"Where's Charles?" Mary sniffled.

"Mother...mother and father had an argument." Susannah wiped her eyes with a lace handkerchief taken from her dress sleeve. "He's locked in the library...he's very upset."

"But—she has no clothes!"

"I...I don't know what happened, Mary, just that poor mother fell over the banister. Oh, it was dreadful!" Susannah burst into tears and ran to the comfort of Mary's arms. "It was so dreadful!" she repeated between sobs.

"We can't let the others see her like this," Summer piped in.

The women, arms entangled around one another, eyes red and watery, stopped their weeping to look at her. "You must do something, Evaline!" Mary said, dabbing her nose with a hankie. "A tragedy such as this—and not one man to help!"

The very last thing Summer wanted was for the others to know the truth of the story. There was such talk already amongst the servants. As she predicted, the news of the soldiers lit emotions like the 4th of the July fireworks. While the few remaining servants yearned for freedom, terror reigned as the Yankees closed in; the smell of freedom filled the nostrils of all, but the fear of the relentless and brutal approach of the Federals was overpowering. Summer was terrified that news of Elizabeth's death and particularly that of Mick Mason, would set off a chain reaction that would only endanger everyone. *Everything in due time.*

"Okay, okay, let me think." She paced the room, the eyes of the women upon her. How she ended up as the one in charge, she didn't know. Elizabeth would be rolling in her grave—if she had one.

Grave! Summer left the women in their state of grief and flew up the grand stairway. She slowed her pace when she came to Elizabeth's room. The door was wide open. She squinted against the gruesome vision that awaited her and stood in the doorway a moment before opening her eyes.

He lay against the headboard, his head folded onto his chest, one foot set on the ground as if he had attempted to rise but was stopped in mid-action. Charles' bullets were anything but tidy. A ragged hole in Mason's chest oozed blood onto the white sheet and lace coverlet. For one split second, Summer realized the appeal of the man; the burly chest, the wide shoulders, muscular arms, the epitome of masculinity down the thick thigh, the bulging calf, and the foot, bare...dead. "Oh, god," she muttered. *How to move him?* She walked to the window. The war had killed the heart and soul of the plantation. Where once the yard was full of activity, children playing, sheep grazing, men with scythes attempting in vain to control the high grass that flourished in the humid summer months, now there was only an empty stretch of yard, its single adornment, the magnolia blossom fountain rising from the pond, ignorant of the ravaged countryside and collapse of the world around it. Mason's horse shuffled in the dirt below at the hitching post.

We have to get rid of the horse and bury Mason, without anyone seeing. We are the law.

She tugged at his feet until his body slid a few inches from the headboard allowing him to lay flat. *I'm tampering with evidence again!* Surely a dead body was evidence of a crime, but what choice did she have? The world was topsy- turvy with the war. There was no law here. *We are the law,* she reminded herself.

Folding the sheets and coverlet over Mason, she was happy to see that the blood had not soaked beneath him onto the mattress— *not yet.* Time was of the essence. She wondered when a dead body stopped bleeding; there was so much she didn't know!

"Susannah!" she called from the top of the steps. "Come up here."

Susannah was obviously relieved to be spared the viewing of the naked and damaged body of her mother's lover. "Oh, Evaline...what shall we do?"

"We're going to bury him."

"But where? What shall we tell the servants? That my father killed him?"

"No, we won't tell the servants. We are going to bury him with the others, you and me, tonight when it's dark. You have to help me wrap him in blankets, if you can find any. Hurry—you must find something!"

"What about mother, Evaline?"

"We don't want Mary to know about Mr. Mason. Try to find blankets, and get extra for Miss Elizabeth, if you can."

With Mason wrapped tight in his cocoon of lace coverlets, sheets, and quilt, the women closed the door leaving his body on the floor, and descended the stairway to the foyer, their arms loaded with what few blankets were left after the carnage of the soldiers.

✳ ✳ ✳

News of Elizabeth's *accidental* death swept the plantation like wildfire. From the tidy cabins along the entrance road, to the ramshackle shanties on River Row, tensions ran high amongst the remaining servants. Not only was Sherman marching across Georgia, burning barns, homes, stealing, raping and terrorizing the countryside, but the mistress was dead; fallen to her death in her own home!

Elizabeth's burial was witnessed by the shrunken population of Magnolia. The family cemetery, a beautiful spot near the Savannah River, bore no less than 20 headstones, some small, some large, representing the Woodfield family from the purchase of Magnolia Plantation in 1803, to this moment.

There were a few murmurs as to the whereabouts of 'the Master' (as Charles remained to be called). It was odd that he should miss his own wife's funeral, but the consensus of the servants was that his will was broken, as well as his heart.

"Ashes to ashes and dust to dust," Susannah read from the bible as there was no possibility of obtaining a proper minister. Elizabeth was laid to rest, the truth of her demise a secret shared amongst herself and Evaline.

20

"What we gonna do now, Evaline?" Lucy rested a fist on each rounded hip. "Ain't no food. Ain't no Miz 'Lizbet. Ain't no Massah what I can tell. Ain't no Mason crackin' his whip at no one. Where'd dat man go? Ain't no work gettin' done. Ain't nothin' doin' nothin'!

Lucy's frustration was felt by everyone in the household, aside from Charles, whose daily routine since Elizabeth's death was to lock himself away in the library. At meals— if a consistent diet of horsemeat could be called that—he sat catatonically, said nothing, ate little, and returned to the library until bedtime. The plantation came to an abrupt halt with Elizabeth and Mason's deaths.

A distant blast rattled the nerves. "Dem Yankees ain't far!" Lucy opened the door and stuck her head out. "Dey ain't out der now, but won't be long 'fore dey ride up here like de apocalypse! Lord help us!" She slammed the door against the unseen enemy.

"Dey's comin' and ain't no Mason here to kill 'em off like he done before." Cherry moaned. "We's in trouble, Evaline. Dem at da Row tellin' us da soldiers done bobbin' all da women; don' care if dey's white or niggah, dey's bobbin' em."

Summer shuddered, the memories of Arthur Ascot and Zach were fresh in her mind. "How do they know this?"

"Da niggahs passin' thru done tell da folks on da Row"

Summer laid her head on the table. This was a good time to return to the 21st century, only she hadn't a clue how! She didn't remember much about the Civil War in high school history class, except for the abolition of slavery, historically a joyful occasion, but the underlying fear and terror of the approaching Yankee soldiers was greatly overlooked in the history books.

"I must feed James," she said abruptly, and stood to leave. Cherry's news struck a chord. They would have to prepare for what was coming. It was no secret that General Sherman was marching to Savannah, leaving a path of destruction in his wake. As long as she was stuck in this time warp, she was not going to suffer at the hands of the Yankees, and neither were Cherry,

Lucy, Susannah, Ruth, Mary, Pompeii or baby James—not if she could help it. They were a starving group at the mercy of brutal soldiers. Charles was useless, and Pompeii was too old for a show of force. If only Juba were alive!

As she made her way to the big house, she cast a glance in the direction of the flower garden and shivered. At night, she often found herself covered in gooseflesh with the memory of the dead soldiers and Mason, all laid to rest beneath the roses and perennials. She wondered if they were really at rest.

Summer tapped on the open parlor door where Susannah sat at a desk, pen in hand. "Miss Susannah?"

Susannah raised her eyes, the darkened circles beneath, a telltale sign of the starvation and fear that now permeated the once thriving plantation.

"We should have a plan." Summer said, trying to control the pitch and pace at which she spoke. At times it was difficult to remember her place.

"A plan?"

"Yes. The Yankees are not far. They are looting and...and Cherry has it from the freed slaves who pass through, that the soldiers are raping women, black...and white."

"Oh, lord help us!" Susannah set the pen down and stood. "What shall we do?"

"I think we should find where Mason hid the soldier's weapons."

"And do we have round balls? We cannot fight off a Federal army with empty pistols!"

"I don't know exactly what weapons Mason took, but I think a good place to start looking is at the cabin."

"Oh, Mercy! Let us go, Evaline!" Susannah floated past her into the foyer and to the front door. "We mustn't tarry!"

Nothing like a threat to a Southern Belle's dignity!

They crossed the large expanse of yard, past the carriage house to the whitewashed overseer's cabin.

Memories engulfed Summer as she crossed the threshold into the cabin. Searching Robert's room, she stopped to touch the bed where he laid, from where he watched her so intently as she brought him back to health. There was no time to cry; the soldiers were not far away, and they were desperate women on a mission.

They searched each room, which did not take long as there were only three. Susannah looked very much out of place in the small cabin. Her wide, hooped petticoat, which she tried desperately to preserve, ballooned her skirt backward and forward, squeezed by the narrow doorways as she entered and exited the two bedrooms. Summer stifled a laugh.

A loud boom shook the cabin. "Oh, Evaline! They're coming closer and there is nothing here!"

Summer fought to control her growing anxiety. *Wake up!* In all fairness, she did not like the idea of leaving Susannah alone at this moment, but she did not bargain for this life-threatening situation when she touched the thumbprint for the second time. After all, this war was done and over with nearly 150 years ago! She could not change history. If she left now, and returned to the 21st century, Susannah would survive, as she did at her moment in time in 1864.

"Let's go," she said, and as they exited the cabin Summer caught a flash of blue in the corner of her eye. "It's them!" she whispered, taking Susannah's hand. A section of the entrance road was visible from the cabin steps, and there, passing between the large oaks, the women spotted soldiers on horseback.

"Too late!" Susannah's eyes grew wide with fright. "We're done!"

It was then Summer noticed, for the first time, the lattice work around the base of the cabin. She tugged hard at the section nearest the steps, and when it came free she hunched over and crawled beneath the house, calling Susannah to follow. Susannah's hoop nearly prevented the task, but when they were both secure in the dark cavity, laying on their stomachs in the dirt, Summer replaced the lattice, leaning it back against the framing.

"Oh, poor father! He doesn't know they're coming!"

And neither do the others. Summer's heart fell. How could they warn the household without putting themselves in harm's way? Would it matter, anyway?

They hushed at the approach of hooves in the dirt, the clinking of metal in motion, and moved further back into the darkness.

"Take a look in there," a soldier ordered.

With his rifle poised and ready to fire, a soldier approached the steps. Summer watched him, first at full figure, then to the knees, then the boots and then nothing but the sound of his boots on the steps. She trembled as the boots clunked overhead, faded toward the back of the cabin, and then to the porch again.

"Ain't nobody here!" he called to the others, and stepped down into the dirt. "No food, no whiskey, no nothin'."

The women watched, taking in the slightest amount of oxygen in small gasps until the men were out of sight. Three soldiers headed toward the slave cabins around the curve of the road, and four toward the big house.

"Damn."

"Evaline!"

"Well, damn, Miss Susannah! What about the others? What about little James? Not only has he missed his feeding, but they're sitting ducks not knowing that the friggin' soldiers are seconds away!"

"Because we are in a precarious position, Evaline, is no excuse to curse! Remember yourself!"

The fact that her breasts were full of milk and she was so far away from James caused a bit of anxiety. All that relieved her was the fact that Ruth had asked her to leave a bottle for James that morning. Perhaps the impending arrival of the Yankees caused Ruth to think ahead to the uncertainty of their future from moment to moment. Summer was surprised to learn that baby bottles even existed in the Civil War days. It was a crude thing that Ruth took out of the cupboard in the kitchen; a glass bottle with an unattractive black India rubber nipple. Summer insisted that both be boiled on the stove first before she painstakingly filled the bottle a third of the way with breast milk.

She pushed the bottle thoughts away and returned to the present situation; lying beneath the overseer's cabin racking her brain for what to do next.

"Wait...what is that?" A ray of sunshine found its way into the darkness of their secret cave and bounced off metal to the left of the lattice work. Summer crawled on her belly toward the spark of light. "This is it!" she exclaimed in a whisper. "The guns! Oh, thank you, Mick Mason!"

They waited beneath the cabin until the cover of darkness, after which they chose only two pistols and a tin of round balls to bring with them, as all the weaponry was too heavy to carry. Susannah's hoop remained an issue, and Summer convinced her to remove it, pushing it back into the darkness of the crawlspace. "You can't be invisible with that thing on!" she scolded when Susannah complained.

"My hoop is precious. I have little left, you know."

"When this is over—and it *will* be over—you can come back and get it...or send someone," she added, thinking that crawling beneath a house in a hooped skirt was a once-in-a-lifetime event for a Southern Belle.

With the greatest care, they found their way to the kitchen, crossing the entrance road and approaching from the side of the house opposite the flower garden. This route passed the outhouses, and they were careful to tread quietly behind them, staying beneath the canopy of trees and moss.

"Der you is, oh heaven be praised!" Lucy exclaimed when they entered through the back door of the kitchen. "And look at da dirt! Where you bin, Miss Susannah? Where yo' petticoat?"

"Where are they?" Summer asked.

"In da big house. Ruth come in shakin' like a leaf. She worried 'bout poor Cherry girl wid dem Yankee soldiers. "

"Cherry's with them?"

"Dey brung rabbit and squirrel. I's fryin' dem up. Dem Yankees waitin' for supper at da big house. Dey give dis one to us." She pointed to skinned rabbit lying on the counter. "I'se gonna cook it up next."

Summer's stomach growled at the thought of fried rabbit.

"Dey brung hard tack too."

"Well, heaven be praised is right," Susannah said. "Not that I want to accept food from those Yankee devils. They're the reason we're all starving in the first place."

Yankees with a heart? My pride is restored! "Fry that up, Lucy, and save me a piece. I'm taking Miss Susannah home. Poor James, he must be crying his little eyes out! I'll bring Cherry back with me."

Summer secretly enjoyed Susannah's attempt at the servant stairway.

"I haven't been on these since I was a child," Susannah whispered.

"Good thing you don't have your hoop on, or you'd never fit."

"This is barbaric!"

"It's a little late for that fact to be recognized. The war is almost over—I think. the stairs won't be used anymore." She couldn't help herself.

"Perhaps I can convince father to improve them somehow when this horrible war has ended."

"Won't be necessary," Summer replied and opened the door to the first floor, stepping into the foyer. Their appearance from the dining room caused great alarm; two of the seven soldiers jumped to their feet and ran for rifles, which were propped against the dining room wall.

"Don't shoot!" Summer yelled, thinking how odd it was to find it necessary to repeat those words twice in her lifetime.

"And who might you be?" The apparent soldier in charge stood from a chair at the far head of the table.

"I am Susannah Woodfield, Mistress of this household, sir, and this is my servant, Evaline. And just who are you, trespassing into our home?"

At'a girl, Susannah!

"I am Sergeant Alex Williams, Ma'am, of General Sherman's army."

"Where is my father?"

"Your father is under guard in the library, Ma'am. He did not take too kindly to our, um, intrusion."

"Nor do I, Sergeant Williams. You may be seated at our dining table, but you are not invited or welcomed guests."

Summer glanced at Mary, who sat to the left of the sergeant, looking as if she could faint dead away. Her white skin shone even whiter in contrast to the black mourning dress. Her hair was neatly secured, but her eyes were that of a wild and startled deer at the sound of a breaking branch.

"Come, Mary," Susannah said. Let us leave these men to their supper. You will excuse us, Sergeant?"

Mary sighed audibly in relief and stood from the table before the sergeant had a chance to give his reply. Cherry stood as still as a statue by the buffet server.

"I'll take Cherry and get the trays, miss." Summer said. Witnessing the look on Cherry's face at the prospect of remaining behind with the soldiers, left her no choice but to temporarily forego visiting the nursery.

In the kitchen, Lucy divvied up the fried meats, setting aside portions for Susannah and Mary. Summer and Cherry gobbled their share immediately before setting out with the trays for the soldiers. As was the circumstance of late, the trays were pounds lighter than in prior times, due to the lack of food. Summer sent Cherry to the second floor bedrooms to deliver Susannah and Mary their portions, while she faced the soldiers alone in the dining room.

"Is this all?" One of the soldiers complained.

"Yes, sir," Summer replied. "Yankees took it all."

"What are we going to do when the rest of 'em get here, Sergeant?"

The rest? The men at the table had her attention. She stood, all ears, by the sideboard.

"First light, we'll check out the slave quarters down by the river, go through each shack. Check all the outer buildings—make sure there aren't any men folk hiding out. Looks like a smokehouse out back. Maybe there's a ham or two they aren't telling us about." He eyed Summer. "You see three soldiers come through here recently besides us?"

Summer's heart skipped a beat. She envisioned the telltale horse haunches hanging in the smoke house. "Only the ones that stole our food about a month ago."

"She talks pretty good for a darkie," one of the soldiers remarked.

"Tell your mistress and the other one to stay away from my men. They been fighting a long time, missing their wives and sweethearts. There's more coming tomorrow…lot's more, and I don't want any trouble. Do you understand?"

Do I ever. "Yes, sir," she answered thinking that she should keep her answers short now to avoid suspicion over her accent. She imagined they wouldn't understand that she was from really from Chicago in the 21st century, that the war was over, and they were long dead and buried.

"We're setting up camp here, so you and the other servants be prepared to take care of the men."

A few soldiers snickered, to which the Sergeant flashed an angry look. "I mean be prepared to cook and serve."

Camp? She eyed the ceiling, thinking of the others upstairs, so frightened and unprotected. It was now that they needed their own men around them, but Charles was useless and the others were dead. She had a fleeting thought of Arthur Ascot, but who knew what was happening at Royal Palms? This was not good, not good at all. The rumors that preceded the soldiers signaled the prospect of total chaos and she shuddered at what awaited them.

21

On December 11, 1864 Summer, Susannah, Mary and Ruth watched from a second story bedroom window as the pounding of horse's hoofs loosened the thick dust of the entrance road, sending it upwards in great opaque plumes of brown, obscuring the moss draped limbs of the oaks. From behind the cavalry came the foot soldiers and wounded, appearing as a mirage through the dust as it settled to the earth again.

This was her home team, and yet Summer's heart pounded hard in her chest with fear of what was to come. She glanced at the splendor of the magnolia fountain below, waterless now, knowing it would soon become the grotesque and ominous shape that greeted her upon her arrival at Tanglewood. Her days were numbered, and fear struck its chord. *What happens to me?* For that, there was no answer.

"Oh, God help us!" Mary raised a lace handkerchief to her nose. "We are doomed! We have no protectors!"

"Just stay upstairs and you'll be safe," Summer promised, not believing a word of it. There were too many soldiers to count; they were most definitely outnumbered.

She left the women at the window and traveled the stairway to the first floor. The Sergeant would be looking for her and she did not want him upstairs. It was important to keep what territory they had left unspoiled by the enemy.

As she assumed, the Sergeant was waiting for her in the foyer.

"Get Cherry, the cook, and that old man and meet me out here." He opened the door and stepped out onto the porch to greet the arriving troops.

When she returned with her crew, Pompeii and Percy were ordered to take care of thirty six horses, not a small task for an old man and a small child. Lucy was chastised for not providing the horsemeat found hanging in the smokehouse and sent back to the kitchen with instructions to cook up everything edible.

"Just where did that horsemeat come from?" the sergeant asked, one eyebrow raised in suspicion.

"Old nag," Cherry quickly replied. "Dem Yankees didn't want no old nag."

"Better be so, woman," he warned.

Tents were set up on the lawn and, as the men set up camp, Summer was surprised at how well supplied the soldiers were compared to their meager pantry. Some knapsacks contained tins of Underwood Deviled Ham and an occasional Van Camps Pork and Beans, which was a surprise in itself. She had no idea that brands familiar to her in the 21st century, existed in the 19th!

When all was done, she counted forty-two tents. Nine wounded were brought into the parlor, the excess spilling out into the foyer floor. Stepping over prone bodies, arms and legs, she and Cherry moved amongst the injured, cleaning their wounds with all that was available—soap and water. The lack of antiseptics, antibiotics and pain killers remained a shock to Summer, so used to the availability of medical supplies and 24 hour drugstores in her real life. Some of the wounds were of a serious nature, red, inflamed, infected and gave worry to gangrene, but many were treatable, even with their pathetic supplies of old rags and soap. Cherry looked at her cross-eyed when she insisted the water be boiled before touching the skin of the wounded.

"To prevent infection," she explained to deaf ears.

"I don't care if deys affected," Cherry replied.

"Maybe you'd better care a little. These men, scary as some of them are, have helped to set you, uh, us, free."

"You don' know dat, Evaline."

"Yes, I do, friend." Still, she could understand Cherry's feelings. Some of the soldiers from the tent area made vulgar comments to them in passing. She didn't know how long the group would remain at Magnolia, but it was too long already. The mood was changing after the third day. The horsemeat disappeared, and stomach's growled. Adrenaline, hunger, testosterone roiled together in a stewing pot of excitement as scouts returned with news of the Sherman's advancement.

On the fourth day, the troops folded their tents, packed their gear and left Magnolia. Their departure was perplexing to Summer. She stood relieved, yet anxious, knowing that the fountain was yet to burn, and she, Evaline, was yet to follow her fate and disappear. When would it happen?

The relief was overwhelming to the women of Magnolia. Not only could the household breathe easier, but Susannah and Mary were free to leave their rooms without fear of endangerment to their propriety.

"And a good riddance!" Susannah said, standing on the veranda. It was an unusually warm day for December; sweater weather and very agreeable to Summer, who had visions of Chicago in December, the icy wind blowing off of Lake Michigan.

"Evaline, send Percy to River Row to see if there are any men left. Maybe there is a man or two in good enough shape to hunt or fish. I cannot believe that every darkie was fool enough to follow the Yankees into Kingdom Come. If we do not seriously work at our food supply, we will all starve. It does not appear that life will get any easier in the near future." Susannah was now master, mistress and overseer of the plantation. Charles was all but useless to them.

Not wanting Percy to visit River Row alone, Summer set off with the boy. Life had changed dramatically since she first arrived at Magnolia. All activity ceased, and even in the light of day, the eerie silence on the approach to the Row was cause for alarm.

"Ain't no sound, Evaline," Percy whispered. The clearing, just ahead at the edge of the bushes, conveyed no sign of life. They slowed their pace.

"Stay here, Percy. Let me take a look first." With trepidation, Summer stepped out of the bushed path onto the Row; empty, a ghost town.

The one time she had visited, at Jamaica's death, the Row had a life of its own; the hustle bustle of a small town was evident. Now, it was as still as the yard at the big house.

Percy took her hand. "Dey all gone?" he asked.

They set off down the road looking left and right at each shanty as they passed.

"Hello?" Summer called. "Anyone here?"

When they reached Jamaica's old shack, a door creaked from across the road and a woman stepped out. It was the same woman Summer spoke with the night Jamaica died. Behind her, came the boy, Moses.

"Where is everyone?" Summer asked.

"Dey gone," the woman said. "Dem Yankees told 'em deys free and dey should go. Ain't no work here, dey say. Dey go off followin' de soldiers."

"I 'member you. You's Evaline, Jamaica's girl," Moses said as he crossed the road toward Summer.

"Are you two the only ones here?"

"Some women-folk stay. Some old folks got nowheres to go, can't walk no more. Dey stay."

"What are you eating? We have no food at the big house."

"We ain't got much, just what we can hide from dem soldiers. Dey took da horsemeat. Dey took what we don' hide. Wha'd you want here?" the woman asked.

"We need help hunting and fishing. I was sent to bring men, if any were here, but, you don't have any. Well...you have one," she said, eyeing Moses.

"Wait," Moses said and hurried back to the shanty.

"He's a good boy, my Moses. De others, dey went off wid da soldiers, but I ain't goin'. I gots a home here. Ain't got nothin' out der. I kin help in da big house, too."

Moses returned with a net secured to a metal hoop closely resembling that of Miss Susannah's petticoat, which still lay beneath Mick Mason's cabin. He also carried a burlap bag, and a fishing pole with a hook attached to the line.

"Moses been catchin' us crawdads an' catfish."

Summer nearly drooled at the words. "Well, let's go fishing!"

She and Percy followed Moses on a different route to the river, south of the bank she knew.

"We need bait," Moses said, standing at the edge of the bank. "Ain't so easy when da water's getting' cold."

He dipped the net into the river and scooped it up after a moment. Nothing. They watched as Moses walked further down river, scooping and retrieving. When he returned, he had a few minnows flip-flopping in the net.

"You hold dis," he said, handing Summer the burlap bag. He then hooked a minnow onto the line and handed Percy the net. "When dat crawdaddy come up, you hold dat net under it in case he let go. We's gonna put it in dat bag real quick like! If you ain't fast, he gonna fall right back into da river."

What followed was a continuous parade of crawdad catching onto the minnow bait. As he pulled the pole up with crawdad attached, Percy held the netting beneath the crustacean so as not to lose it, while Summer raced with the burlap bag to catch it as it let go its stronghold. They worked the crawdad hole until they had a dozen and the last minnow was all but a fleshy bump on the hook. Summer had never tasted crayfish in her life, but anything was sounding good at this point.

With the burlap bag wriggling with crayfish, they moved 20 feet downriver. Moses seemed to know the right fishing spots. From here, he slipped into the river waist high, Summer shuddering against the thought of it.

"Why do you have to be in there?" she whispered. "It's too cold!"

"Gots to noodle da cat."

"Noodle?" Fishing the Savannah required a new vocabulary.

"Keep dat bag ready," he warned. "No noise!"

She and Percy stood still as boulders; the only sound that of the birds in the trees — and the mosquitoes buzzing in their ears. It seemed too cold for mosquitoes.

Moses disappeared beneath the water for what seemed an eternity, before he resurfaced. When he did, there was a three foot-long catfish attached to his right arm.

"Oh, my god!" Summer exclaimed. "It's huge! Are you hurt?"

Hurry!" he yelled, and Summer jumped to, running to the riverbank holding the opened bag beneath the monster. "It's not going to fit, Moses, that thing is a whale!"

"Hold dat bag! Don' let go!"

Summer bent as low as she could, resting the bag on the bank. The weight of the fish made it difficult for Moses to hold. As he lowered the fish into the bag, the bag slipped off the bank, thus sending it, and Summer, headfirst into the river. The cold temperature of the water knocked the breath out of her, but she fought her presence of mind to close the bag, trapping the fish. She realized, for the first time in her life, to what ends she would go for food.

Coming up, she broke the surface and took a deep breath of air. "Hooray! Supper tonight!" she said, slowly making her way to the river bank. "This thing weighs a ton!"

Moses now stood at the edge and took the heavy bag from her. Setting it aside, away from the river, he returned to pull her out of the water.

"You done good, Evaline!"

"Yes!" She was proud. This was the first fish she had ever caught—literally!

"One more," Moses said and slipped back into the water.

Standing still, Summer was fully aware of the air turned cool in her wet state, biting at her flesh. "What will we put the fish in?" she whispered, eyeing the flopping burlap bag 10 feet away,

"I got da net." Percy offered.

"If the next one is like the one in the bag, I don't think the net will do it!"

Standing ready, she shivered and waited, hoping Moses wasn't in trouble. Her teeth began to chatter. She was just about to jump in to see if all was well, when he broke surface with another monster of a catfish attached to his arm. He attempted to remove the fish onto the bank, but it held fast its bite.

"Help me!" he called. Summer and Percy both held the large catfish steady while Moses slid his arm from its jaws.

"That thing drew blood!" Summer exclaimed.

"Ain't nothin'. Me and Mama's eatin tonight!" He pulled himself out of the water.

"Moses, you are a godsend!"

With the fishing session over, Moses returned to the row, proudly bringing supper to his mother and the remaining inhabitants of the row, for surely his catch would feed a crowd!

Summer and Percy literally dragged their catch in the burlap bag, walking slowly along the bank toward the dock where Summer first saw Bruno. "You and me will go fishing again, right Percy?"

"Yes'm. Dat was some fun, huh Evaline?"

"It sure was, and we have something to show for it!"

As they approached the dock, a slight movement at the water's edge caught Summer's eye, and she stopped suddenly.

"What's wrong?" Percy asked.

"Look there," she whispered. "It's that damned alligator. Be still."

"Is dat da one ate Juba?"

"I think so. Isn't it too cold for alligators?"

"Sun goin' down now. He be movin' along."

She and Percy walked away from the bank and edged along the brush until they came to the path.

"I don't like that thing," she said. "It's a bad omen to me."

"What's a 'omen'?"

"A premonition...a signal in your mind that something bad is about to happen."

"Oh, don' scare me, Evaline! Bad things comin' already, like da soldiers."

"The soldiers are gone, Percy."

"Lucy say dey's comin' back again."

Most definitely.

The fish became increasingly heavier, making the last fifteen feet of the journey to the kitchen excruciatingly exhausting. Summer remembered the crawfish in the bottom of the sack and hoped they weren't totally squished due to the weight of the catfish. Lucy would be quite pleased for that little treat.

Dusk settled, the chilling air causing her wet clothing to feel like ice against her skin. Just a few more feet and she could step into the warmth of the kitchen to dry her clothes, but then, just as they approached the kitchen door, a shrill scream echoed across lawn.

Now what? "Percy, call Lucy to get the fish." She dropped the edge of the burlap sack and ran across the yard to the basement door. Up the dark stairway she flew, practically on all fours, bursting through the first floor door into the foyer. The front door was wide open, yet all that was visible through the doorway were two booted feet lying perpendicular on the tile floor of the porch.

"Oh, my God!" she exclaimed, and ran through the doorway to see Mary, comatose on the porch floor. Susannah was not far away on her knees, holding onto the railing. It was a posture reminiscent of Elizabeth's death scene, sending a shiver through Summer. Then, she saw it, the cause of the desperate scene before her. It was not the first time she had seen Charles Woodfield hanging from the fountain, but the shock was the same; he hung from the uppermost bronze branch of the magnificent magnolia fountain. Just as she recalled, his tongue protruded grotesquely from his mouth, his white hair askew and blowing in the slight breeze. If she could cut with a knife the memory of this vision from their minds, she would, for surely it would haunt each and every one of them forever.

22

As Pompeii and Moses dug the grave for Charles Woodfield, Margaret and Arthur Ascot marched from the southerly direction of Royal Palms, across the field of browning grass to the main house at Magnolia Plantation. Summer stood on the porch and watched their approach. Like smoke signals, frosted puffs of breath escaped their lips in the frigid night air.

"Oh Evaline, how could father do such a thing?" Margaret, encumbered by her heavy woolen red cape, lifted her hooped skirt to climb the stairway. Summer wondered if her reference to 'father' included Evaline as a sister?

It was obvious that the woman had cried buckets; her swollen eyes were rimmed in red, with the tip of her nose to match. A hanky found itself in a tight wad at the mercy of her clenched fist.

"This is dreadful! Yankees…Mother…and now Father!" New tears streamed down her cheeks. "We have no horses, no slaves, no food…it's insufferable! How are we expected to live?"

Summer had no answers, no words of comfort; life was also dismal at Magnolia. "We have food today. Moses has caught us catfish from the river."

"Who is Moses?" Margaret asked.

"He's from River Row. When the others left, he and his mother stayed. Some old folks stayed too. They have nowhere to go."

"More mouths to feed," Arthur grumbled. "They wanted freedom, and now they have it. Let them suffer the consequences. Where's Mason? Why hasn't he gotten rid of the bastards?"

"Uh…Mr. Mason disappeared. We don't know where he went."

"Probably turned traitor and joined the Federals. At least he knows where his next meal is coming from."

Summer followed the Ascots into the house where they were greeted by Susannah and Mary, both dressed in the funeral black they had worn since Edmund's death. Death seemed a constant companion to the Woodfield family.

"Who is a traitor, Arthur?" Susannah asked, apparently having heard bits of the conversation on the porch.

"Mick Mason. He's vanished, hasn't he? Otherwise, he should have run the lazy darkies off. Evaline says there are still some at the river."

"We need everyone we can hang onto. Why, Moses has been catching us fish—showing Evaline how to catch the crayfish and catfish."

"Soon as the water turns colder, you won't be getting those. Then what? Then you have a bunch of lazy mouths to feed. Send some over to Royal Palms. I'll put them to work."

"Are you going to pay them?" Summer asked.

"See? This is what the Yankees have given us, back-talking nigger gals…"

"Arthur! Stop, this minute!" Margaret commanded.

Summer breathed a sigh of relief when Pompeii came into the foyer. "Miz Susannah, we's ready."

✻ ✻ ✻

As with Elizabeth, there was no preacher for Charles Woodfield. There were no faithful servants, no slaves, and only a few family members to mourn his passing. Susannah, feeling greatly the loss of both parents, allowed Arthur to say a few words over the plain coffin that Pompeii and Moses had fashioned over the past two days. As the coffin was lowered into its final resting place beside Elizabeth—the woman who destroyed the man who was to lie beside her throughout eternity—the family retired to the dining room in the big house for a meager supper of fried catfish and collard greens. The collards were hardy plants and had grown leaps and bounds in what seemed a few short days. They were grateful for its bounty.

Summer and Cherry remained stationed beside the sideboard, as was their usual position at suppertime. *Old habits are hard to break.* Summer realized that they were technically 'free' and did not have to stand at attention, but it seemed a small thing to do considering the circumstance; Charles was dead, the family was in mourning and needed support. Soon, she and Cherry would clear the table and carry the few dishes back to the kitchen where Lucy was sure to have prepared a small feast for them.

"You are the only one left, Susannah, to deal with this…this house, the plantation. Everything has gone to ruin," Margaret said. "Arthur is here to help, when this dreadful war is over."

"And what are we to do, Arthur?" Susannah asked (somewhat cynically, Summer thought). What money we have is no good. There are no supplies, no livestock, no one to seed the fields, no one to harvest. It is all gone. My brothers lie in their graves for this pathetic end." Susannah's words touched a nerve.

"Your brothers lie in their graves for the cause! They were honorable men and died honorably!"

"The *'Great Cause'*!" Susannah fired back. *'Southern pride'*...to what end? For stealing people from Africa, forcing them to servitude, buying and selling them like cattle? The North moved into modern times with industrialization while we remained tied to our outdated ideals!" Susannah stopped suddenly and laughed. "We are a foolish breed of sops if you take a good long look at us!"

"You are intolerable!" Arthur slammed his napkin onto the table.

"Why?" Susannah shot back. "Because I *think*?"

"Stop!" Margaret ordered, to the best of what southern propriety allowed without seeming crude. "Father is dead, and just hear how you speak to one another!"

Silence, except for Cherry who shuffled nervously by the sideboard.

"Margaret is right, Arthur. Truce."

"Agreed," he replied, after a long pause.

When the trio relocated to the parlor, Summer and Cherry carried the dishes to the kitchen.

"Dey was goin' at it!" Cherry remarked.

"I'll say. I'm glad Miss Susannah has such a good head on her shoulders."

"An' po' Miz Margaret trapped like a fox to dat man...dat bad man, Mr. Arthur."

"We know that, don't we, Cherry? We know how evil that man is."

"Po' Miz Margaret don't even know."

As Summer suspected, Lucy had prepared for them a wonderful dish of catfish, collards and wild onions, and the crayfish, after which Summer retreated up the servant stairway to the nursery to relieve Ruth.

"Supper is ready Ruth. You go on down to the kitchen. Lucy does magic with catfish."

James was growing in leaps and bounds. His eyes remained blue and his hair a sandy brown color, curled and soft. Arthur's dimples puckered his chubby cheeks; a fine looking boy, and one that Summer could barely think of leaving one day—someday—when time called her back to the 21st century. He cuddled himself into her lap and they molded together as darkness approached, snug in the rocking chair as the shadows faded into the black of night.

✳ ✳ ✳

"I want to see my boy."

The voice startled her from a semi-conscious state. It was difficult to grasp the time, but she felt James in her lap and remembered that she had been nursing him and must have fallen asleep.

"Shhh. James is sleeping," she whispered. What are you doing here, anyway?"

"I want to see my boy." Arthur approached with the lantern, shining it on the baby's face.

"He's *my* boy, and you should not be here. Get out."

"I told you I was taking him when he's weaned."

"Like hell you are. You have no say over me."

"Like hell I don't. Yankee rules don't rule us. You don't have a say in the matter, girl."

Summer stood and put James gently into the crib.

"He's a handsome one—nearly white, too." Arthur stood beside her holding the lantern over the crib. "We made a fine fellow; maybe we should make another."

"You'll never touch me again, you bastard."

"You'd better watch your mouth, girl. The war isn't over yet."

"Maybe not, but it will be, and *you* are on the losing end, Mister."

"Evaline and her crystal ball."

"Yes, Evaline and her crystal ball, and I can let you in on a little secret; you will *never* have control of James Woodfield."

"That boy is an Ascot, and I *will* have him!"

"He's only an Ascot by rape, and you don't deserve him. If only the rest of the family knew what a sleaze you are, how you forced yourself on me—and on Cherry when she was only a child—if they only knew Percy was your son. What would they think of you?"

They were so intent on their dispute that they did not hear Margaret approach. She held her lantern low, casting a glow to the black bottom of her hooped skirt, but her face was shaded—her reaction told only in the escape of a breath that first caught their attention.

"How could you?" Margaret rasped, with as much indignation as Summer supposed she could muster. The genteel life of a plantation mistress was drummed into a girl's head from an early age; a proper 'belle' would never show her outrage in public.

"What are you doing up here, darlin'?" Arthur said, finally, as if nothing out of the ordinary had taken place.

"How could you!" she repeated, and disappeared from the doorway, the light from her lantern fading down the stairwell.

"Now you've done it!" Arthur retreated to the door.

"You did it all by yourself," Summer retorted. "Finally, the truth exposed!"

"Don't think you're off the hook," he warned. "I'm coming back for my boy, and I won't rest until I have him!"

Arthur hastily followed after his wife, while Summer took the servant stairway to the second floor and waited to hear the goodbyes. They were quite speedy in coming, as Margaret must have been totally shocked by the discovery of her husband's fatherhood, and eager to leave. The Ascots had at least a mile to walk to Royal Palms.

The servant stairway, which had for so long been a consternation to Summer, was now a sanctuary, a way to creep unnoticed from floor to floor. When she opened the door to the foyer, Susannah stood on the porch watching her sister and husband walk across the grassy fields in the moonlight toward their path through the woods. The lack of horses had made foot travel the only means of communication between the two families.

Susannah turned at the sound of the door opening. "Margaret is acting so strangely, Evaline. Whatever could be wrong? She went to look for Arthur, and when she returned she was beet red and said she had to leave. Do you know why?"

To tell, or not to tell? "I do know," she answered, deciding in favor of the truth. She approached the veranda and walked to the banister, joining Susannah. Looking at the magnificent magnolia fountain, she wondered when it would burn. The anticipation and dread where overwhelming.

"Well?"

"Mr. Arthur came to me in the nursery. He...he said he wanted to see his son."

"His *son*? Whatever do you mean?" She look incredulous as the truth dawned across her face. "You mean James? James is *Arthur's* son?"

"Not by choice, Miss Susannah. He attacked me one night—in the servant stairway. He said he would kill me if I told."

"My God, that man is an animal! And here we thought James was Robert Mason's son!"

"I only wish...." Robert. What has happened to Robert?

"You poor thing, Evaline. All this time and we didn't know! You should have told us...me, at least."

"That's not all," she continued. "Percy is Mr. Arthur's son, too. He raped Cherry when she was just a girl. He and I were arguing upstairs in the nursery, and Miss Margaret overheard. That is why she left in such a hurry."

"Oh, mercy." Susannah leaned against the banister. "I cannot believe it. My poor sister. I never trusted that man to begin with."

"Mr. Arthur says he's going to take James from me when he's weaned. He says Miss Margaret hasn't given him any children, so he's taking James from me."

"Over my dead body!"

It was a relief to hear those words. At least she had a friend in this place, not knowing how long she would stay and when she would have to leave James behind.

"Miss Susannah, about Robert. I don't understand how he can be so completely different from his father."

Susannah looked at her quizzically. "You are a mystery, Evaline. Surely you remember when he first came to Magnolia; why, he was just a boy of sixteen."

"I...I guess I was too young to remember."

"I don't know what made Mr. Mason so attractive to my mother. He was illiterate, uncouth, and downright mean. My mother was raised a Southern lady from a genteel family. I never understood her, and now it's too late. Apparently, Mr. Mason charmed another young woman from a genteel family in North Carolina. The rumor is, that he seduced the planter's daughter. She gave birth to Robert in great shame, but he was, nevertheless, raised by the family. The family went to ruin through unpaid debts, the boy's mother died, and the destitute and elderly grandparents sent him to Mr. Mason. Thank heavens he had a proper upbringing before destitution sent him to his father."

"I just hope he returns before I..."

"Before you what, Evaline?"

In the silence that followed, the sound of horse's hooves caught their attention.

"No...it can't be!" Susannah shrank from the railing.

Summer's heart fell, when out of the darkness the full moon shone on Yankee uniforms—more infernal soldiers trotting up the entrance road. *This is it. This is the end!* Sadness enveloped her as the troops rode around the circle stopping below them, an officer in the lead.

"Glad to see you ladies are up," said the officer. "We'll need some assistance setting up camp."

23

The horror of the war for the women on the home front continued that night. Summer, Susannah, Mary, Cherry and Lucy were put to the task of settling in the soldiers, while Ruth was allowed to remain in the nursery to care for James. Pompeii and Percy were again the designated stable boys. Pompeii, already weak from age, was put to the test of endurance. Poor nutrition and hunger had depleted his strength and Summer sorrowed to watch him lead horses away, two by two, stooped, unsteady, and shoulders slumped in defeat. He was a free man at last, but now age kept him prisoner at Magnolia.

Percy, with the exuberance of a child, sprang to his duties with relish after his initial fear of the soldiers diminished. With good-natured cajoling and treats of candy from some of the more fortunately supplied soldiers, Percy found his stable-boy job quite rewarding. He was a sight, his dark body leading the powerful animals away to pasture. Far removed from Percy's mirth were the spirits of the women—especially Summer and Cherry, whose good looks gathered much attention and remarks from the men.

The newly pitched tents poked into the night sky, the moon highlighting the peaks of canvas roofs that stretched the entire front of the great yard. The young women were sent to fill canteens with water from the pump. They lost count of how many soldiers, and therefore, how many canteens they filled as the hours passed and legs became weak with trips from the tents to the pump and back.

"The soldiers say they're going hunting tomorrow for squirrel and raccoon, and whatever else they can find." Summer sat totally exhausted at the table in the kitchen. "Be prepared to cook for the officers, Lucy."

"Ain't I always?"

"Just thought I'd warn you," she said and raised her weary body off the chair. I'm off to bed." Soft snores were heard from Cherry, who had already collapsed on her pallet in the small room behind the kitchen. Percy and Pompeii slept in an empty stall in the barn, caring for the horses.

Wearily, Summer left the kitchen, crossing the yard to the big house. The thought of sleep was so sweet. The officer in charge, Capt. Williams, gave her permission earlier to feed James, and then return to the duties he bestowed upon the women. She hoped James had fallen asleep and would stay that way for the next several hours. She desperately needed sleep if she were to contend with the mass of soldiers in the morning.

Just as she stepped through the doorway to the basement, she was jerked backward by the back of her blouse.

"What have we here?" asked a gravelly voice. The face, in the moonlight, was grizzled, unshaven and smelled of a strong mix of body odor and alcohol.

"It's one of them pretty darkies," spoke another voice from behind.

Her brain raced for a plan to eject from the situation immediately.

"Hey girlie girl, where you goin' in such a hurry?"

"None of your business," she blasted, and made an attempt to push her captor off.

"Oh, a feisty one, ain't ya?"

More like terrified.

"Ain't nobody back here to stop us, Jake." The owner of the other voice moved within view. He was taller than Jake, but just as grizzled and unkempt, as near as she could tell in the moonlight.

"I say we do her, Tom."

Fighting trembles, Summer frantically eyed the left and right of nightfall for an escape route. "You aren't touching me, you low-life, smelly pigs. You should be ashamed of yourselves. I always thought the Yankees were the good guys."

"We got you free, didn't we?" Tom asked. "Now's the time to repay the debt, wouldn't you say, Jake?"

"Yeah, I say so." Jake pushed her through the dark doorway of the basement. "In here," he said to Tom.

Summer stumbled onto the dirt of the basement floor. *Oh God, no!* This was a nightmare inside a nightmare. *Wasn't Arthur enough? How much did poor Evaline have to endure?* Reminding herself that this wasn't really happening to *her* was no consolation. It *felt* real, and she really was here at Magnolia; it was *most definitely* happening.

"Don't you dare," she growled from the dirt.

"Ha! A regular spitfire!"

"I'll spitfire you!" Lucy yelled.

Summer heard a frightening 'crack' and grunt before one of the soldiers fell beside her onto the dirt floor. She jumped to her feet to witness Lucy, standing in the doorway outlined in the moonlight, threatening Jake with a cast iron frying pan.

"Hold your horses, woman!" Jake said. "Put that thing down!"

"I ain't doin' no such thing. You get dat man and get outta here."

Tom groaned as Jake struggled getting him to his feet.

"Land sakes, woman. You probably broke his head."

"An' I's gonna break yours too, if you don' get outta here *now*."

Lucy stepped away from the doorway and let the men pass, Tom leaning heavily on Jake's arm while holding the back of his head.

"Lucy, you are an amazing woman, and I love you!" Summer hugged her tightly. "I hate to think what would have happened—I was so scared!"

"Me, too, precious. Dem soldiers, dey's a bad lot. Sometin' bad gonna come from dis."

Lucy's words were haunting. Summer knew something bad was going to come of it, but didn't know exactly what, or when—just that she was about to disappear.

✳ ✳ ✳

In the morning, as the soldiers hunted, Lucy scavenged the garden for whatever cold-weather crop was growing, but it was slim pickings. They couldn't keep any food for themselves, regardless how large or small the crop; every time something sprouted it went from the garden to Yankee mouths.

"I jes hope dey bring sometin' fo' us." Lucy set her empty basket on the kitchen table, much to the disappointment of Summer and Cherry who sat resting from the morning activity; a yard full of hungry and tired, yet rowdy, men was not an easy thing to deal with. The younger women were run ragged tending to the wounded who were again spread about the floors in the parlor and foyer. With buckets of water and bars of soap, they cleaned wound after wound. Bandages were running short. The last petticoat was literally pulled out from beneath Mary's skirt. She was not happy to see it go.

At four o'clock in the afternoon, the hunting party returned with their bounty, delivering the carcasses to the kitchen.

"Oh, this is disgusting!" Summer moaned. You never could have convinced her back in Chicago that she would one day be sitting outside a Southern plantation kitchen expected to gut and skin rabbits and other wild critters. "Argggg," Her throat closed in disgust, causing her to gag. "I don't think I can do this!"

Cherry made a few decisive cuts on a squirrel and somehow pulled the skin up to its shoulders. A few more fancy slices, removal of feet, cracking of bones, and a squirrel skin was laying next to Summer's feet. When Cherry sliced the animal open and twisted the guts into a bucket, Summer ran off to the closest bush to vomit.

Cherry laughed. "You's useless, Evaline!"

"Give me something else to do, but not this," she moaned. Her stomach was tied in knots and another bout of vomiting was imminent if she were forced to watch Cherry whittle her knife like a professional butcher.

"Such a baby, Evaline."

Summer was sure that she could never again eat the animals once they were cooked and disguised, now that she was witness to the process of getting them from the woods to the supper table.

"I'm sorry, Cherry, this is one job I can't do." Feeling foolish and ashamed in the face of such gnawing hunger, she returned to the main house, leaving Cherry to sit behind the kitchen with her tedious and gruesome job.

Back at the big house, cleaning the bandage of a soldier's gunshot wound caused Summer to ponder how she could even play nurse without vomiting. Were the raw, bleeding and sometimes putridly infected wounds of the soldiers easier to deal with, than the skinning and gutting of a dead animal that would feed their gnawing hunger?

✳ ✳ ✳

It was becoming old hat to carry a tray of odd animal parts up the servant stairway to the dining room where, on this night, Captain Jarvis and four other men were seated. Excitement was on the rise, as Sherman's men were on the edge of Savannah.

"We'll be pulling up and out of here soon," Capt. Williams informed the men. "Fort McAllister and then Savannah. Won't be long before the Rebs are tossing in their kepi caps."

"I'd like to blow a few off before then," a soldier replied.

"I'm sure you'll get your chance," the Captain replied.

Mary and Susannah had remained upstairs throughout supper, leaving Summer and Cherry alone with the soldiers. There was no privacy on the first floor of the house. The wounded had the luxury of sleeping on the floors of the parlor and foyer. Susannah and Mary preferred to hide upstairs when possible. Mary's ears, especially, were unaccustomed to the profanity and advances of the worst of the men.

At their stations next to the sideboard, Summer listened intently to the latest news. She wished the men would pack up and leave this night, as it was nerve racking to have them here. Not only were she and Cherry at the soldiers beck and call, but they were worried about their own safety, as the rowdier soldiers did not stop their lewd taunting.

"I wish dey'd go away." Cherry grumbled as the two women made their way down the stairs to the basement. The trays were loaded with dirty dishes and glassware, and Summer marveled at how accustomed she had become to the trickery of balancing a loaded tray while traversing the narrow treads.

"You heard them say they'd be leaving soon."

"Ain't soon enough."

The women stepped out of the basement onto the lawn. It was dusk, and the air, chilly. *Winter creepeth*, Summer thought. How different from the previous winter when Elizabeth had her stoking fireplaces day in and day out. It felt strange without Elizabeth. *Perish the thought, the woman was a lunatic!*

The world went dark. It took a moment for Summer to realize that someone had thrown a bag of sorts over her head. Cherry shrieked behind her. The trays clanged to the ground, the sound of breaking glass pierced the night. A strong arm around Summer's waist squeezed the air out of her, while Cherry's muffled screams faded into the distance, setting her heart to racing.

"Let me go!" Summer screamed. This was *not* going to happen, of that she was determined. With all her might she kicked, punched, elbowed and screamed for Lucy. In her frenzy, she hit the jackpot. Not knowing exactly where she had caused her abductor pain, she was suddenly released. Tossing the bag from her head, she ran like the wind, screaming toward the kitchen.

"Stop, you bitch!" the man called from behind.

The kitchen door flew open, and Summer literally ran into Lucy's arms.

"You git, you no good Yankee piece of misery!" Lucy yelled.

Summer turned to see the man disappear behind a corner of the kitchen. Gone. Her heart beat like the proverbial drum; Boom! Boom! Boom! Her chest quivered from the pounding inside. The tears came. She was so terrified during those moments, and Cherry—what became of her?

"Lucy! One of those men took Cherry!" The revelation was horrifying. "Oh, my god, we must find her!"

"Les go," Lucy said, grabbing her frying pan.

"Better yet…" Summer said, disappearing into Lucy's bedroom where the Yankee's stolen weapons were now kept. She returned with a pistol and a handful of mini-balls. "I've had it with this nasty bunch. Just call me 'armed and dangerous'"

The women set out in the direction the soldier had gone, Lucy with her frying pan, Summer with the pistol. With a lantern in tow, they walked along the edge of the woods calling Cherry, but the only sound returned to them was the sound of nightfall. Defeated, they returned to the kitchen when the lantern could no longer guide them adequately in the final veil of darkness.

"You gots to tell Ruth her baby got stolen."

"I can't bear the thought of it."

"She gots to know."

✳ ✳ ✳

A sorry group gathered at the kitchen table. Summer, Lucy, Ruth and baby James formed a vigil for Cherry. Susannah chastised the captain severely for allowing his soldiers to behave in such a 'deplorable and animalistic manner', and the Captain promised that he would punish the two men severely—if he discovered which soldiers they were.

"Oh for a Starbucks," Summer lamented. "Not even a friggin' cup of coffee to get us through." She was beginning to hate this place…this war. It was as if she never existed in the other world, this world was so real. Her pain was real, her worry for Cherry was real, and her love for James was real. Her love for Robert was a dagger in her heart, knowing that she was destined to never see him again. She adored Lucy, Percy, Pompeii and Ruth, too. Would she ever return to the 21st century? Did she ever exist in the 21st century? The question haunted her.

The night stretched on until, alas, a fumbling at the kitchen door. It opened and Cherry stumbled in, bruised, scratched, disheveled...and sobbing.

"Oh, Mama," Ruth caught her in her arms. "Dos' men...."

"It's okay, baby. You's home now, you's safe."

While the women tended to Cherry's wounds, Summer's anger flowed like hot lava through her veins. She left the kitchen, the hairs on her neck standing on end as the crossed the yard in the dark, ever on guard of the marauding bastards who tormented them. She marched through the basement and up the stairs to Susannah's room.

"You need to come and take a look at what those animals did to poor Cherry." She had entered without knocking, the heat of anger overriding propriety and manners. "Something must be done about this! Those men need to be punished!"

Susannah wrapped a fringed shawl around her shoulders. "Let's go," she said, and followed Summer out the door. "Oh, no, not that way," she said when Summer led her to the servant stairway.

"She's bloody and bruised and crying her heart out," Summer informed her Mistress as they took the grand stairway to the main floor where Susannah sought Captain Jarvis.

"I can't believe Yankees would behave in such a disgusting and vile way," Summer said, following Susannah as she wove her way through the sprawled bodies laying on the foyer floor.

"Why ever can you not believe it, Evaline? These are our *enemies*."

"Never mind." She gave the soldiers the dirtiest look she could muster. She couldn't explain that the North was her home team.

"Captain Jarvis." Susannah found him standing on the veranda overlooking the yard full of tents. "I demand that you punish the men responsible for abusing my servant, Cherry. She has returned from God only knows where, bloody and bruised at the hands of your soldiers. We are defenseless women without men, and perhaps your soldiers feel that fact gives them the right to pursue their...their carnal lust without consequence. I *demand* that you punish the perpetrators!"

"Ma'am," the Captain said, removing his hat. "I apologize for the bad behavior of my men. I would not hesitate to punish the men responsible if you could point them out to me." With that, he spread his arms out to the vast peaks of roofs before him. "Point them out to me, and I shall punish."

✳ ✳ ✳

That night, Summer awoke to the sound of heartbreaking sobs. For a moment, she thought Cherry was somehow nearby. She lit her candle and followed the sound to the attic door. Opening the latch, she held the candle before her to shed light into the stairwell. Even before she looked, and even though she hadn't seen Evaline's ghost in a long while, she knew it was Evaline. Without fear, she peeked around the corner of the doorframe to see first, the feet hovering over the treads, then the translucent skirt, and, as the light rose to the upper torso and head of the vision, there appeared Evaline in a state of great despair. There were no tears, and yet she sobbed. It wrenched Summer's heart, for the sadness filled her own body until she wanted to scream from the misery and pain of it. *The end is coming....* surely that was the message.

24

Tent roofs disappeared as if in a game of dominoes. One by one, they fell as the sun rose higher in the sky. December was warmer than usual—or so Summer imagined. There was a mugginess in the air. Magnolia was a hub of activity with Percy and Pompeii retrieving horses. The women bandaged the wounded for the last time, while the able-bodied solders packed their tents and gear.

As instructed by Captain Jarvis, the women lined up on the veranda around noontime, except for Cherry who was mentally incapable at the moment to do much else besides lay on her pallet in the little room behind the kitchen.

"If you bring your servant Cherry to me, she can point out the men who did her harm."

"Cherry is broken, Captain," Susannah divulged. "She is bruised, battered and incapable of speaking. I will not force her to endure an encounter with the beasts. I can only hope that the worst in life befalls them. I shall pray every night for that end."

"Then please gather the baby, anyone else in the house, and your personal belongings. We are instructed to destroy all dwellings when we leave."

"No!" Susannah shrieked. "You will not destroy my home!"

"War is not a pretty thing, Ma'am. I am under orders by General Sherman, himself."

"You should be under orders from God! We've been hospitable to you, and you have thanked us by raping my servant, eating what little food we have, and now you want to destroy the roof over our heads! Have you no decency?" Susannah was nearly hysterical. "Have you no family? No women, no children at home? You should be ashamed to leave us without even a roof over our heads!" Susannah held a hankie to her red nose, tears streaming down her cheeks.

I love this woman. Summer was awed by Susannah's perpetual courage in the face of this frightening and foreign enemy.

Captain Jarvis stood quietly a moment, deep in thought, and then turned to the nearest soldiers awaiting his orders. "Gather the furniture from the house and pile it up in that fountain there." He turned to the women. "I'll spare your home, ma'am, but that's all. It's serious business to disregard the orders of a commanding officer." He tipped his hat and walked away.

"Good heavens!" Susannah exclaimed. "Beast!" she called after the Captain.

"Shhh." Mary grabbed Susannah's arm. "We don't want him to change his mind."

"They cannot burn the furniture, Mary. What more do we have? Nothing!" she cried. "They leave us with nothing!"

By the time the women entered the foyer, soldiers had already hefted items onto their backs, lugging them out the door, down the steps to the grand fountain. The wounded were gone, but the parade of men carrying chairs, sofas and cherished memories continued nonstop. The women stood in the middle of the foyer while Susannah declared every passing piece a 'family heirloom'. She cursed the captain, as her cries went unheard.

When the first floor was emptied, Summer couldn't imagine fitting anything else into the magnolia fountain; it was full to the brim and then some. Chests, tables, chairs, mattresses, all poked their legs, drawers, doors and corners at odd angles protruding from the fountain.

"Upstairs, men," one of the soldiers shouted.

The women, under Susannah's direction, raced to create a barrier on the sixth step.

"Move aside, ladies," the soldier said.

"We will not!" was Susannah's retort.

"We'll knock you over," he warned, and then did. He stepped between Summer and Mary and pushed them aside. Like bowling pins, Mary bumped Susannah and they topped over onto the steps.

Under Susannah's orders, the women scurried up the steps after the men, and barricaded themselves in Elizabeth's room.

"They cannot have it all," Susannah growled. "I won't let them."

"Look!" Summer shouted, observing a black stream of smoke from outside the window in Elizabeth's room.

"Oh, no!" Susannah put her hand to her heart and braced herself against the sill as all three women peered from the second story to the scene below;

the furniture piled up in the fountain was now a blazing bonfire. "All of our things!" she cried.

The soldiers continued piling more furniture into the roaring fire.

Concerned for James' safety, Summer flew up the servant stairway to the third floor. Ruth was at a window watching the fire with baby James in her arms.

"Hurry, Ruth!" Summer grabbed the blankets from James' crib along with his few articles of clothing. The women raced down the steps, stopping to pound on Elizabeth's door. "Let us in!" Summer called.

Barricaded again in the room, the women stood mesmerized, watching the contents of Magnolia, piece by piece, burn to ashes.

"Open this door!" The heavy pounding broke the trance. The knob turned and the soldier on the other side shook the door violently. Mary screamed.

"Open the bloody door!" the soldier repeated.

"No!" Susannah was adamant. Summer wondered for a moment if her reluctance to comply was putting them all in further danger.

"She ain't budging," they heard the soldier say.

The women screamed when the door began to thud and shake.

"They're trying to break it down!" Mary yelled.

Summer scanned the room and ran to the fireplace. Choosing a poker from the fireplace tools, she motioned Susannah to open the door. Ruth clutched James to her bosom as Summer stood behind the door, the poker ready to swing like a baseball bat.

"Stop!" Susannah yelled to the marauding soldiers, then took a breath and unlocked the door, opening it to hide Summer's presence.

"You have to leave, ma'am." The soldier seemed to have tamed his anger in a hurry.

"We will not leave! Surely you have a mother at home...a wife, a sister. Is this how you want to picture them, helpless against foreign troops? Would you want them shrinking in fear as the enemy burned their homes, their belongings? I beg you to leave us this little bit of furniture...sir."

The soldier looked as his companion in crime and shrugged. "Wha...?"

"Leave it," the other soldier replied. Everything else is gone—just leave it."

Susannah nearly fell to the floor after the soldiers retreated down the stairs. "Oh, I thought surely they were to bully us out of here!"

"You are one brave Southern belle, Susannah Woodfield!" Summer beamed with relief and admiration for Evaline's half-sister; the one Woodfield she was proud to be related to—next to James.

"What about my Cherry?" Ruth asked.

"Oh, Lord," Summer exclaimed, remembering that Cherry was alone on her cot in the kitchen house. She looked at the group huddled again around the window, watching the fire; Mary, her face white with fear, Ruth, anguished over Cherry's safety, yet holding onto James for dear life.

James—sweet James— she loved him so. She looked at Susannah, knowing in her heart it was for the last time. "Please take care of my boy. You're a fine lady, and I know you'll do good by him."

"Whatever are you talking about, Evaline?"

"Just remember my words...take care of my sweet James." She ran through the doorway, tears streaming down her cheeks at the thought of never seeing James again. The servant stairway was the safest way in which to avoid the Yankees, and she descended quickly in the dark, each step ingrained into her memory from her many trips up and down its narrow route. Before leaving the basement, she poked her head out the door, searching in both directions for danger before stepping out into the grass. She ran quickly across the yard toward the kitchen, but stopped when she heard a familiar voice.

"Hey, girlie girl, where you goin' in such a hurry? Where's that Cherry girl?" Summer turned quickly toward the garden side of the house and saw that the man was not alone, two other soldiers stood next to him, roughly twenty feet from where she stood.

"Is she in the kitchen, there? Go get her, Hank," he said to one of the men. "We're gonna have some fun before we ride outta here."

"She's not there." Summer fought to keep her voice steady. "She's where you won't find her, you pig."

"Pig, eh? Well we'll have a pig load of fun with you girl, when we catch you."

Summer ran like lightning toward the outhouses on the opposite side of the house. She turned behind to see all three men running to catch her. They were somewhat encumbered by their uniforms and weapons, and not as quick as she. By the time she arrived at the front of the house she was out of breath, sharp pains jabbed her chest with each intake of air. There was such a crowd of soldiers hollering and watching the fire that she wove herself into the mass, hoping to hide.

The crackling of the burning furniture mingled with the excited shouts of the men. The flames shot into the air, nearly reaching the third floor of the big house. Summer glanced up at Elizabeth's window hoping for one last look at her friends and family at Magnolia, but saw nothing through the black smoke.

"The fountain is melting!" someone cried. Sure enough, the bronze magnolia blooms that graced the limbs of the unique and beautiful fountain, were now withering, shrinking in the heat of the flames. Branches, that just an hour ago reached gracefully upward and outward, now drooped in the sadness of the occasion. Legs of furniture, blackened and charred, poked grotesquely from the pyre.

"Ain't no Magnolia Plantation now!" a soldier cried. "Ain't nothin' but a bunch of tangled wood! Huzzah, boys, trample the South!"

'Trample the South' rose in chorus of male voices, driven—forceful—fearful, sending shivers up Summer's spine.

A hand gripped her elbow. "Thought you'd get away, huh?"

She shook off the hand and broke through the crowd, running quickly toward the garden side of the house, stopping only when a tremendous explosion rocked her eardrums. Turning to look at the inferno behind her, new flames rocketed into the sky and she wondered if one of the burning cabinets contained ammunition, to cause such an explosion. Her pursuers stood with their backs to her now, also mesmerized by the explosions and horrific flames.

My chance, she thought, and took off in the direction of the river. The sun was low and the opportunity to hide greater than before. It was important to keep the men from Cherry, who was traumatized enough through this hell...this war...these evil men.

She heard their voices behind her as she ran. Reaching the river, panic set in. *Where to now?* With the onset of winter, the leaves of bushes and plants were not as thick as during the summer months. *The dock*. She knew she had to take cover or they would spot her. *If only it were dark!* Slipping into the cold water beneath the dock, she snuggled closely to the muddy bank. The water was deeper here—nearly four feet. She thought of the ugly, gigantic catfish, and hoped one didn't think she was 'noodling' and grab her leg.

"Damn," one of the men said. "We gotta pull out and I wanted some fun before we left. It may be the last time."

"Shit."

The men did not leave, and she fought to keep her breathing inaudible, though her lungs screamed for air.

"Maybe she was lyin' 'bout that Cherry girl. We should look in the kitchen. Hope that woman ain't there with the frying pan. She gave Tom a lump the size of Texas." The men laughed as they retreated from the river.

Oh, no! Summer couldn't bear the thought of Cherry suffering another bout at the hands of the brutal soldiers! She had to help her—somehow. Getting into the river was one thing, but getting out was another thing all together. She waded to where the bank looked more receptive for exit. *Slippery damned mud.*

"Wha…." The pain was unbearable. Her left thigh was gripped in a vise. For a moment she thought it was a catfish, but the monster released its jaws and clamped again. "No!" *This can't be the way it ends!* She clawed at the muddy bank, scrambling for dear life while the deep, muddy grooves from her fingers carved the story of Evaline, as they trailed downward on the bank. She screamed, the terror overwhelming. *So stupid!* How could she have forgotten Bruno? "Help!" she screamed, but the cold water filled her lungs as the grooves left by her fingers disappeared below the water line; it was a battle written in the passages of time and could not be won.

25

"Summer!" She heard the voice calling from behind. *'Summer'? What an odd thing to call me,* but everything was odd with the blasted war. She couldn't let them catch her! Poor Cherry was done for if that were the case

The dock...I'll hide beneath the dock. She reached the riverbank, out of breath and gasping for air. Slipping into the water, she found it not as cold as she expected—or remembered; she couldn't tell which. Why had she expected it to be cold? She pressed her body against the muddy bank below the planks of wood overhead. Oh *God, don't let them hear me!* Her heart beat in rapid succession.

"Get out!" the man's voice sounded alarmed. "Hurry! Get out of there!"

They know I'm here! She was terrified. She pressed harder against the mud, hoping to become invisible.

"Behind you!" the man called.

She looked over her shoulder and was horrified to see the alligator, his eyes gliding on the surface toward her. She screamed.

This is not the way it ends!

A *splash!* and the man was beside her in the water. "Get out!" he said, and gripped the top of the dock with two hands. He brought his knees to his chest, and just as the gator approached, he kicked his legs out with all his might—the water a force against him—and hit the alligator in the snout. It swam off to the side and circled around.

As the creature swam back to them, she looked it in the eye and suddenly realized the danger. "Guy! What are we doing here? Get out!" she screamed. She was frantic and hadn't a clue of how she got into the water. Knowing that the gator was there, she *never* would have climbed in unless she was under some kind of voodoo spell! Guy lifted his knees to his chest again, and gave another shove at the gator's approach.

"Now!" he yelled, and, as the gator circled again, he lifted himself onto the dock, then Summer after him. Seeing that his meal was beyond his reach, Bruno headed south down the river.

Sitting on the dock, her nightgown clung to her small frame, her nipples outlined and erect. She crossed her arms over her chest. "Oh, my God, it's coming to me."

"What in the world were you doing, Summer?"

"I *am* Summer, now," she said, more to convince herself than Guy.

"I know you're Summer. What the hell were you doing in the river? If I hadn't seen you running, you'd be that gator's dinner by now."

She shuddered. "I know what happened to Evaline."

"Well, tell me later," he said, standing. He reached a hand out to help her up. "First, let's get you into some dry clothes."

She was too shocked to speak, anyway. She followed Guy back to the big house, not saying a word, just reflecting on poor Evaline's demise. *Is this what she wanted me to know? That she didn't leave by choice?*

After changing into dry clothes, she sat with Guy at the kitchen table. He had apparently been working in the garden, as the red bandana around his forehead was wet with sweat, and his fingernails dark with dirt.

"There is just too much to tell," she said. "I don't' think I'll ever be going back to Magnolia, and I'll never know what happened to Cherry. The damn Yankees were headed back to the kitchen and she was there, lying on the cot...."

"Now, who is Cherry?"

"It's strange that Jesse never mentioned Cherry. She must have been her great-something-or-other grandmother. She *must* have survived. Oh, it's just too much! I can't believe I'll never know what happened!"

"Drink your tea," he said, pushing the steaming cup toward her.

"Come with me, Guy." She stood and walked to the back door. I have to show you something."

He obediently followed her around the side of the house to the garden.

She stood at the northeastern corner of the picket fence. "If you dig in this area," she spread her arms in a circle, "you will find bodies...skeletons by this time."

"What?"

"There are three Yankee soldiers buried here. Mick Mason killed them. We had to bury them out of sight because the Yankees kept coming back. I think they suspected us, but they never discovered the truth. And, we ate their horses."

"What?"

"We were starving. You just can't imagine how horrible it was. There was no food and, whatever we had, the Yankees took. The horses had to go, or the Yankees would have known."

She walked to the southeastern corner. "If you dig here, Mick Mason is buried in this spot. Perhaps you'll want to move him, give him a proper burial. He didn't have one."

"Why is he buried here?"

"Charles Woodfield killed him when he caught him in bed with Elizabeth. He...he killed Elizabeth too."

"Jesus. I thought she had an accident on the stairs. Is she buried here, too?"

"She fell over the second floor banister after Charles Woodfield shot her. I saw the whole thing. She's not buried here, though. She had a proper burial in the family cemetery. Only a few of us knew the truth...where are you going?" Summer asked, as Guy walked toward the side of the house.

"To get a shovel."

He returned with the shovel and entered the garden. The roses over the Yankee graves were blooming, so he started digging out the weeds that covered the spot Summer designated as Mick Mason's grave.

After an hour of digging in the humid heat, and after drinking the pitcher of iced tea that Summer brought to him, the shovel hit an object. Guy stood five feet below ground with Summer standing over the gravesite. She watched as he tugged on something. A piece of cloth tore off and he passed it up to her. She turned the decaying fabric over in her hands.

"Oh! I think this is part of Elizabeth's bed sheets! Mick Mason was naked when Charles killed him and we had to roll him in sheets and blankets—whatever we could find."

Guy continued solemnly to dig. Summer was uneasy over his silence but convinced herself it was understandable, considering the deceased was Guy's ancestor. Or, maybe he didn't believe her?

She watched as he leaned over in the dark pit, and then turned to face her. His face was white against the blackness of the hole as he raised a skull upward for her to view. "You're right. I guess this is him."

"It's him," Summer whispered, the shock of seeing Mason's skull causing her to step away from the pit. So recently had she seen him in the flesh, and now he was just bone. The distance of years between was now unquestioningly clear.

Guy set the skull on the side of the grave and hefted himself out of the hole. "I'll get the rest of him, but I don't know how I could tell the authorities about this. Explaining your time travel knowledge would most likely not go over very well."

"Then leave him where he is."

"It seems heartless."

"He was a heartless man, but he did save my—Evaline's—life. A garden of flowers is not such a bad place to be buried."

"What about the three soldiers? Were they naked too?" He grinned.

"You look so much like Robert," she said, feeling a stab in her heart.

"Do you love me, like you did Robert?" They stood on opposite sides of the picket fence, his hands suddenly covering hers on the vertical rails.

Her stomach flip-flopped. "I do," she said, right before he kissed her.

The trip to Aunt Ada's bed did not take long.

❉ ❉ ❉

"Are we nuts?" Summer stretched her naked body hither and yon on the bed. "In the middle of grave digging, we stop to make love!" She flushed in remembrance of the passionate moments just passed.

"I can't think of a better way to rest between digs. I'm just sorry I brought all this dirt with me."

"I'm not. There's something sexy about the dirt, the sweat and the bandana. I felt it from the beginning. Guess I'm just a dirty girl." She laughed. Leaning on her side she traced invisible hearts on his chest. "Maybe you don't want to hear this, but…but the love I feel for you is so deep. I feel like I've loved you for a long, long time."

"I understand," he said, staring at the ceiling. "I feel the same, like I've known you a long time and that this is the way it's meant to be."

"Does it scare you?"

"Not in the least. I guess I've been waiting for you—waiting for you to come home to me."

She leaned her head on his chest. "Home. Yes, I've come home."

26

"I need to tell you about Cherry and Percy." Summer and Jesse sat on the veranda sipping mint tea. "Cherry was a beautiful girl, and sassy! Such a figure too! She was in love with a slave named Juba, but he's the one who was killed by the alligator."

"Oh, such drama!"

"Cherry was heartbroken afterwards. It took her a long time to get over Juba. Unfortunately, once she recovered from the loss of Juba, she was raped by two Yankee soldiers. The last I saw of her, she was recovering from that ordeal. I don't know what happened to her though…it drives me crazy. Cherry and I were very close."

"I get goose bumps listening to these stories."

"Now, hold onto your hat."

"Oh, oh."

"When Cherry was thirteen, she was raped by Arthur Ascot. Cherry gave birth to the boy, Percy, and he may be your ancestor. Percy, was the son of Arthur Ascot."

"What? You have got to be kidding! You mean *da boss is still da boss?*"

"Yes, and I can't wait to tell Blaine. Cherry was the daughter of Ruth, and I'm surprised you never mentioned her."

"I don't know anything about Cherry, just Ruth. I never heard of her or Percy, either. I thought Ruth's child was sold off."

"Have you ever searched at the library?"

"You know the records of slaves are very slim."

"Just start with yourself, and go backwards; write down you parent's names, grandparents, etc. Maybe we can find out what happened to Cherry by doing a genealogical search. And poor Evaline, now we know what happened to her. I think Evaline was out there—waiting in limbo—and when I came along she had the opportunity to free herself from purgatory, so to speak. She sure got my attention. I just wish she and Robert could have been together in life; she really loved him, and he loved her."

"Now you've got my curiosity up about Cherry and her boy. I wonder what happened to them?"

"It kills me to not know. I'd love to know what happened to *all* of them. They were my friends, my family."

✳ ✳ ✳
One Year Later

"And you thought you couldn't do it," Guy said as he and Summer walked across the yard toward the old overseer's cabin.

"Here I am, after one year, the official mistress of Tanglewood…oops, let's make that 'Magnolia'. The new fountain arrives next week, magnolia blossoms and all. I'm so excited!"

"So, what is it we're doing on this venture? You know we all believe your story already. You don't have to prove anything else."

"I know, but I just remembered something and I need to prove it to myself. I lived as Evaline, and still it seems like a dream…a dream that I must continuously prove to be the truth and not imagined."

"Well, here we are," he said, stopping at the steps to the old overseer's cabin.

Summer immediately proceeded to tug at the lattice. Old, chipped and frail as it was, it held tight to its frame.

"Somebody repaired this since I was here last—nearly 150 years ago." They both laughed and Guy stepped to the rescue. After two tugs on each nailed corner, the piece separated from the frame.

"Now what?" he asked.

"Here goes," Summer got on all fours and crawled beneath the house.

"You are a piece of work!" Guy called after her.

"I know it's still here!"

Memories flooded her as she crawled in the dirt beneath the floorboards, bits of sunlight filtering in to light her way. She felt her eyes fill with tears. *They were my people;* it had a very special meaning for someone alone in the world. She was now bonded to the land, to the dirt, to the descendants of Magnolia. She was *connected*, and it felt so good. Her only regret was that she didn't know what happened to Cherry and the others. Evaline's death was a heartbreaker, and she hoped that Cherry fared better.

Her hand bumped something and she groped like the blind, eager to feel something familiar, something to bring the people back to her in any small way. The object was hard and narrow and, as she fingered it, she felt another band, and another. *The petticoat!* She opened her mouth to call Guy, but stopped, holding the petticoat frame to her chest, remembering her days at the *old* Magnolia. Then, feeling silly clutching an ancient petticoat, she crawled toward the opening dragging the relic behind her through the dirt. "I have it!" she yelled.

Guy took the petticoat from her and held it out in front of him, parts rusted, the fabric eaten away by time. "*This* is what you crawled in the dirt for?"

"Yes. It's Susannah's."

"It *was* Susannah's, you mean."

"It was, it is, it always will be."

"What will you do with it?"

"Hang it in my closet. I only know that I'll always keep it with me."

✳ ✳ ✳

Guy took a small box from his pocket and set it on the table next to Evaline's journal.

"What is this?"

"Just a little reminder of how much I love you."

"May I peek?"

"In a moment. First I need to ask you something." He rose from his chair and knelt beside her, taking her hand. "Summer Woodfield, you are one brave lady. You have endured a journey to a strange land and time; you have endured slavery, Yankees, murder...and even alligators. You have loved and lost a man, and gained another. Considering your bravery and ability to defeat adversity, I think I need you in my life to safeguard my passage the rest of the way." He smiled. "Therefore, it would honor me beyond belief if you were to accept this proposal of marriage."

She grinned from ear to ear. "It was a damn fine day, Guy Mason, the day I drove up to this rickety old house in Blaine's limo. You bet I will!"

He stood and pulled her to him. "I love you Summer Woodfield."

A 'thud' interrupted their kiss and they turned to see that the journal had fallen open on the table—on its own accord. After a year of no response from Evaline, three words appeared on the page:

Love Springs Eternal.

Summer's hair stood on end as a thumbprint appeared beneath the words. Then, beside that, appeared another thumbprint...smaller...softer... sweeter....

✳ ✳ ✳

Renovations on the new 'Magnolia' progressed rapidly. Summer and Guy spent hours removing old wall paper, sanding floors and painting walls. It was on one of these busy days while Summer concentrated on painting the baseboards in Evaline's old room, that she heard it:

Scratch...scratch...scratch...

Goose bumps raised her flesh. The hairs on the back of her neck prickled. *No, it can't be!* She rose off the floor, paintbrush in hand.

Scratch...scratch...scratch...

Her first thought, as she approached the attic door, was that her impression of the last note in Evaline's journal was wrong...*Evaline is still unhappy!*

Her heart fell at the thought; all this time she thought that Evaline and Robert were together at last!

With her hand on the familiar latch, she paused long enough for another trio of scratches to send chills up her spine. Taking a deep breath, she opened the door to the darkness of the attic; no candle, no lantern, no flashlight, just a paintbrush in hand. She didn't need a light, for when she peeked around the corner and up the stairwell, a glowing figure hovered toward the top, its fingers beckoning her to *come*, to *follow.*

Summer slammed shut the attic door and braced herself against its aged wood. She stared across the room at the floorboard she had left half painted, and tried to collect her composure. Was she relieved? Apprehensive? Mostly, she was shocked—surprised—and then, reconciled. Alas, the words left her mouth: "Cherry! Cherry needs me!"

THE END

<u>Jocelyn Miller</u> divides her time between the Eastern Shore of Maryland, and Sanibel, Florida—when she isn't seeking adventure in other parts of the world. Her keen interest in the lives of pre-20th century women, has inspired her to write of the adventures and adversities faced and fought by fictional women on the outside fringes of the social circles of their time.

www.jocelynmiller.com

Made in the USA
San Bernardino, CA
17 November 2013